# ASHES
*ashes*

DOWN WE GO BOOK TWO

# KYLA FAYE

Cover design: Books and Moods

Formatting: Books and Moods

Editing: Cruel Ink Editing & Design

Proofreading: Zainab M. at Heart Full of Reads Editing Services

*To my lover,*
*It'll always be you*

# WARNING

If you have any triggers, this is not the book for you.
Seriously. Do not proceed unless you're prepared to read about some fucked up shit.
Triggers include mentions of domestic violence, blood/knife play, sexual assault, torture, graphic sex scenes, graphic language, dub/non-con, breath play, mentions of suicide, and much more.
Proceed with caution and at your own risk.

# PROLOGUE

'm always watching.

I was watching her then, and I'm watching her now.

I've never stopped watching her.

Watching and waiting.

Always watching and waiting.

I remember the first day I met her. She was young, but her eyes betrayed everything she'd seen and experienced.

With one look into her breathtaking, turquoise eyes, I could see the darkness that lurked within. Her demons called out to me, and I answered the call. Every time.

We're connected in a way I can't explain. I'm drawn to her like a magnet and have been ever since that day.

I lost her nearly six years ago when she decided to marry *him*; the bastard that beat her and bruised the delicate body that should've been worshipped. I stayed away because she looked happy and wore a bright smile in every photo. I should've known she was miserable. Her smile never met her eyes, and I know her well enough to know how much her eyes light up when she's genuinely happy.

I should've known, and I should've saved her from that hell.

Because I'm always watching, I know what's happening with her now, and where she's at. I've been tracking her and waiting since she was taken from that alley at Confess nightclub. Just watching from the background and waiting for my chance to come out of the shadows and go to her.

The Triad tried to save her and failed. *He* failed, and he will pay for it.

I love her, and unlike him, I won't fail.

She's mine. She's been mine since the very beginning, and it's time she comes to be with me where she belongs.

I wait across the street, hidden in the shadows of the night, watching the scene that rolls out in front of me.

I watch when they go inside the house.

I watch when they brawl in the street.

And I watch when they drive away, leaving her behind in the house. A house I knew she had been at for the last four days, but I didn't have the opportunity to get inside. I guess I have them to thank for that.

But the difference between me and those Triad fuckers is they gave up on saving her, but I won't. I never will.

I wait until the coast is clear, then run across the street and into the red brick house, searching for her. She isn't hard to find.

I follow the smell of the smoke, which leads me into the basement. Getting to her is easy—way too easy.

The closer I get to her, the more my anger stirs within me. It stems from the fact that they let her down.

*He* let her down.

They didn't even try to save her. They left her behind in the burning basement, bleeding out and chained to the wall.

Since I'm the savior she needs, and the only one who truly cares about her, I rescue her from the flaming house that threatens to steal her from me.

I risk myself to save her because that's what you do for those you love. So, I take what's mine, and get the fuck out of there.

For her, I'd walk through the flames of hell. I'd do anything for her, no matter the risk.

It doesn't matter that she's without a pulse or cold and blue.

I have her back. And that's all that matters.

She's mine, dead or alive.

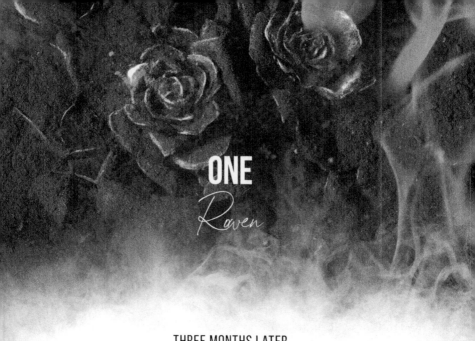

# ONE
*Raven*

**THREE MONTHS LATER**

How do you live when your heart has been ripped out of your fucking body?

I don't feel like I'm living. I barely even feel alive. Numbness consumes me.

I'm so tired of feeling like this. It's been three months since that night in the basement when we turned our backs and let the smoke swallow Tate's body. She was already dead when we left her, but that doesn't stop me from feeling like I do right now. We turned our backs on her.

*I* turned my back on her.

I listened to the voices of others when I should've listened to my own. Now, I can't stop thinking about how different things could've been.

I should've trusted her; I should've known better.

But it's too late now. There's no going back in time. I can't change the decisions we made…the decisions *I* made. I've been shunned and forced to live in my own personal form of hell.

I can't sleep. I can't eat. I can barely even fucking breathe.

I hate living without her. I shouldn't be living without her, not like this. This is too permanent.

Why do I get to live and she doesn't? She had been through hell just like I have, and I'm still standing, while she's not.

I don't want to live in a world where she doesn't exist.

My desperate need to feel something brings me back to the same place five nights a week—an underground fight club.

I'm in the ring every chance I can get. I never fight back, even though I know I can take my opponents and win. But I don't want to win. I need to feel something, and the pain of getting my ass kicked allows me just that. This is the only time I feel alive.

The fight club is where I'm at tonight. I'm sitting on the sidelines and waiting for the current fight to end. The octagon ring in the middle of the room is now occupied by two others fighting. It will continue until one of them passes out, and I'll get my chance to step in and take on the winner.

They're both smaller than me, and I could take them on easily, but I need to be hit. I need the pain of a fist connecting with my face or any other part of my body. I fucking need it as much as a junkie needs their next fix.

I never fight back. I'm afraid if I do, the beast within me will be unleashed, and I'll likely kill whoever I end up getting my hands on. There's too much anger and regrets to risk my rage. For now, I'll bury it down and let it fester.

Soon, I'll get my revenge on the person who deserves it the most.

"We have a winner! Vixen is undefeated for the twentieth fight in a row!" the busty pixie-cut blonde announces into the microphone as she walks around the ring, showing off the winner.

Vixen. *What a stupid ass fucking name.* But she's right. He's been undefeated for twenty fights in a row. I don't think it's because he's good, but because he's a twisted bastard who always goes for the cheap thrill shot. There are no rules down here, and he always goes for the punch that'll bring his opponent to their knees. This gives him the opportunity to knock them out. He's lucky I don't fight back.

The woman's voice fades into the background as the crowd erupts into roaring cheers. I'm next, and my heart is already beating with the anticipation of getting to feel the physical pain. I'm fucking craving my next fix.

I stand from the bench I'm sitting on and chug down the water in my bottle. My eyes narrow in on Vixen, who's walking around proudly in the ring; no doubt waiting for me.

Then I stretch out my aching joints and jump around a few times to shake off the stiffness. I'm still bruised and aching from the beating I took the night before last, but I'm not going to let that stop me from being here tonight.

I'm about to take a step forward when I feel a hand grab my shoulder and stop me in my tracks. I turn, facing one of the two people I don't care to see or speak to.

"What the fuck are you doing here, King?" I snap, shrugging away from his grip. We haven't spoken much since *that* night. The three of us still have our businesses together, but we avoid each other at all costs.

I haven't seen King or Eli in weeks. I haven't been able to go back to the cabin where King stays or the penthouse Eli lives in. I've been staying at one of the other apartment buildings we own. Communication between the three of us hasn't been necessary, so I haven't talked to either of them.

The two of them disgust me. They act as if she never even existed.

King keeps himself locked in the cabin doing God knows what, and when he's not home, he's at Sinners getting private shows and drinking himself to death in a private room.

Meanwhile, Eli is back to bending his assistant over his desk. I know this because I caught him once. I'd gone to see him at his office two weeks after the fire. I'd walked in without knocking, and he had Elena bent over his desk. He was thrusting into her with the most stoic expression I'd ever seen.

What the fuck is wrong with them? Tate existed, and we killed her. They set her death into motion, and now they're living seemingly without a care.

We always vowed that nothing and no one would ever come between us, but that vow was broken the minute she came into our lives.

Back into *my* life.

I always knew she would be capable of being our undoing, and I was right.

I stare at King, aware that my brows are pulled into a deep frown. There's no reason for him to be here. There's nothing he can do or say that will change the way I feel toward him. The resentment I feel can't be undone.

"There's been a fire." Those four words were the last I expected to hear from him.

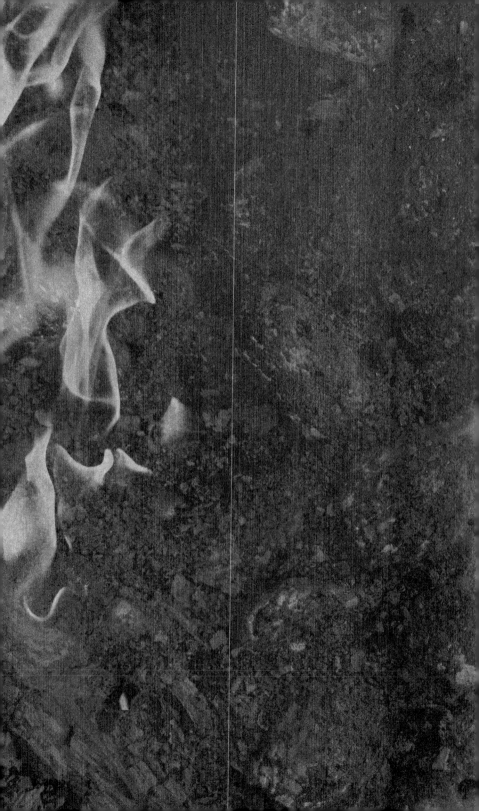

# TWO

*Eli*

"**A**t this time, the police do not have any suspects. They are asking for help from the community to identify those responsible for the fire at Luigi's Pizza." The newswoman's voice fades into the background as I lower the volume of the television. I grip the remote so tightly my knuckles turn white, and I nearly crush it in my grip.

Luigi's Pizza is the second Triad-owned business that has caught fire within the past two weeks. According to the news anchor, the police still have no suspects.

Someone is intentionally burning our businesses, and we still have no fucking idea who.

When I was notified of the first fire, I'd called King. We hadn't spoken in weeks. He'd dragged Rowen out of that underground fight club where he likes to go to wallow in self-pity, and the three of us were quick to jump into action and step into business mode. It felt nice to come together again with my brothers. Terrible circumstances, but it felt comfortable having them by my side again.

We haven't been the same since Tate died. With each passing day, I know that we're drifting further and further apart, and we may never be who we once were.

I always knew she was capable of being our downfall, and look how fucking right I was. We're not the same anymore because of her. We allowed pussy to weaken us, and we let a woman come between us. We all did.

Rowen and King both blame me, and that's how I know how truly weak they are. But she's dead, and I'm over it. I have to be. At least that's what I tell myself.

One of us has to be strong and in control.

I wish they were able to get over it too.

Now that we're at risk, our enemies are starting to creep into our city and put down roots. Word has spread quickly through the underworld about the Triad being vulnerable, and we're proving them right by letting others set up shop within our city limits.

When the Westside Disciples were dealing in our city, we should've killed them to send a message instead of trying to make a deal. If we had, we wouldn't be in this fucking situation right now.

We should've done what we did best and eliminated them. Instead, we devised a ridiculous plan to kidnap and trade Tate for them to leave the city. I knew that plan was stupid, and I should've stopped it. Especially once I realized that there was no way that Rowen would be able to let her go. Not again.

I should've known, and maybe if I had come up with a different plan, she'd still be alive. Maybe I'd have my brothers by my side again. I have regrets. Many, many regrets.

My anger is boiling as I throw the remote to the coffee table. The battery cover pops off, and the batteries spill out. I grab my phone and scroll through my contact list until I reach Detective Roberts's cell number.

He answers on the first ring, and I interrupt before he has the chance to complete his opening. "Tell me you have some information."

"Eli. I'm good, how are you? Would it kill you to try to make small talk?" He chuckles, probably thinking he's the funniest fucking guy to exist.

"I don't have time for small talk. Do you have any goddamn leads?" I growl. I'm losing my patience each day that goes by without any additional information.

Two weeks. Two fires. No fucking suspects.

"You're a lot more unpleasant these days," he mutters. "The answer is no. There are no leads on the fire at Luigi's. We have no further information on the destruction at the warehouse or on the fire at that house." The first fire was at a warehouse we own. Luckily, it was empty since we had just purchased it and hadn't decided what to do with it yet.

"What about similarities between the three?"

"Yeah, there's one similarity. They all fucking burned. I said I'll call you if we find anything." He ends the call, only causing my anger to amplify. *Bastard.*

He seems to forget who pays for that lovely, big house of his.

When the warehouse caught fire, I thought about the fire that had started at Tyson Holbrook's house three months ago. The fire that killed Tate.

Right after the fire at Tyson's that King and I escaped from, I asked Detective Roberts to look further into it, and sure enough, he did. He confirmed that three bodies had been found, two men and one woman.*Her.*

Her body was discovered, yet I can't shake the feeling that somehow, I received false information.

Now I can't help but wonder about the person who started it. Tate may be dead now, but I don't, for a second, believe that the threat to us is over—even if Rowen and King are naïve enough to believe it.

This fire proves it. Someone is coming after us. They're launching a personal attack on the Triad. There will be hell to pay for the sorry fucker who believes he can come after us and succeed. It's time we come together and take back the control of our city. Starting with the person responsible for setting fire to our businesses.

I'm pacing back and forth the length of the living room at the penthouse when the front door clicks open, and in walks King and Rowen. They're each wearing a deadly expression that's aimed right at me. It pains me that this is what has become of my brothers and me. Once so close, and now we're barely able to be in the same room as each other.

"I've been on the phone with Vlad and Maverick, and they're looking into it. Whoever set the fire was careful. They wiped the video footage, so they're trying to see what they can recover, if anything," King explains, making himself comfortable by getting a beer from the fridge and throwing himself on the couch.

Meanwhile, Rowen stays where he is, hands in his pockets and eyes narrowed in on me, and me alone.

Of my two brothers, Ro is the one taking Tate's death the hardest. He's the most guarded, and Tate was the first woman that he's ever lowered his guard for and let in completely. He's glaring at me, but I don't have time to cuddle him. It's been three months; it's time to move the fuck on and get on with life.

I dismiss him with my eyes; my attention turning toward King. "Another fucking fire," I growl. "This is unacceptable. Two of our businesses have gone up in flames. We need to take better security precautions."

*ashes*

"Already a step ahead of you. Security has been increased at our most popular businesses, and we are working on getting extra employees involved so the rest of our businesses are protected," King says from his spot on the couch, beer in hand, looking mighty fucking calm. His calmness enrages me.

I'm so angry and lost in my fury that I don't even hear Ro's phone ping. I don't realize what's happening until King pulls me out of my head by slapping my shoulder and shoving Rowen's phone toward me.

I read the text on the screen, frowning.

> Unknown: You help me, I'll help you.
> Give me what I want, and I'll give you
> what you want.

"What the fuck is that supposed to mean?" I snap, handing the phone back to King, who then tosses it to Rowen. "What the fuck does he want?"

"Three months ago, he wanted Tate. He took her, and now she's dead. What else is there for him to want?" King replies, shaking his head in disbelief.

"Reply to the text. Ask what he thinks we want," I say, making eye contact with Rowen for the first time in weeks. He doesn't speak, only nods, then begins typing on his phone.

A few minutes later, it chimes again, and he turns the screen to allow King and me to see the response.

> Unknown: Sebastian.

Rolling his eyes, King stands before speaking. "How the fuck does he expect us to know what he wants? He already got what he wanted three months ago."

"It doesn't make any sense. The texts stopped completely. Two of our businesses are burned to the ground, and the texts start back up," I say, pacing the room. "That's not a coincidence. This fucker is responsible." Pulling my phone from the front pocket of my jeans, I dial Travis, a member of our tech team who's able to dig into anyone we need him to.

He answers quickly, and I blurt out, "Travis, I need you to track the last number that texted Rowen's phone. See if you can find anything out. Report back immediately."

"Will do. Is it the unknown number again?"

"Yes. I know you couldn't find anything last time, but it's been three months since that last text, so I'm hoping the bastard got sloppy. Maybe we can get a location. Let me know right away if you find anything."

"Yes, sir."

"I'm going to Luigi's and the warehouse. I'll see if there's anything left behind that we—or the police—missed the first time we were there," Rowen says, not waiting for a response before he walks out the door, letting it slam behind him.

"I see he's still got a stick up his ass."

"What do you expect, Eli? He loved her, and you know that. You know their history, so I'm not sure why you're so surprised that he's taking it as hard as he is," King scolds me, his eyes narrowing into a glare.

"He needs to get over it."

"We can't all be heartless assholes like you. Sorry you've never been in love and don't know how it feels." His words pause me.

Like Rowen, King follows his footsteps and walks out of our penthouse, leaving me with the guilt I try to keep buried.

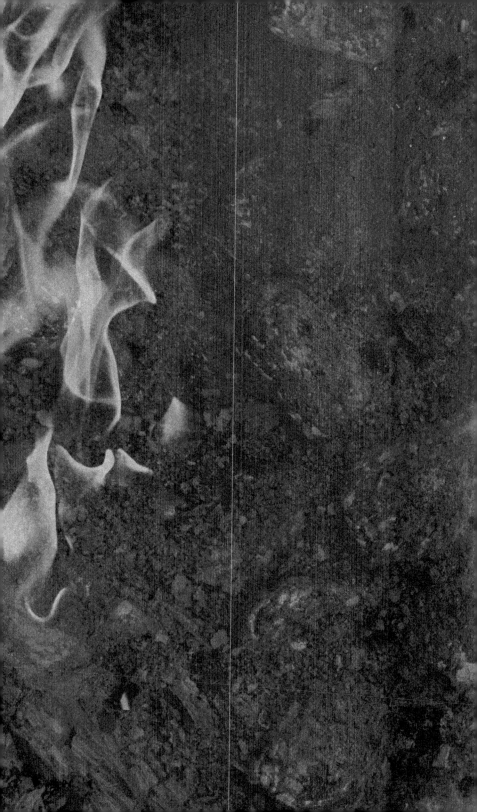

# THREE
*King*

Three months of radio silence from the unknown fucker, and now all of a sudden, he's back. I'm assuming this "unknown fucker" is a male.

Since the day we received the first text a few months ago, we've spent countless hours trying to trace the person on the other end of the phone, hoping to get any information possible to help us find out who's responsible; unfortunately, every attempt we've made has been unsuccessful. The number doesn't trace back to anyone. It's frustrating as fuck, considering we pay our tech and security team more than enough to figure this shit out.

When we received the most recent text yesterday, Eli called Travis to trace the number, and as expected, it was another dead end.

No matter how much our tech and security team digs, nothing's ever found. Every attempt for months comes up short. Whoever this fucker is, he's damn good at covering himself.

He's so good that not even Travis, the best hacker we have, can trace the number and nail it to a specific location. According to him, it's an untraceable burner phone.

I'm in the middle of a workout at the cabin when my phone chimes. I instantly shelve my weights, frantic to read what this motherfucker has to say.

I've been waiting for this.

I know who's texting before I even look at my phone, considering no one else texts me anymore.

Since we realized how easy it is to hack phones and even send false texts, we've all decided to stick to calling so we can hear each other's voices and know our conversations are legit. We've been taking every possible precaution. I had suggested we all get new phones and numbers, but Rowen had a feeling that we'd be hearing from the faceless fuck again and said we shouldn't.

Snatching my phone from the floor where it's sitting beside my water bottle, I grab my towel and wipe away my sweat.

I stare at my phone, my jaw clenched as I read the words.

**Unknown: Ding dong, you have a delivery.**

I stare, confused by the words, but I'm not confused for long because with my next breath, I hear it—the doorbell. I angrily throw my towel to the floor with a huff, jogging my way up the stairs and toward the front door.

Our cabin is secluded, and no one *should* know where the fuck it's located. We sure as fuck don't have deliveries out here. Mail gets delivered to Eli at our office in the city.

Only those in our inner circle know where our cabin is.

Once upstairs, I grab my gun and carefully make my way to the door, gun loaded and ready to be used if needed. With a quick breath, I pull open the front door, scowling at what I find on the other side.

Rowen looks up at me with an expression that matches mine. He stands, holding an unmarked manila envelope in his hands.

"I just got a fucking text," I explain, lowering my gun.

"I just got here. I saw this at the door but didn't see anyone around." He brushes past me, rushing into the house with the envelope in his hands. I follow behind him, eager to find out what the fuck is inside the envelope.

"What did your text say?" he asks, setting the envelope on the kitchen counter and pulling his phone from his pocket. This is his first time in the cabin since we lost Tate. He's refused to step foot on this property until today.

Setting my gun on the counter, I toss him my phone, allowing him to read the text. "What are you doing here, Ro?" I ask.

"To talk, but that can wait. Let's open this up."

"Fine. I'll call Eli, and then we'll open it," I say, reaching for my phone.

"No, fuck that. Let's open it right now. I'm not waiting for Eli, and I will no longer bow down like a bitch to him. I'm done doing whatever he wants, jumping every time he says to jump, and trusting him blindly.

Look at what happened last time we trusted his word." He shakes his head. "We're supposed to be equals, but we're anything but." A smirk tugs at my lips at his words. I'm glad my brother is just as done with being a bitch boy as I am.

Things are about to change, and Eli can either accept it or fuck off. "Glad to hear you say that, brother. Let's open this shit." I grin, slapping him on the back. Rubbing my hands together, I reach for the folder and look it over carefully. There's no address, meaning it didn't arrive via the postal service. It was hand delivered, which is worse, because that proves this unknown fucker knows our location.

I'm ready to open the envelope when I realize something. "This fucker had to come here to deliver this. I never received a notification from the alarm. Can you check it? We need to check the cameras too. We'll see if we caught anything." Rowen nods while I carefully open the seal and pull out the contents. "What the actual fuck." My thick brows pull together as I look over the photograph.

"What the fuck is that?" Rowen hisses, grabbing the photo from my hand. Shaking my head, I lean down to pick up the paper that fell out of the folder and read it as adrenaline pumps fast throughout my body.

*Bring her to me, and I'll tell you where you can find him.*

What the actual fuck?!

"Look at this," Ro says, shoving the photo at me. He takes the note as I study the photo. My fingers twitch with the need to be wrapped around the fucker's throat. The picture is of Tate's piece-of-shit husband, Sebastian. It's a photo of him standing beside his car, pumping gas. The picture was taken from a distance, but there's no doubt it's him.

"I thought Eli was still having someone keeping tabs on him? We should know his whereabouts; we don't need to get information from this shithead. And who the fuck is he talking about? Bring *who* to him?" Rowen sighs, running a hand through his dark hair.

He makes a good point. Months ago, Eli assured us that Sebastian would be watched. Eli said when the time was right, he'd make sure Sebastian was delivered to us so Ro and I could give him a taste of his own medicine. Something tells me that Eli failed to keep good on his promise.

With twitching fingers, I grab my phone and dial the man in question. His calm voice answers on the second ring. "King, brother, what can I do for you?"

"Hey, bro, I just wanted to check in and see if there's been any updates or movement from Sebastian," I say, trying to keep my voice calm, careful not to alert him. I don't fucking trust him anymore. "Ro and I are thinking of showing up at his house tonight. He still home?" Eli had told us that he had our tech team hack into Sebastian's home security system. He even showed us the indoor cameras, allowing us to see inside the ridiculous, oversized glass house.

There's a long silence that tells me what I already know. Eli isn't keeping tabs on Sebastian. "Eli, please tell me that you've kept tabs on that soon-to-be dead piece of shit." His sigh fills the silence.

"We have more important things to worry about than the husband of a dead woman. She's gone, and it's time we focus on our business," he says unapologetically.

I can practically feel my blood boiling in my veins. "When did you stop watching him?"

"The night of the house fire." Her body was barely even cold when he stopped watching Sebastian. "Come home, brother. We have work to do."

Doing my best to refrain from freaking out on him, I force out a simple, "Sure." After hanging up, I meet Rowen's gaze.

"What did he say?" he inquires.

"You're right. We can't trust Eli. We're on our own, and we shouldn't tell him about receiving this picture or the text." He nods.

"Do you think we should trust this anonymous fucker? Trust that he's a step ahead of us and knows something that we don't?"

"Right now, we may have to. His message makes it clear that he knows something we don't," I say, picking up the photograph again, staring at the fucker responsible for hurting my butterfly. The bastard used to beat his wife, and because of that, I'm going to give him a taste of his own medicine. Right now, I've got revenge on my mind.

Revenge will come to the man who hit his wife. And vengeance will come to all the other pieces of shit in Tate's life that hurt her. I know that Ro, Eli, and I are also responsible for hurting her. We played a role in her death, and we will face the consequences of our actions. One way or another, I know we will.

"We need to meet with this person, and then we kill him. If we have to play his game to get close to him, then oh well, we have to do it. We'll kill him and Sebastian. In the meantime, we need to keep this to ourselves. Don't let Eli in on anything," I say, earning a nod from Rowen.

"You're right. We can't trust him, so this stays between us. He's worried about the fires, so let's be the good little puppies he thinks we are and help him figure out who's starting the fires," he says, taking the photo from my hands and sliding it back into the envelope. "Maybe it'll lead us closer to the faceless fuck. He's probably involved anyway."

Only months ago, the three of us were closer than ever; nothing and no one would've ever been able to come between us. And it's all Eli's fault.

The trust is broken. Our bond is broken.

It would take a miracle to restore it.

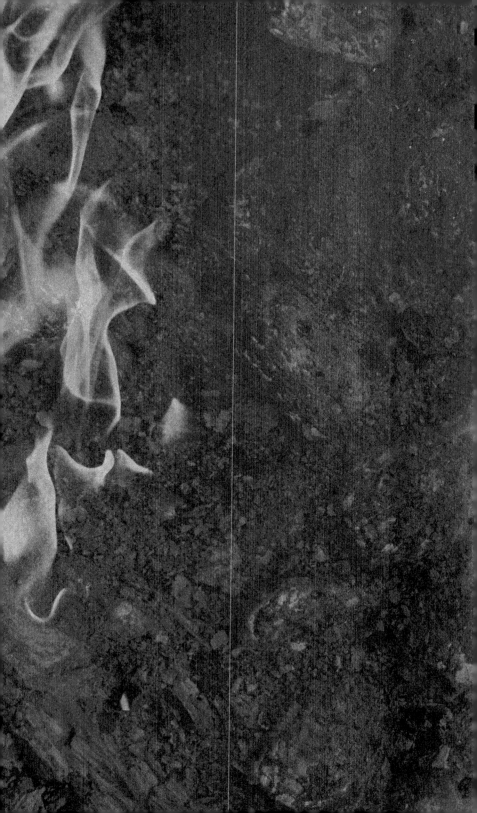

# FOUR
## Raven

I t's been a week since King and I received the text and photo of Sebastian. It's been silent ever since. As we suspected, our security system had been hacked, and the camera footage at our cabin was deleted.

We had Travis and Maverick come over that night to replace the system and ensure it would be secure. We even added more hidden cameras around our property and connected them to different servers. If the fucker returns, he won't be able to hide. One of our many cameras will capture him.

I've taken it upon myself to dig yet again into Tate's background. The faceless bastard once referred to her as *Lee*, so I've been doing my due diligence and spending countless hours with Travis, digging into every piece of her background. It's been tricky, considering she had help from her friend, Ace Jackson. He helped to erase her background and reinvent her.

Travis has also been digging into Ace. I find it odd that his background seems as bare as hers, except for a few details that seem to be planted. For example, he's a great hacker, yet he let the date he moved to town, his address, and his bank information be known.

That's not a coincidence.

At one point, Tate believed that he'd never do anything to hurt her. She said Ace couldn't possibly be responsible for anything, but I think otherwise, which is why I'm having Travis dig further into him.

Sooner or later, we're going to uncover all of her secrets, and I genuinely fucking hope that it'll put us closer to discovering the identity of the unknown sender.

This morning, we received another delivery from him. This time, it was to our office, and thankfully King and I hid it before Eli had a chance to see it. This time, there wasn't a text along with it; just a photo of a brunette woman holding a blonde child—probably three or four years old—in her arms. The child's face was hidden in the crook of her neck as the woman walked out of a grocery store. When we flipped the photo over, there was something on the back.

Not just something.

Names.

**Rachel and Olivia Hollis.**

That's it. That's all the information we were given. We immediately began searching the names, hoping to get answers as to why this photo was sent to us and what's so special about the mother and child in the picture.

The note that came with Sebastian's photo said to *bring her*, so I'm assuming the *her* he's referring to is the woman in the photo.

It's now 5:00 p.m., and I'm still sitting inside the nearly empty office I claimed as mine a few years ago when we started our business. King and I are rarely here, as we prefer to be doing groundwork rather than wearing a suit and sitting in an office all day, as Eli prefers.

That's why he makes a great CEO. He enjoys being front and center and navigating the business world, while King and I prefer to get our hands dirty and navigate the underworld. It's what we're best at.

The only reason I'm still here is because I've been doing some digging of my own, putting the information I know about Lee to use, and doing a search of my own. Also, I've been waiting for one of our tech or security guys to get back to me with the information I requested on Rachel and Olivia Hollis.

Speaking of which, a tap at my door tears my attention away from my computer screen that is currently loading a search regarding one of the foster homes that I knew Tate/Lee had been in. "Come in!" I call out, watching as the door opens and Malcolm appears.

I hired him four years ago after he'd been discharged from the military, and he's always been the most loyal to me. I trusted him with the photo and to remain discreet and not tell Eli what he's doing for me.

"I don't have much." He clears his throat, getting right to the point. He closes the door before speaking. "Rachel Hollis is thirty-seven years old. Olivia, her daughter, is ten. The photo is a few years old and was taken in Florida, which I confirmed by the car license plates in the background of the picture," he says, walking to my desk and extending a thin file toward me.

Taking the folder, I open it, and my eyes scan over the few pages. "As you can see, there's not much there. Besides age, there's nothing to be found on either of them. No record of birth for either, no employment, bank accounts, or mortgage. Rachel and Olivia Hollis do not exist."

Their pasts have been covered up for a reason. Their identity has been concealed for a fucking reason, just like Tate's has been covered up. I'm convinced now more than ever that this woman has something to do with Tate, and I will figure it out sooner rather than later.

"Thanks for looking into them, Malcolm."

He nods, pointing toward the file in my hands. "That's her address. Don't ask how I got it because it was not the legal way." I make a mental note to give him a raise. I won't ask questions; I never do when it comes to him because I know he uses less than ethical means to get his information.

I have an address which is good enough for me. The faceless fuck wants Rachel, and now I know where she lives. I'm going to visit her, but before I use her as bait, I plan to find out about her connection to Tate.

It's time I get some of my fucking questions answered.

"Thanks, man, I appreciate it. Actually, can you look into something else for me?" He nods, awaiting instruction.

"Remember that house fire three months ago? Look into the bodies that were recovered. The bodies were badly burned and had to be identified with dental records. Look into it. Make sure the three people's identities are correct, and run a full background on them. I want to know everything there is to know."

"You got it. Anything else?"

"That's it. Remember, this stays between us."

Malcolm nods. "Yes, of course." With that, he's gone, leaving me alone with a smug grin about the fact I have Rachel's address and am now one fucking step closer.

After a few minutes, I call King, and he answers on the first ring. "Hey, brother. What did you find?" he asks.

"I have an address. I'll arrange our travel plans and make sure we can leave without Eli noticing. We're going to get some answers," I say, unable to keep the excitement from my voice. This is the best news we've received in a while.

"Fuck yeah!" King shouts through the phone. "Let's do it, brother. It's time to lure out the faceless fucker and end him for good."

That's exactly what we're going to do.

Game fucking on.

# FIVE

*Ace*

M ommy always said I damage pretty things. I've always broken pretty things.

She's a pretty thing, and if *I'm not* careful, I'll break her, too, even though I *don't* want to. I *want* to be gentle, but I also *want* to know how it would feel to hold her life in my hands. I *want* to reach inside her chest and rip her heart out so I'll know how it feels to have the heart of a pretty girl.

Mommy was always afraid I'd do something terrible and break another pretty thing, and that's why she never let me go to school and be around other kids. I've always been big for my age. My hands are too big, and I'm too tall. Kids my age are scared of me because of my size. I have my father's size instead of my petite mommy's size.

My mommy was pretty, and I broke her. Just like she always said, I ruin all pretty things, even if I don't mean to.

I hadn't meant to kill Mommy; it just happened. I should've listened when Father told us to stop running in the house and to pick up my toys. I hadn't meant to leave my toys scattered, but when Mommy started playing a game of tag with me, I forgot to put the toys away. Despite my father's warnings, we kept playing.

We kept playing until I broke another pretty thing—my mommy.

She tripped over one of my toys and fell down the stairs, hitting her head. The crimson liquid that pooled out of her head was so pretty that I just had to coat my hands in it. It was warm and sticky, and it wasn't my fault that my young cock swelled in my pajama pants.

I knew what to do when my body reacted and got aroused; the porn videos I watched had taught me. Plus, I'd seen Father and Mommy have sex enough times to understand. I'd seen him wrap his hand around his swollen cock plenty of times.

The smell of my mommy's blood, the feel of it on my hand, and the gurgling noise she had made were too much for me. So, I pulled down my pants, coated my cock in her slippery blood, and wrapped my fist over my shaft until heavy ropes of white cum shot out all over Mommy's heaving chest.

She stopped breathing just as Father found us. He was disgusted at the sight of me with my pants down, bloody hands and cock, and my dead mommy beside me, covered in my cum.

That was the day he locked me away in the attic and stopped loving me.

Then one day, Father got a new family. He loved his new wife and stepdaughter more than me. He loved his stepdaughter so much that he visited her bedroom late at night after his wife was asleep.

I hated my stepsister. She wasn't pretty, but at least she kept Father from visiting my room, as he used to after Mommy died.

My new stepsister wasn't pretty, and I only hurt pretty things, so she had nothing to worry about, but her mother thought I was the one visiting her room at night instead of Father.

They sent me away. Father didn't want me anymore, and neither did his new family. I went into foster care because of them.

My foster siblings hated me and were scared of me, but who could blame them? I didn't speak, and I towered over everyone. No one wanted to be my friend, talk to me, or even say anything nice about me.

No one wanted me until her.

The pretty girl with turquoise eyes, a halo of blonde hair, and a smile that made me want to smile too.

Her caseworker brought her inside of the house, and instead of looking at me with fear like everyone else, she looked at me and smiled.

One smile from her, and I promised myself that I'd never break another pretty thing for as long as I lived—as long as she continued to give me her smiles.

She's here because she was unwanted, too, but not anymore.

I want her. She'll be my pretty thing, and I'll protect her.

Lee will be the only pretty thing in my life that I'll never break.

# SIX

*Ace*

### THREE MONTHS AGO

"The police have confirmed that three are dead due to a house fire a week ago. They are still investigating but have no reason to believe that foul play was involved. The police have not yet released the names of the victims."

I sit on the floor in front of the TV with my legs crisscrossed in front of me, watching the news report with a wide smile that reaches from ear to ear. I'm giddy like a child at Disneyland for the first time. I've never been to Disneyland, but I'm sure my excitement is similar to how a child would feel.

The police don't need to release the victim's name. I already know who died. It wasn't accidental. They found what they were supposed to find, and the rest went according to plan. I love when things work out perfectly.

A sound coming from within my house has me turning the volume down on the TV. The news lady's voice fades into the background with each click of the volume button. I stand, stretching my limbs as

I reach my full height of six-foot-six. I'm tall and fucking love it when people are forced to look up at me.

My steps are quick and heavy as I stalk down the dark hallway searching for my pretty thing who thinks she can run from me.

I hear the light footsteps running away from me, but I'm quicker than my prey. I have the advantage of having long legs and knowing every hiding place within my house. The house has eyes, and there's nowhere to hide.

With three giant and quick steps, my eyes settle on my prey. I lunge forward, wrapping my muscular arms around her small waist. She lets out a yelp as I lift her from the ground. She struggles to twist in my arms until we're face-to-face.

At the sight of her, a wide, sinister smile spreads across my face. "Are you trying to run from me? You should know by now that you can run, but you'll never be able to hide from me." She shakes her head quickly; droplets of water splashing me in the face from her dripping wet hair that's been freshly cut and colored. Her once long black hair is gone, and now her hair is shoulder length and platinum with streaks of silver and violet roots.

"I'd never run from you." She smiles, wrapping her limbs around me like a koala. I always have to be careful when it comes to my pretty thing. I don't ever want to break her. As much as I'd love to drown in her blood and have the warm thick liquid coat my skin, I'd miss her too much if she were broken.

She's the one thing I cannot break because my life would never be the same without her. I need Lee as much as I need to breathe.

I haven't been breathing while she's been away, but now that she's back, I'm never letting her go. Not again. I made that mistake before, and I'll forever regret it.

"On second thought, maybe you should run from me. It makes

my dick hard." To prove my point, I grip her hips tightly and pull her body down my torso until my hard cock is poking her barely covered bottom.

Lee throws her head back, exposing her creamy throat to me, and laughs. "What doesn't get you hard?" She sneers, unwrapping herself and climbing down from my body to stand in front of me. "You get hard whenever I *breathe* around you. I'm beginning to think that your dick never goes down, and you're hard twenty-four seven." She's right. My dick hasn't deflated once since I rescued her from that house. It doesn't help that she smells sweet, has a warm body, and she looks at me like she wants me to destroy her.

As much as I want to bend her over the couch and force myself into her tight little pussy, I'm not sure I'd know what to do with her.

I've watched enough porn to know the basics but have never known what it feels like to be inside a wet pussy.

I dream of how it would feel to have a warm cunt wrapped around me and be able to feel the pulsing of her walls. I imagine it's the most wonderful feeling, and I bet it would be even better than using my own hand.

My thoughts cause my engorged cock to throb with desperate desire. Slowly, I wrap my hands around Lee's beautiful neck, admiring her milky skin. She's so fucking flawless, even more so with cuts and bruises on her body; God fucking knows what she had to endure in that basement.

Her pulse quickens under my thumb, but she's not afraid. I can see it in her blue eyes. She's excited to find out what I'm going to do next.

"When I fuck you for the first time, I want your blood on my hands. I want to smear the beautiful crimson all over your pretty little body and fuck you until you're begging me to stop making you bleed."

I search her eyes for a response, knowing I'll never find any judgment because she's just as fucked up as I am.

Her pupils dilate. "Ace." She practically moans my name.

"If I were to slip my hand inside your panties, how wet would you be?"

"Soaked." She clenches her thighs together.

"I want to gag you with your wet panties while I fuck you and make you bleed. That way, you can't scream. Instead of begging me to stop, you'll have to take it. You'll be forced to endure everything I want to do to you." One thing I love about her is that she never pressures me into taking the next step.

Lee knows I'm a virgin. She also knows about my fetish for breaking pretty things. With her, it'll be different. I'll be making love to her and doing something I've never done before.

We both want it, but I'm scared. I can tell her what I want and need, but when it comes to having to do it, I'm fucking terrified.

My biggest fear is that I'll lose all control and kill her, and that's not what I want. She's not like the other women. They weren't special, and they were disposable.

The women who formerly satisfied my needs were prostitutes I picked up on the street. They got into my car and went to hotels with me willingly. They were willing...up to the point I started making them bleed so I could use their blood to coat my hand before wrapping it around my cock.

I loved watching them die while I jerked off, then came on their chests. The sight of my white cum mixing with their blood was such a beautiful sight. That sight alone always urged me to come again.

It's been six months since I've satisfied my needs. Now, the urge is back, and I need to be inside of Lee before I explode.

"Ace," she whispers my name, pulling me from my thoughts. She wraps her arms around my neck as her warm body melts against mine. "Don't be afraid. We're not going to do anything you're not ready for."

"I love you, my pretty thing. Do you know that?" I wrap my arms protectively around her body. "You are mine now. I will always protect you, even if that means protecting you from me." I don't expect a response. It's hard for her to use those three words, and with her history, I understand.

Every time I look at her, I see her flaws and her trauma that's wrapped inside a beautiful exterior package. She is so fucked up that it fascinates me to learn precisely how fucked up she is.

She's endured an abusive childhood, both physically and sexually. She was in an abusive marriage, too. She's been through much more than I could ever imagine. Still, she's standing tall as ever. She looks at me like I'm her savior, despite all the shit she's been through. She should be afraid of me and be frightened of the things I want to do to her, yet here she is.

Two weeks ago, I rescued her from that burning building. When I went inside, the flames had already been extinguished, but it was smokey. She had passed out from the smoke, but I was able to get her out of there. After having her properly cared for by a doctor and countless breathing treatments to clear her lungs, she's good as new. Her gunshot wound is healing nicely, as is the rest of her. She's perfect, as always.

"I have a plan, and I would love your help with it."

My curiosity piques. She's been resting for two weeks and is already up to something. "I'll do anything for you. What is it?"

"I want revenge."

"On who?"

"On everyone," she states, matter-of-fact. "I want revenge on all the piece-of-shit foster parents I had who used me as a punching bag and the foster fathers who thought they could touch me." The thought of anyone touching her without consent angers me beyond belief. I'd love to rip those mother fuckers to shreds with my bare hands. "I want revenge on my piece-of-shit husband who made me feel worthless. I want revenge on everyone who has ever made me feel weak." Her eyes sparkle with her bloodlust. "And, I want revenge on the three that made me trust them, then shot me and left me to burn alive."

Eli, King, and Rowen.

My pretty thing wants revenge, and that's exactly what she will get.

"Okay," I agree, willing to rip my own heart out and offer it to her if she were to ask. "Tell me how I can help you." With a devious twinkle in her eyes and a smile on her face, my pretty thing tells me everything she's been thinking about since the night of the fire.

How lucky I am to have someone who trusts me so deeply that she's willing to ask for my help with her evil plan for revenge.

"Who are we starting with?"

"With them." Her hand slips between us, and she grips on to my hard, pulsating cock that seemed to have gotten even harder when she began sharing the details of her plan with me. "They'll never see it coming." I press my lips against her hungrily, sealing the deal with a kiss.

Ready or not, my pretty thing is coming for the Triad.

# SEVEN

*Lee*

## THREE MONTHS LATER

Everyone says death is painful, but I beg to differ. Death is easy; it's living that's hard. I've been dead before, twice actually, and both times it was easy. It's easy to pretend I don't exist, conceal my identity, and become someone else. I did it when I faked my death to escape my bastard of a husband, and I did it again when the men I loved left me for dead.

I was foolish to allow myself to fall for their words and false promises of security. I should've known better. After all, I've experienced broken promises of love and safety time and time again.

Like a fool, I had too much faith in Rowen, King, and Eli.

Especially Rowen. I believed that our past meant something, that we were brought back together for a reason, and that he was still the same boy that protected me from our foster father all those years ago.

I've always been a pushover and too forgiving. Too naïve and desperate for a happy ending, I've consistently ignored the red flags waving in my face. Sometimes, I wondered how many times my trust would have to be destroyed before I learned my lesson and stopped trusting people.

Unfortunately, the answer came to me the night I was left for dead in a burning house. I saw the haunting look in King's eyes and the cold look in Eli's when they walked away. At that moment, I knew I'd been too trusting again and put my faith in the wrong people.

I don't believe in God, but I remember praying for a miracle. I prayed for someone to save me, to love me enough to rescue me, and to have one person, just one person, that I'd be able to trust wholeheartedly who would never betray me.

My prayer was answered, and I was rescued by the person I least expected.

The only person who has never let me down or betrayed my trust. One person who, in my desperate time of need, came to my rescue yet again. He's saved me more times than I can count and might be the only person on the face of the earth that I can say I trust completely.

After all, he knows everything about me, including my biggest secret I'd die to protect. A secret that I'd risk myself and my safety to keep protected. And I know he'd do the same.

It had been years since I saw him, but I felt instant relief. Honestly, I thought he had forgotten everything about me and moved on. Instead, I learned that he's been watching after me all along.

If only he would've been able to rescue me from Sebastian...But better late than never.

I was nine years old when I met Ace Jackson in foster care. He was three years older, tall and lean, and a total introvert. He was too shy to speak to anyone, and the girls in our home hated him because he stared.

For a while, everyone thought he was mute. Then one day, two weeks later, he surprised me by giving me a rose he'd picked from our foster mother's rosebush. She whipped him with a belt for picking it, but he didn't apologize. That was the first time anyone heard him speak, and all he said was, "Pretty things deserve pretty things."

At the time, I didn't understand what he meant. But a few days later, he called me his pretty thing, and it made sense.

Since then, Ace has been my best friend.

When Rowen killed Greg, I ran away and called Ace, and he promised to help me. He was sixteen and had no money, but he had an aunt who was registered as a foster parent. After one call to her, his Aunt Willa picked me up that night. She wouldn't take Ace, claiming her house was too full, and he was too old, but she accepted me. We thought it would be a good idea, but little did we know we were opening the door to hell.

Ace didn't know what his uncle and cousin were doing to me—the things his aunt ignored.

Willa told me that Ace didn't care about me and stopped calling me. Meanwhile, she told Ace that I had a boyfriend and was succeeding with ballet and didn't want anything to do with him anymore.

After I killed his family and left their burning house with a baby in my belly, there was only one place I could go and one person I desperately wanted to talk to.

Ace and I reconnected when I was seventeen. He was twenty and making serious money by hacking online poker games. He had enough money to support us both, so for a while, we lived together.

Eventually, I wanted to move on with my life and asked that he reinvent my background, which he did.

He had always been good at computers, but over the years, his hacking only got better.

Ace never blamed me for killing his family, but he never stopped blaming himself for what happened to me while in their care. He was always so fucking remorseful that it ended up driving us apart, so I moved out to continue my ballet career. We spoke occasionally. He kept a protective eye on me, but we were never the same.

Then one day, I met Sebastian, and Ace backed off completely. He believed I was happy and left me alone until the night of the fire.

Before that night, I hadn't seen him in years, but he was there when I needed him the most.

Now, we've spent the last three months sharing every detail of what our lives have been like over the past few years. He admitted that when I killed Lee and left Sebastian, he followed me here, staying in the shadows and watching over me as I became Tate.

When he saw me with Rowen, he assumed I was safe because he knew that I was safe with Ro years ago.

Little did I know that all this time he's been twelve feet away watching me, trying to redeem himself for the mistakes made in the past.

Two days ago, Ace informed me of the photo of Rachel and Olivia that was sent to King and Rowen. He played his role well, acting as if he didn't know who they were. When Malcolm asked him to assist with digging into both mine and Sebastian's backgrounds to search for the names, he did, but of course, nothing came up.

Rachel and Olivia do not exist on paper, and there's no record of me ever being connected to them. So, how does *he* know about them?

I'm not worried about King and Rowen seeing their photo. I'm concerned about the fucker that sent them the picture and why. I know exactly who it was; it's the same person that used to call me little bird and bring me white roses after every ballet recital. The same person responsible for me being held in that basement.

The bastard is supposed to be dead, but clearly, he's returned from the grave to torture me a little bit more. As if he didn't damage me enough while I lived in his hell hole of a house.

I'll never regret the day I set his house on fire and smiled while his family burned. The news reports said three bodies were found, and he was one of the deceased. Just like me, the dead has a way of rising.

It's him. I fucking know it.

He knows about Olivia and Rachel, meaning he's been following me for much longer than I've been aware of. That's the only possible explanation of how he'd know about them.

It's been years since I've seen them, but I assume he must've followed me the last time I visited them and discovered they were important to me. I can only fucking pray that he hasn't put two and two together and figured out exactly who Olivia is. I'll risk my life to keep her safe.

It took two days for Ace to clear his schedule so he could take me to see them. He's working for the Triad and told me how hectic things have been within their organization. They're busy looking for a rat in their empire and trying to find the person responsible for setting fire to their businesses. Meanwhile, the rat is sitting at the table across from them, and they don't even know.

Considering Rachel lives ten hours away and we have to drive, we decided to leave during the night so we'd be able to arrive in the morning and have as much time as possible to pack up Rachel and Olivia and move them since their location has been discovered.

It's my fault. I should've never been naïve enough to believe they'd be able to stay safe and hidden. My past has a way of coming back to bite me, and I should've been prepared for it.

"Do you want me to come in with you?" Ace asks, stealing my attention away from my thoughts. I stare, unblinking at the small gray house with the white picket fence, watching as Rachel moves around in the house. I have a clear view of her from the open window.

Clearly, she's gotten comfortable as well because she used to never leave her blinds and curtains open. I've been sitting in front of her house for nearly twenty minutes, and she's yet to notice.

"No, I'll be okay. Stay here and keep watch." I exhale a breath I wasn't aware I was holding, then quickly lean across the middle console to steal a kiss for support. I try to pull back, but Ace wraps a hand around my head and tightens his fingers in my hair, twirling my short strands of platinum hair between his rough fingers.

"My pretty thing," he groans against my lips, his touch calming my racing heart. "Go." He pulls back, hits the unlock button with a click, and lets me out of the car.

I've barely unlatched the white gate and started walking up the driveway when the door opens, and a little blonde-haired beauty comes running full speed toward me. "Aunty Lee!" she screams, throwing herself into my arms.

I'm an only child, and I don't have a niece. I just hope she'll never know that.

"Oh my goodness, Olivia, look how big you are!" I can't help but smile happily whenever I'm around the almost ten-year-old spitfire.

She looks up at me, her bright blue eyes matching mine perfectly. "Mommy is inside. Let's go." She grabs my hand, leading me inside the small house.

Fear and worry flash in Rachel's brown eyes when she sees me. She quickly looks around and draws the blinds and curtains like she should've already fucking done.

"Aunty Lee, want to see my bedroom? Mommy got me new furniture, and it's awesome!"

"In a minute, sweetie. Let me talk to Mommy for a little bit, okay?" I take her small hands in mine and study her features carefully. The same features that mirror my own. She may not notice it now, but I worry that as she gets older, she'll realize she looks more like me than the woman she calls Mommy; she might ask questions. As far as she knows, Rachel is her mom. That's how it needs to stay.

My sweet, innocent girl doesn't know any better. She believes the lies she's been told since birth.

For what it's worth, Rachel is her mother. She may have grown inside my body, fed from my breast, and look exactly like me, but I'm not her mother. I'm just the woman who brought her into the world. I didn't raise her, teach her to walk, talk, or kiss her cuts and bruises.

I may be her birth mom, but Rachel is her mother in every other sense of the word.

"Go to your room, honey," Rachel says. Olivia sighs and nods. Turning around, she disappears into the hallway. I stand and Rachel opens her arms and pulls me in for a tight hug.

Rachel and I met during my time in foster care. I had gone to a foster kid support group, and she was one of the volunteers. She's ten years older than me, but she took me under her wing and, in a way, became my family. We kept in touch as much as we could over the years, and when I was nine months pregnant, I showed up on her front step after setting fire to my last foster home with the family inside.

She took pity on me, gave me a place to live, and when Olivia was born, I begged her to take her and raise her, and she did. Rachel isn't able to have children of her own, so Olivia is the only child she'll ever have.

Thanks to Ace, Rachel Hollis has been erased from all records. She and Olivia are ghosts, and I hate that they have to live this way. Ace ensures there is always money in a bank account he set up for Rachel since she can't have a regular job.

She gave up so much to help me and raise Olivia, but I know that she doesn't regret it. Plus, she's told me plenty of times that she doesn't regret anything because I gave her the chance to be a mother.

I owe Rachel everything.

"What's going on, Lee? You never visit anymore unless you have bad news." Worry laces her tone. I hate how true that is, but it hasn't been safe for me to visit. Besides, I don't want to confuse Olivia by having me around constantly.

Plus, it's hard for me to watch my vibrant, beautiful daughter call someone else Mommy. I don't regret my decision to give her to Rachel, but I'd be lying if I said it wasn't painful at times.

"Come, let's go in the kitchen and talk," she says, taking my hand and leading me into the small white kitchen. I sit at the table while she rushes through, making a new pot of coffee. We wait silently for it to brew, the bitter aroma filling the air.

Once she brings two mugs and a bottle of French vanilla creamer to the table, I hedge, "Do you remember me telling you about the last foster home I was in? With Willa and Bill and their son, Colton?"

Her eyes widen. She remains silent but nods. She knows what happened, and she knows one of them is Olivia's biological father.

"Well, the dead has risen, and you and Olivia have been discovered. You have to move. Ace is helping me set up a safe house for the two of you." Silently, she pours a little creamer into her coffee, then slides the bottle across to me. I happily pour nearly half of the bottle of creamer into my coffee, laughing to myself at the fact she remembered how I drank my coffee and that she gave me a nearly half-empty cup.

"Olivia has moved six times in nearly ten years. It's not fair to uproot her life again when she's comfortable here." She sighs and takes my coffee to the microwave to heat up since it's now cold from all the creamer I added. "I don't understand how you can drink so much creamer," she mumbles, rolling her dark brown eyes. "Is Ace with you?" she asks, returning to the table with my cup of hot creamer and a splash of coffee.

"He's outside. He brought me here." I sip the hot white liquid carefully. "Look, Rach, I know it's not easy to uproot your lives again, and I'm sorry, but it's not safe here anymore. Pack only the necessities, and I'll be back to help you move tomorrow morning."

She looks at me, her eyes glossy with unshed tears. "Of course, we'll go. I'm so sorry that you have to live your life always looking over your shoulder." She reaches across the table and takes my hands in hers.

"Who came back from the dead, and how do you know?" she asks, sipping her coffee.

"Colton. Too much has happened, and I know it's him." She nods, not asking me to explain any further. "Please, Rachel, pack what you can tonight, and I'll help you with the rest in the morning. I want to see Olivia before I go." She nods as I stand.

I've just opened the door to Olivia's purple-painted bedroom when my phone beeps in my back pocket. Olivia is sound asleep on her bed, hugging her teddy bear. She must've fallen asleep while waiting for me.

Quietly, I close the door and pull my phone from my pocket.

**Ace: Your Triad fuckers are here. I'm around the block waiting.**

Fuck. Fuck. Fuck!

What the fuck are they doing here?!

On high alert, I rush to where Rachel's standing at the sink, washing our cups. I grab her shoulders and make her face me. "There are some men outside who will be knocking in a second. Do not tell them I was here, and do not act suspicious. You are a normal woman and have a husband who will be home any second." She nods, knowing better than to ask questions. "Pack your stuff, and I'll be back. Keep the doors locked and the curtains closed."

"Lee, I understand. Now, hurry up. You can explain later." The doorbell chimes, and her eyes widen.

Giving her a quick hug, I slip into the laundry room where the back door is located. I unlock it carefully, just as Rachel answers the door and I hear the voice that I haven't heard in three months.

Silently, I sneak out the back and run away from the house, going down the street to where I know Ace is waiting.

The moment I reach our car, I yank open the door, climb in, and Ace speeds away, not wanting to chance staying a second longer.

"Did you know they were coming?" I ask, reaching into the backseat to grab my black backpack.

"Fuck no. I knew they'd become aware of their existence, but I never heard any of them saying they would be making a trip here. Last I heard, they were trying to gather information on Rachel and find out how she's connected to you."

"I think it's time to say hello to Rowen."

"Why? They all think you're dead. Why would you want to make it known that you're alive? How can you get revenge if you announce that you didn't die in that fire as they thought?"

I shrug. "My plan is on pause. It's only a matter of time until they figure out who Olivia is, and I need to protect her. She's what matters right now." He doesn't say anything else, only nods and places his hand on my thigh while we drive in silence.

Rowen and King were led to Rachel and Olivia for a reason. If cutting my revenge short and letting them know I'm alive will keep Rach and Olivia safe, then it's what I have to do, whether I like it or not.

My plan has ended. Now, I'm winging it and hoping for the best.

# EIGHT

*Raven*

"Are you sure this is the right address?" King asks for the hundredth time as he stares at the small house. His eyes are squinted as he compares the house in front of us to the house in the photo that Malcolm sent over.

"Yes, I'm sure. Malcolm confirmed this is where the woman in the photo, Rachel Hollis, lives."

"Fine. Let's make it quick. I'm starving and tired," he whines.

I chuckle, slapping him on the back. "We'll find out what she knows, then we'll go check in to the hotel." Rolling his eyes, he smashes his finger against the doorbell, taking a step back so I'm front and center.

The door creaks open, and in the doorframe stands Rachel Hollis, the woman in the photo. It's clear the picture is several years old, but she still looks the same. "Hello? Can I help you?" she asks, her eyes looking us up and down. She's trying to hide her nerves, but it's obvious she's afraid of the two burly men showing up at her door unannounced.

"Hello Miss, sorry to bother you, but we're having car trouble. Neither of us has cell reception. Do you have a phone we could use?" I ask, flashing a bright white smile, doing my fucking best to ease her mind and keep her from slamming the door in my face.

Out of my brothers, Eli is the charmer, but considering he's out of the picture due to my lack of trust in him, I'm left to charm Rachel Hollis. I'm just hoping she's dumb enough to let us inside her home or reveal something useful.

To be completely honest, I don't have a plan. I'm going rogue. I've had two days plus the drive up here to be thinking of a plan, but instead, I spent the time thinking about how the hell this woman is connected to Tate and why the unknown fucker wants her.

King and I plan to use her to lure him out of hiding, but that can be difficult, considering she has a child that will most likely be in the home. We may not live by the greatest moral codes, but we'd never hurt a woman or child; at least, not willingly. Not again.

We learned our lesson when we attempted to trade Tate months ago. This time, we only need unknown to *believe* that we're going to give him Rachel Hollis when we truly have no intention of doing that, considering it's likely he'd kill her since we already know what he's capable of.

"There's a mechanic about a mile up the road on the left. Start walking. You can't miss it," she says, pointing in the direction she's telling us to walk.

"Do you mind if we use your phone?" King chimes in, attempting to flash a friendly smile, but instead, it comes off creepy and untrusting.

I knew she wouldn't allow us inside or spend much time speaking with us. Why would she? It doesn't take a genius to figure out we're dangerous men. One look at us with our tattoo-covered hands and necks and untrusting aura about us will tell you that.

Rachel opens her mouth to speak, possibly to tell us to fuck off when a small voice comes flowing from down the hallway. "Mommy! Where did A—" The woman shushes her, stopping her from saying anything further.

We can't see the child from where we stand, and Rachel begins closing the door. "Go to the mechanic shop." She slams it shut, and through the door, we hear her sliding multiple locks into place.

With a smirk, I turn and follow King toward our parked SUV.

"That was pointless," he complains after we're both inside, and I'm driving toward our hotel.

"No, it wasn't."

"How do you figure?"

"She has several locks on the door but was trusting enough to undo every one of them and open the door to two strangers when I'm sure she saw us through the peephole. Based on the number of locks, I'm assuming she's the only adult in the home. It's just her and the child," I say, sharing the small details I noticed during our brief encounter. "We'll go back tomorrow morning. And when we do, she won't have a choice but to come with us."

King gives me a nod of approval, rubbing his hands together. "Can't fucking wait."

"I'm ordering room service, then passing the fuck out," King says as we arrive at our hotel. We drove straight here and haven't slept in nearly twenty-four hours. I'm just as exhausted. I'm hoping Malcolm will have answers for us tomorrow about Rachel Hollis's identity, but for now, we need to rest. We know where she lives, and tomorrow we'll be returning to get answers to our questions.

King and I played nicely today, but tomorrow it's unlikely we'll be so kind. My patience is running thin. There's a reason why Rachel and Olivia Hollis don't exist on paper, and I want to know everything I can about them. Especially why they seem to be significant enough that the unknown fucker would send us their photo.

I have too many questions and not enough answers. It's as if I'm being given all the pieces to a puzzle, but the pieces aren't fitting together. I can't connect the dots. So, I'm hoping after a nice meal and a good night's rest, I'll be able to think clearly and connect some of those dots tomorrow.

"Goodnight, brother." King waves, stepping off the elevator once we reach his floor. The hotel we're staying at only had two rooms available, and they're on different floors. I wave him off, then ride up to the next floor.

Entering my keycard into the lock, I push the door open and flick on the lights, stepping inside my empty hotel room. After throwing my duffel bag onto the bed, I strip out of my clothes and walk into the bathroom to take a long, hot shower. The feeling of the scorching water loosening up my tight muscles and relaxing my tired aching body is long overdue.

After finishing up, I wrap the plush towel around my waist and open the bathroom door. I'm immediately met with a gust of steam from the warm and cold air mixing together. A chill from the sudden change in the air temperature causes a shiver to run down my spine.

Walking over to the bed, I dig inside my duffel bag, pull out a clean pair of boxers, and quickly shrug them on.

I'm zipping my bag when the hair on my arms stands, and a sense of awareness washes over me.

*I'm not alone.*

Carefully, without making it obvious, I reach into the side pocket of my bag and pull out my gun. Inhaling, I quickly turn around, raising the weapon at the one person I never expected to see again.

My jaw nearly fucking drops as I look into those crystal blue eyes of hers. Eyes that are always so blue that they almost seem unnatural.

"Tate," I whisper. There's no fucking way it's her. My mind has to be playing tricks on me. I must be fucking dreaming.

She sits on the couch across the room, her eyes never leaving mine. Slowly, she stands and walks toward me until the barrel of my gun is pressed against her forehead.

"Hello, Rowen." Her silky voice has the same baritone I've heard in my mind every night for three months. I've replayed the night of the fire in my head every single night when I close my eyes. I imagine doing things differently and finding a way to protect her. I imagine saving her and her surviving.

After a long moment of silence, the relief I feel seeing her again is washed away and replaced with anger.

So much fucking anger.

She's alive. Tate's alive, and I'm finding out three months later.

What the actual fuck?!

"You're supposed to be dead." I glare, not lowering my gun from where it's pressing against the middle of her forehead.

"Surprise." She shrugs carelessly as if it's no big deal that she's alive when I've spent the last three months thinking I've lost her forever.

"How?" She doesn't know what the fuck I've been going through. What King and I have both been going through. The guilt that we've felt over her death. "I guess I shouldn't be surprised. I should know by now that you're a master of faking your death. You did it to Sebastian. Why not to me too?"

Her lips thin. "That's not fair. You knew why I did what I did with Seb. With you, it wasn't planned. Let's not forget that you, King, and Eli left me for dead. You three abandoned me when you could've easily saved me."

"I should kill you right now. Put a bullet in your brain. That way, at least you won't be a liar anymore. No one will even know you're alive or here."

A smirk spreads across her mouth. "You could, but you won't. Plus, someone knows I'm here." My eyebrows furrow in confusion.

Sighing, I remove the gun from her head, keeping it at my side. "What do you mean? Who knows you're alive?"

"Me," a deep, familiar voice sounds from the side of the room. Turning, I see Travis entering the room and shutting the door behind him.

"Travis? How the fuck did you know she's alive?"

"Ro, I'd like you to meet Ace Jackson," Tate says, quickly taking the gun from my hand and tossing it onto the bed.

My eyes widen in disbelief. "Travis?" I'm genuinely confused. Travis has worked for us for nearly a year, and he came highly recommended by a trustworthy source. From my understanding, he's never been in contact with Tate, so I'm not sure how the fuck they know each other. Then it registers in my brain what she just said. "Ace Jackson?"

Travis nods, walking toward us. "Yes, Ace Jackson, my former foster brother that you, King, and Eli believed was out to get me," Tate says with a smirk. She takes a seat on the edge of the bed.

"You lied to us." I look between the two of them. "You betrayed our trust." I clench my fists at my sides, doing my fucking best to keep myself from connecting my fist with his face for lying. We did a background check, and we also checked his fingerprints, which clearly shows he's a better hacker than we've been aware of since he was able to connect his fingerprints to an entirely new and made-up identity.

"I did, but I won't apologize for it. I needed to keep an eye on Lee, and I wasn't certain that the three of you had pure intentions. It turns out I was right, considering where I found her," he snarls, stepping up to me until we're standing toe-to-toe.

The man I've trusted for twelve months has looked me in the eye and lied. The man I know as Travis is actually Ace and has known Tate all along. He's got a pretty good poker face. We've discussed her several times, yet he's never let it slip that they're not strangers.

Unable to deal with him right now, I step away and turn my attention to the woman sitting at the foot of my bed, taking her in.

For the first time in three months, my eyes connect with her clear turquoise orbs, and I'm unable to breathe. She stands slowly, never disconnecting our gaze. Clenching my jaw, I rush toward her and grab fistfuls of her short platinum and violet hair, yanking her head back, so she's forced to look up at me.

"Do you have any fucking idea what I've been through, thinking you were dead?" My fists tighten at her roots, yanking her head further back. "I thought you were fucking dead!" I yell in her face, my anger taking over me.

She's silent, allowing me to do and say whatever I need to right now.

"I thought I lost you! I fucking blamed myself for not protecting you! And come to find out, you're alive and perfectly fucking fine!" Spit flies from my mouth and lands on her cheek. Still, she doesn't move. But maintains her stormy gaze on me.

Slowly, Tate wraps her arms around my waist, bringing our bodies close together, allowing me to feel her warmth on my bare chest. "You left me, Rowen. You fucking left me. You don't get to be angry when I'm the one who was left for dead." Her nails rake painfully down my back.

I open my mouth to speak, but she stops me by speaking first. "I needed you. You weren't there and didn't even try to save me."

"How? How the fuck did you get out of that house?"

"Ace saved me," she says, her body flush against mine. I break our eye contact by turning my head to the side to look at the man in question. She must not like that because she sinks her nails deeper into my back, scratching so painfully I'm confident I'll have welts and blood drawn soon. "Look at me, not him. Look at me—the girl you left for dead." My eyes land on hers yet again. Glaring at me, she moves her hands to my chest and forcefully shoves me away from her. It's unexpected, and I nearly lose my balance, but I am able to keep myself upright.

"Fuck you, Rowen. I thought I could trust you!" She steps toward me, shoving me away again. Damn. She's feeling fucking feisty tonight.

A smirk spreads to my lips as I watch her small hands shove and slap against my hard chest. She must not like my smirk because she surprises me by raising her hand and slapping me across the face with all the strength she has. Not going to lie, it stings, and my jaw feels tight.

I'll give it to her. She doesn't back down from a fight, even when she knows that's what she will get; even when she knows that she's dangerously close to unleashing the beast within me.

I'm balancing on a thin line between being grateful that she's alive and being so fucking angry that she's lied and put me through hell these last three months that I've spent thinking she's dead.

Then she slowly backs away from me, knowing damn well that she's succeeded in pissing me the fuck off.

Without caring that we're not alone in the room, I rush toward her, take her in my arms and toss her petite body onto the bed, climbing on top of her, pinning her underneath me, and caging her in.

"Fuck you!" she hisses, her eyes now narrowed into slits as she glares at me. I don't give a fuck that she's angry. Her anger is nothing compared to what I've been feeling.

"No, fuck you. You let me believe the worst, and instead of coming clean and coming to me, you've been hiding for fucking months. So, fuck you!"

"Why the hell would I come to you? You, King, or Eli could've saved me. None of you did, so you don't get to be angry and act like you've been betrayed. I'm the one who was betrayed by the ones that I trusted the most." She wiggles beneath me, causing my cock to stir and come to life. "You don't get to be upset and go all caveman on me."

Grabbing her wrists in one hand, I raise them above her head, pinning them to the mattress. "You're right, angel. You can be as angry as you need to be, but don't tell me that I don't have an equal right to be angry too. I thought I had lost the love of my fucking life, which hurts. Every day I've lived with the guilt of knowing that we failed to save you." I lower my head, pressing my forehead to hers. "I'm so fucking sorry, angel," I whisper, pressing a kiss to the tip of her nose.

Tate raises her hips, grinding against the solid rod that's tenting my boxers, earning a groan from us both.

"What do you want, Ro?" she asks breathlessly. "How can I make you feel better and forgive me?"

"It's going to take some time to forgive you." I press my lips to her, stealing her breath. Her body relaxes beneath mine, and her lips part for me, allowing me to slip my tongue into her mouth. Letting go of her hands, I move mine down to her ass and raise her to me, grinding my cock along her core, earning the sweetest moan I've missed hearing.

We work together to tackle removing her clothing and then my boxers quickly. Once we're naked and pressed together, skin on skin, she spreads her legs for me, wrapping one around my waist and her arms around my neck.

"What do you want, Rowen?" she asks again, smirking.

"I want to see how loud I can make you scream," I answer as I force myself into her tight wet pussy, pushing into her until I bottom out. I need her so fucking bad, and I can't be gentle right now. She doesn't deserve gentle after all she's put me through.

Tate looks over my shoulder, her eyes no doubt landing on Ace, who, until now, I had forgotten was even in the room. His presence isn't going to stop me from fucking my angel. I need her, and I don't give a fuck that we have an audience.

"Eyes on me," I warn, thrusting my hips against hers. "Keep your eyes on me while I reclaim this tight pussy." Her lips part as her eyes become dark with lust. My head falls in the crook of her neck. "Fuck, angel, I have missed you."

One of her hands tangles in my hair and pulls at the roots while the other moves down my back and painfully claws at my skin. "You could've saved me. I thought I could trust you, but you failed me," she says breathlessly, her pussy strangling my aching cock.

I'm fucking furious at her for allowing me to spend months thinking she was dead and blaming myself for it. I'm a fool for fucking her instead of getting answers, but right now, I'm thinking with my cock and not my brain.

"You don't get to enjoy this. This is for me, not for you." I firmly wrap a hand around her throat, squeezing just enough to cut off her air supply. She claims she doesn't trust me, yet I'm holding her life in my hands, and she doesn't even flinch.

Her pupils dilate, and her bright blue eyes turn dark with lust as her pussy squeezes around me in a vise grip.

Looking over my shoulder, I make eye contact with the man who has worked for me for months and lied to my face every single fucking day.

"Either leave or sit the fuck down and watch. Don't just fucking stand there like a creep," I grunt, quickening my thrusts into Tate's tight warm center.

Turning my attention back to the woman underneath me, I move my hand away from her neck, allowing her to suck in gulps of air as she struggles for oxygen to moan.

I don't hear the door close, so I'm assuming Ace chose to stay, not that it matters to me. I'm not embarrassed to have him watch me; if anything, his wandering eyes turn me on even more.

Leaning forward, I bite down on Tate's right earlobe roughly, whispering into her ear, "Has he fucked you too?"

She quickly shakes her head in denial. I want to believe her, but I'm struggling to trust her. The only thing I trust her with right now is taking my cock and the load of cum I'm going to be filling her with, if I choose to.

"I think you're lying to me, angel. I think you let him fuck your tight little pussy."

"N-n-no, I haven't!" she cries out, her nails digging into the skin of my ass.

"Ace, get the fuck over here." Like a lost fucking pussy, he quickly obeys, standing beside the bed. His dark eyes are transfixed on the sight before him.

"Have you fucked her?" I ask, leaning back onto my knees so I'm no longer covering her, and her body is on display for him. I grab her legs and spread them further apart, moving enough out of the way so he can have the perfect view of her pink glistening pussy being stretched by my cock.

"No. I've never fucked her," he grits out, his jaw tight, eyes never leaving where we're connected. I can see the growing bulge in his pants, but he does nothing to adjust himself or even resolve some of the pressure I'm sure he must be feeling.

"You're missing out. She's the best fuck I've ever had." I pinch her sensitive clit, earning a yelp from her. "So fucking tight, and always fucking ready." I slide out of her, allowing him to see the way her pussy clenches and pulses with the loss of me. Smirking, I raise a hand and bring it down, slapping her right on her pussy.

Tate yelps, her body jerking as I repeat the process, slapping her pussy until it's hot and red. "Such a shame you haven't fucked her. This pussy is magic." Pressing my tip against her entrance, I surge forward, bottoming out inside her heat easily with one thrust of my hips.

To my surprise, Ace leans down and presses his lips against hers, stealing the moans I'm giving her with his mouth.

His hand roams down her body, but instead of touching her like I expected him to do, he cups my heavy balls, massaging them in his hand, causing a familiar ache to warm my spine.

The gesture takes me by surprise, and I should stop it and demand he gets the fuck away from me because he lied about his identity, but I don't because it feels too fucking good to have his hand massaging my tightening sack.

With a loud groan, and sooner than expected, I empty myself inside of Tate's pulsing body, roaring my release into the heavy, sweat-scented air of my hotel room.

"Fuck, I have missed you." I pull out, collapsing on top of her body. I can feel the frustration radiating off her because she didn't get to come, but I already told her this was for me, not her. If she wants me to make her cum, she'll have to earn it.

Ace pulls back, leaving her lips swollen from his kiss. With a smirk, I quickly kiss her lips, then pull back and climb off the bed.

"I'm going to go clean up." Without a second look back at her, I walk toward the bathroom to pee and clean up the mess we created.

God, I really have fucking missed everything about her. I should be angry, but I'm not. I'll never be able to stay angry at her. Not anymore.

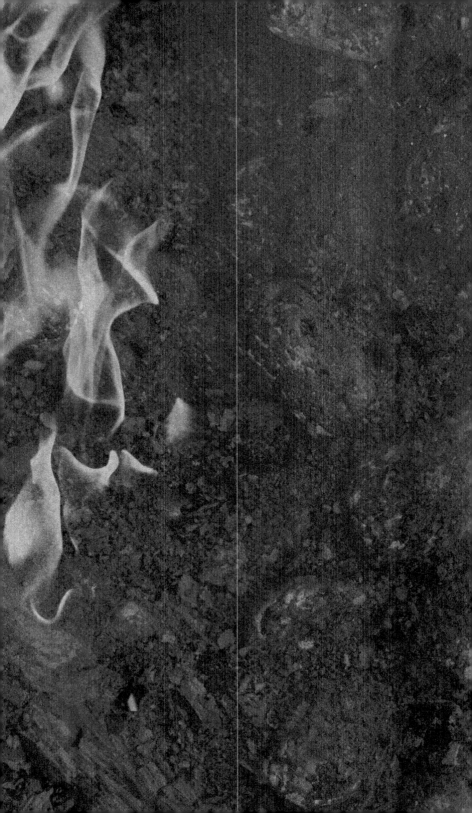

# NINE
### Raven

"Why did you choose to rise from the dead now? Better yet, why are you here?" I ask, putting on a clean pair of boxers once I return to the room after cleaning myself up.

"I'm here because of Rachel. I wanted to get to her before you or anyone else had the chance," she says, confirming what I already knew. She knows Rachel, and I'm about to find out how.

She must know my next question because she continues talking, answering my unasked question. "Rachel is a...friend. Ace has been helping me keep her and her daughter safe over the years. When you received the photo of them, Ace told me, so I came here to keep them safe."

"How did you know where I'm staying?"

"I was there when you and King showed up. We waited until you two left, then we followed you. I rode up in the elevator with you, and you didn't even notice," she says, standing up from the bed and walking naked toward the bathroom, closing the door behind her.

A few minutes later, she returns wearing the plush, white bathrobe from the closet.

I replay the moments in the elevator and vaguely recall seeing a blonde in the corner. I didn't notice her. That shows how distracted I've been. I'm slipping, not properly checking my surroundings like I need to. Better safe than sorry.

"Tell me how exactly you know Rachel. Saying she's a friend doesn't explain anything."

She rolls her eyes, brushing her hair out of her face and behind her ears. "I'll tell you tomorrow. I want to get some sleep."

"Go to your room and sleep, then."

She waves her arms around the room. "I'm already in my room. The hotel is sold out, so we're staying here tonight."

"The fuck you are. I'm still pissed at you."

"Oh well…" She shrugs. "You'll have to get over it. We're staying." She turns her attention to Trav—Ace. Referring to him by his real name instead of the name I know him as will take some getting used to.

"I want answers right now, Tate. One of you better start talking and tell me what fucking role Rachel Hollis plays in all of this." I'm desperate for answers, and it's beginning to show. Tate's mind has always been fascinating to me. I've always loved learning how the wheels turn in her brain, and if I'm being honest, I always thought it would be excited to rip her open to see how her pieces all fit together and how her brain is connected.

She's kept her secrets close to her, and I want nothing more than to dig inside her brain and learn everything she's been keeping to herself for far too long.

Her mind is such a beautiful thing, and her secrets are deadly. Most likely, it'll be me dying, trying to figure them out.

"Ro, please. I've had a long day and don't want to talk about any of that right now. Let's get some sleep, and we'll talk in the morning and figure out a plan."

"A plan?" I scoff. "We'll talk right now. And I'll tell you what *my* next move will be."

She crosses her arms over her chest and glares at me, pinning me with her infamous deadly look. "Your tough guy act isn't getting us anywhere. You seem to forget that I know you so well, Rowen." I hate not getting what I want, especially when it comes to unanswered questions.

I hate loose ends, and I'm anxious to learn her connection to Rachel Hollis. I don't understand why that woman is so important, and she is; Tate wouldn't have come out of wherever she was hiding otherwise.

"Come here," she says, holding her hand out toward Ace. He goes to her instantly. "The bed is big enough for the three of us."

"I'm not sleeping with the two of you. Don't forget that I don't trust either of you anymore."

"That's wise." She grins. "You can sleep on the bed with us or on the floor." She walks toward the bed and pulls the blankets back. "The least you can do after fucking me is share a bed with me." She sighs, climbing to the middle of the bed. "By the way, I don't trust *you* either. Not since you left me for dead."

Ace clears his throat. "You may find this awkward..." He begins stripping out of his clothing, tossing everything to the floor with a silent thud until he's standing fully nude before me. "But I'm not uncomfortable, and it was a long drive." He joins Tate on the bed, claiming the side closest to the door. Why would I find sharing a bed with him awkward when he just helped me come?

If I weren't so annoyed, I'd laugh at how much he reminds me of

King in this moment. He, too, doesn't give two fucks in situations that may be awkward or uncomfortable, and he loves going commando as well.

"I will tell you whatever you want to know tomorrow," she promises, her words not providing me any comfort or reason to believe her.

Rolling my eyes, I refuse to continue arguing. We're going in circles and beating a dead horse. Right now, I have a lot of resentment toward her for not telling me she's alive sooner, and I'm pissed at Ace for pretending to be someone he's not.

It looks like we just figured out who our fucking rat is.

Admitting defeat and refusing to sleep on the floor or the couch of the hotel room I'm paying for, I join them on the king-size bed.

Tate scoots closer toward him as I climb in, putting her directly in the middle of the bed. "Keep your fucking hands to yourself. I don't want to wake up to you touching my dick. Either one of you," I scold as I lie down and face away from them.

Tate giggles, and my fucking heart tightens at the sound I've missed for months. "That would be a sight to see. You two can fuck out your problems, and this time, I can watch." Her laughter fills the room.

"Don't be like that. I know that Ace helped you…get off."

Reaching forward, I click the lamp off, encasing the room in complete darkness. Her warm body presses against my back, and her lips press against the back of my shoulder. She snakes her arm around my waist, grabbing on to my cock that's now fully erect, thanks to her.

"Seems like you liked it," she whispers in my ear, biting down on my earlobe.

"Tate, shut the fuck up and go to sleep," I hiss, shoving her hands off my body and her mouth away from my ear.

"Yes, sir, whatever you say." Her laughter fades into the background as exhaustion takes over.

# TEN

*Lee*

"S hhh." I press my finger against my lips, silencing Ace as we tiptoe around the dimly lit hotel room.

The only light in the room is from the sun that's peeking in from a gap in the curtains that haven't been shut all the way. We need to get out of the room as quietly as possible without waking Rowen.

It was great to see him again—and being intimate with him was incredible—but I still don't trust him; especially when it comes to knowing the truth about Olivia. That's why I told him I'd explain everything in the morning. I won't be here when he wakes up to keep good on that promise. A few months ago, I would've trusted him enough to tell him anything he wanted to know, but things are different now. That fire changed me.

Actually, I was changed before that. The night I jumped out of the bathroom window at Confess nightclub, and King shot me...that was when my faith in them began to flicker. They'd betrayed me and believed that I had betrayed them. They should've known I would've never done anything like that, but instead, they chose to believe the lies Colton fed them, and the three of them fell right into his trap.

When King and Eli showed up at the house, I was so hopeful they would save me and take me back to the cabin where I could be safe. Instead, they chose to save themselves when the fire started. They sealed their fate that night, and I added them to my list of revenge.

I know the unknown bastard who's been texting them will try to get to Olivia through them. I'm not positive that he's her father, considering it's possible his father could've also impregnated me, but they're still related. They're either father and daughter or brother and sister, but it doesn't matter. I want that sick bastard to stay as far away from Olivia as possible.

I know what he's capable of. I know how demented and twisted he really is, and I'll never let him get his hands on her, even if that means I'll spend the rest of my life running and looking over my shoulder.

I'll do anything to keep her safe.

Ace grabs my bicep, pulling me away from my thoughts and the hotel room. Yet again, I got so lost inside my head that I hadn't realized what was happening around me. He's already packed our bags, and there's no trace of us in the room anywhere.

Rowen will soon wake to an empty room and be furious that I slipped through his fingers, taking my secrets with me once again. I don't care. That's what he gets.

Ace leads me out of the room and carefully closes the hotel room door behind us, so it doesn't slam. It closes with a click, and then we're rushing toward the elevator in a hurry to get to the car; we need to get to Rachel's before we run into anyone else.

While he steps outside to pull the car around for me, I slip into the dining area to take advantage of the continental breakfast.

I take two bottles of water, two muffins, and two yogurt cups.

I'm desperate for a cup of coffee, but I doubt I have time to open two dozen tiny creamer cups to get my coffee to the level of sweetness that I prefer. Hopefully, Rachel will have a pot ready when we get there.

Rushing out of the hotel, I practically sprint toward the car and jump in once I see it. Ace speeds off before I can even get the door closed and my seat belt on.

"I've already called Rachel to let her know we're on our way back. She said they're ready to go," he says, glancing over at me.

I nod, leaning my head against the headrest. "Thanks. We need to make this as quick as possible. As soon as Rowen wakes up to an empty bed, he'll know we took off, and then he and King will be coming straight here."

"Why didn't you tell Rowen who's been sending them those texts?" he asks, taking me by surprise.

"If they would've unchained me from that basement, I would've told them. I knew who was behind the texts the minute the man in the basement called me little bird. Only one person ever called me that, and I wanted to tell them who it was," I explain, hating that my relationship with Eli, King, and Rowen ended the way that it did. "Colton has had it out for me before those texts even started. He's the one who put the hit out on me that they responded to. The only reason they didn't turn me over to him like they were supposed to is because Rowen and I have history, and he and King fell for me…and then Eli did, too. Although I'm sure, he'll never admit it." I smile to myself, remembering the moments I spent with Eli and the rare times he let his gentle side show.

He likes to keep it hidden and pretend to be some intense hard ass, but I know the real him. If Eli didn't care about me, he wouldn't have built me the ballet studio; he knew I loved to dance and had been missing it so he brought one to me.

Only someone who truly cares about you would do something like that.

"Do you think I should've told him?"

"No, why should you? You're right. They failed to protect you, so they can continue to play whatever game Colton wants to play."

I smile and reach across to place my hand on his thigh. "So, about last night. Looked like you had a nice time feeling up Ro," I say with a knowing grin.

"I'm not gay if that's what you're asking."

"I never said you were." Ace doesn't like titles. He likes the human body, and that's nothing to be ashamed of, and it doesn't need to be labeled. "All I said was it seemed like you had a good time." I know that Ace finds Ro attractive. You'd have to be blind not to, but even at that, his voice is attractive too.

Ace has told me many times about his attraction to all three of them. Eli, King, and Rowen, and if I'm being honest, I've had a fantasy about the four of them together. I secretly wonder if I'll ever be able to make that fantasy happen.

A girl can dream.

When we arrive at Rachel's, I hurry inside while Ace agrees to remain outside, keeping watch in case Rowen or anyone else shows up.

Rachel opens the door as soon as I knock and greets me with a weary smile. "We're packing only the necessities, as you said. Olivia is in her room, but we're almost ready to go. Be warned, though. She's unhappy about leaving behind her newly decorated and painted bedroom," she says before turning her back on me and walking toward the kitchen to finish packing.

With a sigh, I walk down the hallway to Olivia's room. The door is open, and she's sitting in the middle of the room, hugging her backpack as fresh tears stream down her porcelain face. The sight is heartbreaking.

"Aunty Lee, I don't want to move. I like it here, and so does Mommy. We don't want to leave."

I squat in front of her. "I know, sweet girl, but I miss you guys so much and want you to be closer to me," I say, taking her small hands in mine.

"But Mommy is leaving her boyfriend, and I'm leaving the friends I've made. It's not fair that we have to go. Can't you move here with us?" I raise my eyebrow at the mention of Rachel having a boyfriend. This is the first I've ever heard of someone being in the picture.

With a sigh, I sit on my bottom, pulling Olivia closer. "I'm sorry, sweet girl, but you have to come with Ace and me. I promise you'll make new friends, and we'll even give you a better bedroom than this one." Her bright blue eyes light up with so much hope.

Looking at her is like looking in a mirror. She's my twin and looks exactly as I did when I was her age. The difference between us is she's sweet and innocent; the world hasn't tainted her and stolen her innocence like it did mine. When I was her age, I was already jaded and had experienced horrific things. Things that I never want her to know about or ever have to experience herself. That's why I try so hard to keep her and her mother safe—I want to keep her pure and innocent for as long as possible.

"Do you promise?" she asks, raising her little pinky to me. With an easy smile, I nod and hook my pinky around hers.

"I promise. You'll have the best bedroom ever, and I bet if you ask nicely, Ace will even take you shopping and let you pick out whatever you want to decorate it with."

She jumps up, her wide smile spreading from ear to ear. "Okay, Aunty Lee, I believe you."

"Good girl. Now, help your mom finish packing, and I'll start taking your stuff to the car." She nods, shoving her backpack toward me before she sprints out of the room, yelling for her mother.

My chest aches every time I hear her call someone else mom. I don't regret my decision not to keep her, but it's still painful to hear.

After carrying the bags from Olivia's room out to the car, I go back into the house to find Rachel in the living room. "So, Olivia said something crazy, and I can't help but wonder if it's true."

She looks at me skeptically. "What did she say?" she asks, taking the photos down from the wall and packing them away into a box.

"She told me that you have a boyfriend." She pauses for a moment, silently giving me the answer I dreaded. "Shit. I was hoping it wasn't true."

Rachel tapes the box closed and passes it to Ace when he walks in with a chatty Olivia who's busy talking about something that happened at the park last week.

"I've been alone for so long, Lee. Don't judge me and get mad for finding someone after being alone for over ten years. It's not like I was trying to meet anyone. It just happened."

I shouldn't be angry. She's right. She gave up having a normal life to raise Olivia and has never once complained about it. Six months after I had Olivia, in order for them to remain safe with no questions asked, they moved from city to city once a year.

Eventually, I met Sebastian and felt it was safe enough for Rachel and Olivia to settle in one place for a while. When I learned how evil he was, I had to stop visiting them because I feared he'd find out about them and hurt them. Once I left him, I told Rachel to move again in case Sebastian learned about them.

For years, they've been running, never understanding why they couldn't stay in one place for very long and why it wasn't safe. At one point, Rachel thought I was being paranoid, but I knew differently. One day, someone from my past was bound to catch up to me and threaten Olivia if they found out.

I was right. Except the person coming after them is the last person I ever expected. It's Olivia's father or brother. The verdict is still out on that one since Colton and his father both liked to rape me, and I got pregnant during the same week they'd both paid late-night visits to my bedroom.

"Are you okay?" Rachel asks, stealing my attention away from my thoughts. Clearing my throat, I nod as she sighs. "I understand that you don't trust easily, Lee, but Mike is a good man, and Olivia adores him."

"Have you told him you're leaving?"

"I told him I was going to visit a family member, and we'll be back in a couple of weeks," she says, her eyes snapping to Ace and Olivia when they appear in the living room.

"The car is packed. Are you ready to go?" he asks, earning a nod from Rachel.

"As ready as we'll ever be," she says, pulling her car keys from her pocket.

"Actually, you can leave your car here. We'll get you a new one later," Ace explains. He takes Olivia's hand and leads her outside.

Rachel grabs her purse, tosses her keys inside, and leads me outside to our waiting SUV that's packed with their belongings. She climbs into the back with Olivia, and I sit in the front with Ace who drives away the moment our seat belts are clicked into place.

I turn in my seat and look in the back toward the two passengers. "We have a long drive ahead of us, so whenever either of you need to stop, let us know." Olivia looks up from her iPad and smiles happily.

"I love road trips, and I'm super excited to decorate my new bedroom."

"Sweetie, put your headphones on and watch a movie. The drive will be long and boring, and you won't like the grown-up talk." Rachel reaches inside the purple backpack and produces a pair of rose gold headphones. She helps Olivia connect them to the iPad and pick out a movie before she puts them on her small head, her attention stolen by whatever she's watching on the screen.

Looking at me, Rachel asks, "What's the plan? Where are we going?" I open my mouth to speak, but Ace beats me to it and answers her question.

"We have a safe house that you'll stay at." I turn around and sit correctly in my seat. He places his hand on my thigh, tracing lazy circles over my bare skin exposed by my shorts. He knows I'm anxious right now, and his touch is helping to soothe me.

"Wake me when we stop at a gas station," Rachel says through a yawn.

We'll stop somewhere soon to refill our gas tank and get food, but we need to drive farther away to be safe and ensure we aren't followed.

Right now, it's not just Rowen and King we have to worry about. It's Colton, too, and I wouldn't be surprised if he's near, watching and waiting like the fucking predator he is.

He knows about Olivia, and he knows that Rachel has her. I'm just not sure what his plan is or if he even knows where they are. He sent King and Rowen after them, but that doesn't mean he isn't also aware of their location.

When it comes to Colton, anything is possible, and I wouldn't put anything past him. He likely knows precisely where they lived but wanted to play a game and have someone else do his dirty work.

He always loved to play games.

The worst thing about Colton is how charming he is. He can charm the pants off anyone and get them to do anything. I know because I've seen it before. It's how he charmed me into being alone with him years ago, and his charm kept me quiet about what he was doing to me late at night when he'd sneak into my room.

He's out there somewhere, and I won't rest until he's found and put down with a bullet in his brain. It's the very least he deserves.

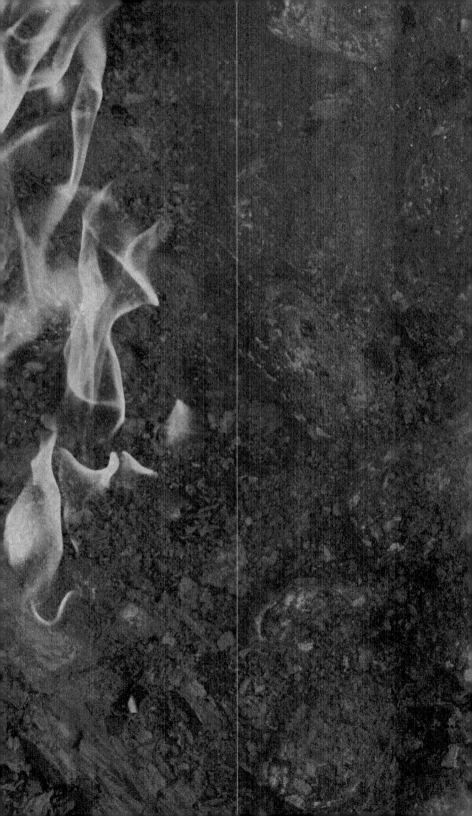

# ELEVEN

*Ace*

One look at Lee and it's easy to see how anxious and afraid she's feeling. It's always one thing after another, and I wish I were able to ease her mind, make her life easier, and take away some of her fears.

She's spent her life looking over her shoulder and being afraid, not knowing when she'll ever have the chance to be "normal" and live without fear.

It's been one thing after another since the day she was put in foster care and placed with parents who had no business having children in their homes. Even when she aged out and married Sebastian, her nightmare never ended.

My heart breaks every time I catch her staring off with a sad look on her face or playing with her fingers, like she does whenever she gets nervous. She thinks I don't notice, but I do.

I notice everything about her. I *know* everything about her.

She puts on a brave face for me and everyone else, but underneath her mask is a scared little girl who was forced to grow up so fast and has never truly been protected. She hates being a victim, but I don't think there's anything wrong with being one.

She's a warrior. A fucking queen for living through all she has, but she's also a victim. I wish I could take away her fear and promise her that everything will be okay, and that one day she'll have to stop looking over her shoulder.

I don't know when or if that day will ever happen, but I sure as fuck hope that, for her sake, it does.

I hope that one day she'll be able to heal and live as normal of a life as she can.

It's what I want for her. She deserves it.

"Ace?" Lee's voice cuts through my thoughts. Blinking, I turn my head and glance at her.

"Hm?"

"You okay?" she asks, rubbing my hand that's holding the steering wheel.

"Yeah, I'm fine. What did you say?"

"I asked if we could stop at the upcoming exit," she asks, pointing toward the sign showing the exit coming up.

Nodding, I switch lanes, getting closer to the right so I can take the next exit.

Perfect timing, too, because we have fifty miles remaining with the gas we currently have.

Parking at an empty gas pump, I turn toward Lee. "Get me water and a snack, please?" She agrees with a smile, and we get out at the same time.

While I begin pumping the gas, she wakes Rachel and Olivia, and the three of them go inside the small convenience store to load up on snacks.

We still have hours to go until we're back in the city and at the safe house. When Lee told me she wanted to move Rachel and Olivia, I immediately checked the house to ensure it would be safe for them.

It's temporary until we find somewhere else to move them to for a more extended period of time, but for now, it'll have to do.

"They didn't have ranch corn nuts, so I got you regular," Lee says, holding up the white shipping bag as she walks toward me, a carefree smile lighting up her beautiful face. "I also got you FIJI Water and a Vitamin water."

"Do you know it's not healthy just because it says *vitamin*? It's still loaded with sugar." I chuckle, removing the gas nozzle from the car and hanging it back up once the vehicle is full.

She rolls her eyes and leans against the car. "I thought you might like something besides water. You're such a health freak." I'm not a health freak. I just watch what goes into my body and workout. I don't enjoy fueling myself with junk.

Well, that's not entirely true, considering I always have a craving for ranch corn nuts. They're my guilty pleasure and one of the few indulgences I allow myself to have.

I can count on one hand the things I allow myself to give in to.

Ranch corn nuts.

Vanilla ice cream.

And Lee.

She is the main indulgence that has my sweet tooth aching whenever she's near, and she's the one thing I haven't yet enjoyed.

One day, when the time is right, I'll taste her sweetness. I'm positive she'll taste just like my favorite flavor.

*Vanilla.*

Smiling, I turn toward her. "Thank you. That was thoughtful." I grip her hips and pull her small body toward mine, and she presses her chest against me. "How are you feeling?"

"I'm good, yeah, I'm okay," she says, but her eyes give away her lies. She's not okay, but she's trying to be strong and not let it show that she's afraid.

Afraid of not knowing what's going to happen next.

I'd love nothing more than to take away all her worries, but I can't, so instead, I'll do what I can and try my best to provide her comfort.

"Let's go. We need to get back on the road. We still have a long drive ahead of us," I say, placing the gas cap back on.

Once the four of us are back inside the car, I pull out of the parking lot and head toward the freeway, driving farther away from the small town where Rachel and Olivia had been living for the past year.

As I drive, one question remains in my mind.

*What'll happen next?*

# TWELVE

*King*

"How the fuck did we lose them?" I shove my hands into my hair and tug at the roots, kicking the air as I pace back and forth inside the house that only hours ago contained Rachel Hollis.

Rowen came pounding on my hotel room door this morning, telling me we had to hurry and get to Rachel's. The fucker was in such a rush that I couldn't even enjoy the complimentary breakfast spread out downstairs. Hell, I barely had time to get dressed before he dragged me out of the room.

He'd been quiet during the drive to her house, refusing to speak or even look at me. I know my brother well enough to know that something is bothering him, but he won't tell me what's wrong. Instead of talking to me and telling me why he's fuming, he's shutting me out and holding his anger in.

"Fuck!" Rowen roars so loudly that it startles me. Her car is parked in the driveway, so we assumed she was home. We knocked for five minutes before I picked the lock and we discovered the place was empty.

They're gone. Rachel is fucking gone. We lost the only chance we had to find out how she's connected to my butterfly—not to mention why the unknown fucker wants her so badly. Now, we're back to square one and have no fucking leads. No fucking information and nowhere to turn from here.

"Where the fuck could she have gone? Her car is outside." I drop my hands to my sides, pacing around the living room. Still, Rowen remains silent.

Rolling my eyes, annoyed at his silent treatment, I search the house again, hoping to find a clue as to who Rachel Hollis is and where they could've gone.

The first room I enter is a child's room. The twin bed in the middle of the room has a purple canopy over it, and the bedding is ruffled as if a child had been sleeping there and never made the bed. The closet door is wide open, and all that remains inside are empty hangers.

Inhaling to calm my nerves, I exhale slowly. "What the fuck?" I whisper to myself, still unable to believe this. Walking out of the child's room, I visit the next room, which I'm assuming belongs to Rachel.

The queen bed is unmade, and the closet door is open and empty. Groaning, I sit on the edge of the bed and lean forward to rest my elbows on my knees. My head hangs between my shoulders, my focus falling to the wood floor.

Something under the bed catches my attention. Reaching down, I grab the item and pull it out from under the bed, revealing a photo album. It's filled with photos of Rachel and the child. There are countless photos of who I assume is Olivia, as a baby, and a few through the years as well.

I continue flipping through the pages until I land on one photo that causes my breathing to stop and my heart to sink into my stomach. The photo is of my butterfly. Her long blonde hair is pulled onto the top of her head in a messy bun, and in her arms is a tiny baby wrapped in a pink blanket that she's staring at lovingly.

*Holy fuck.*

Unable to breathe, I turn to the last page in the album and I'm met with a recent photo of Olivia. Her bright blue eyes stare back at me on the paper, her smile wide as she stares at the camera. I've seen those blue eyes before. I'd know them anywhere.

Olivia is the spitting image of my butterfly.

"Find anything?" Rowen asks, walking into the room, disturbing me from the newest revelation I've made. Unable to control my trembling hands, I hand the album to him.

"Look at this." I flip toward the photo of Tate holding the baby, then flip toward the last page, where the most recent picture of Olivia has been placed.

"Oh my God," he gasps, his eyes going as wide as saucers. "Olivia's her daughter."

"Did you know she had a baby?"

He shakes his head. "The child is too young to be mine and too old to be Sebastian's." Tate had told us that she'd been pregnant before. I knew she had once been pregnant by Rowen when she was barely a teenager, and then she'd been pregnant before by her bastard of a husband. Both pregnancies resulted in miscarriages. She never mentioned a third pregnancy, a pregnancy that she carried to term and resulted in a daughter.

"Rachel Hollis must be the woman that Tate has raising her child. Why wouldn't she tell us?" A frown curls on my lips, my eyes glossy with unshed tears. My butterfly didn't trust us enough, didn't trust *me* enough to tell me about her daughter. She didn't tell me she had a daughter, and I don't understand why. "We need to find out who the father is. Olivia is ten, right?" I ask, wiping my fallen tears. My heart aches at the fact that she felt she couldn't trust me enough to tell me something important.

Knowing where I'm going with my questions and train of thoughts, Rowen grabs his phone from his pocket and takes a picture of the photos in the album. "Ten years ago, she was seventeen. That's the same time her foster family died in that fire." His phone chimes, signaling that he's sent the photos in a text message.

"The father must be either her foster brother or father. She told us that they'd both hurt her. The timeframe matches."

"But they're dead," I deadpan, shaking my head. I know what Rowen's thinking, and there's no way either one of them is still alive or responsible for wanting Tate kidnapped months ago.

"There was a fire, yes, but that doesn't mean they died. We've never looked that much into her last foster family. Eli discovered they died in a fire. Tate confirmed she set the fire, but that's it. We never looked any further." He brings his phone to his ear. "I think it's time we look into it. Let's go." He walks away, carrying the album as he begins speaking into the phone.

I follow him, listening to him speak on the phone. "Malcolm, I sent you a few photos of Olivia Hollis. Look into her and the Adamson family that died ten years ago in a fire at their home. I want a full report on all three family members, including a list of all their living relatives and any close friends they had. Also, look closer into Rachel Hollis. See if she has any friends or known associates. I want to know everything about her and her daily routine." After a few more words, he ends the call, shoving the phone into his front pocket. "He'll report back on what he finds. Let's get back to the hotel until we hear something."

We don't know where Rachel and Olivia disappeared to, but I fucking hope that the unknown fucker isn't responsible for their disappearance. Now that I know about my butterfly's connection to Olivia, I know I have to do everything I can to protect them both.

We don't know where they are. If they left willingly or if they were taken. Tate would want to see them safe, and I'll ensure they are for her. Based on the condition of the house, I'm assuming they left willingly since their clothing is gone, along with whatever photos had been hung on the walls. The album being left behind was clearly a mistake.

Rowen and I go through the remainder of the house, searching for anything else to give us some insight into who Rachel Hollis is and where she and Olivia could've gone. Unfortunately for us, there's nothing left behind that can help us. Besides the photo album Ro's placed in our car, there's nothing important left in this small house.

The drive back to the hotel is quiet, much like our drive to the house. Only this time, I don't bother with trying to make small talk, because I'm fuming over the fact I didn't know she had a living child. I wish she would've told me. What we shared was special, but this reminds me that I don't know much about her, and she still has many secrets that I'm more determined than ever to uncover.

We stop at a drive-through and grab burgers for lunch. Once we're back at the hotel, I offer to come to Ro's room to eat with him, but he declines and lies to my face by saying he's going to take a nap and eat later. I've known him long enough to know when he's lying.

Once I'm back in my room, I set my greasy bag of food on the coffee table and collapse onto the sofa, setting the photo album beside my food. Tears stream down my face.

I've slept in Tate's room in our cabin every single day for three months. I've fallen asleep by hugging her pillows that still smells of her vanilla coconut shampoo. I've never missed anyone as much as I miss her. The feeling is new to me. The longing I feel is unbearable, and sometimes it feels like my heart is going to literally break.

I miss her. I miss her so fucking much, and I'm living with so many regrets.

At first, I was angry with Eli for playing a role in me turning against her and believing whatever he was saying. Now, I realize that he was right when he said we don't know her. This trip proves it. She has a fucking child, for crying out loud, and no one knew about it.

My butterfly had been keeping secrets. Luckily for me, secrets don't stay buried for long, and they have a way of exposing themselves when you're dead.

Sooner or later, I will uncover everything she'd been keeping to herself.

# THIRTEEN
## *Raven*

King doesn't know that Tate's alive, and I can't tell him. Rachel and Olivia are gone, and there's no doubt in my mind that Tate and Ace are responsible for their disappearance.

I now understand why she didn't tell me about them when I asked last night. She was trying to protect them since she doesn't trust me, but that doesn't make it any less painful. Like I've said before, I can't blame her. Eli, King, and I have given her nothing but reason after reason not to trust us.

The only difference is that I don't have to live with it. There's still a chance I can make it up to her and earn her trust again. I don't yet know how, but I know that I will. I have to.

When King discovered that Olivia is Tate's daughter, I thought about telling him that she's alive, but seeing his reaction to knowing his precious butterfly kept that big of a secret from him, I knew I couldn't break his heart even more. We've both been hurting for months, and I don't see that ending anytime soon.

Guilt is weighing heavily on me. Keeping secrets from each other is the type of shit Eli does, not what King and I do. No matter how ugly the truth has been, we've never kept secrets from each other. I trust him with my life and know that he'll never lie to me; I hate that I looked him in the eyes and lied to him.

I looked my brother in the eyes and carried on as if I hadn't learned an explosive secret. Truthfully, I'm doing it to protect him. If I tell King that Tate is alive and she came to see me and not him, he wouldn't take it well. He loves her. She's the only woman he's ever loved. The sick bastard found his equal in her, and then he lost it. He lost her.

No, I can't tell him. Not yet, anyway. I'm not sure what he'd do if he found out. But at the same time, I know the longer I wait to tell him, the angrier he'll be when he finds out—and I'm not foolish enough to believe that he'll never find out. Secrets have a way of uncovering themselves.

For his own sake, I hope it's later rather than sooner.

For my own sake, I hope I don't have to tell him. I'd rather her visit him just like she did with me. He'll find out that I knew and didn't tell him, and he'll be upset, but it would be best to come from her.

If I tell him, he'll look for her, and I need him right now.

Once I'm inside my hotel room, my phone rings, and Malcolm's name appears on the screen. I answer it quickly, eager to find out what he's learned.

"Talk to me," I say, pacing the room as I hold the phone to my ear.

"Rowen, I wanted to give you a heads up that I'm not the only one looking into fires today. Eli had Maverick pull the reports from that house fire a few months ago. I'm not sure why, but they've been huddled up working on something. Apparently, a mistake was made with one of the bodies identified."

The hair on my arm raises. Fuck. Why the fuck would Eli be looking into the fire that we believed killed Tate? As far as I'm aware, he thinks she's dead, so why is he looking into it?

Hopefully, he's only searching for clues to connect that fire with the fire that claimed two of our businesses.

"Thanks for letting me know. What do you have on the Hollis' and Adamsons?"

"Olivia Hollis, enrolled at Byer Elementary. Just turned ten years old and will be going into the fifth grade. Great student, straight A's, perfect attendance. I reviewed her medical file from her doctor's office. Rachel Hollis is *not* the biological mother of Olivia, but I've not been able to find any record of adoption." I hear clicking in the background; he's most likely reviewing the information on his computer. "The birth certificate at her school lists Rachel as the mother and someone nonexistent as the father. The birth certificate is fake, and I'm currently working on digging up the real one. That'll take some more time." He takes a breath. "As for Rachel Hollis, she was born with the name Angelina to parents Doug and Jasmine Miller. Both died in a car accident when she was eight. She lived with her grandmother until she died of cancer when Angelina was sixteen. She was placed in foster care for two years, and during that time, the poor girl had twenty-seven hospital visits. Broken arm, leg, nose, all kinds of shit," he says with a sigh.

"Once she reached eighteen, she filed for a change of name, officially becoming Rachel Hollis, and that's where the trail on her ends. There's no record of employment, no lease, no bank accounts, nothing. There is no life under the name Rachel Hollis. She did volunteer at a youth center for foster children several years ago, but one day, she stopped showing up."

"This is great. Thanks, Malcolm."

"Now, for the Adamsons…" Excitement fills his voice now. "Willa and Bill Adamson were licensed foster parents who fostered children for nearly twenty years before they died in an accidental house fire that was started by a candle. During that time, they did not have any foster children in their care. Their twenty-one-year-old son, Colton, was home visiting from Harvard University and was killed along with his parents." He's not telling me anything I don't already know about them.

"Do they have any relatives?"

"Willa had a sister named Mariah Winters Jackson. She died years ago after she hit her head due to a fall down the stairs."

"Her last name was Jackson?" Alarm bells begin to go off in my head.

"Yes, she married James Jackson, and they had one child. A son named—"

"Ace," I cut him off before he has the chance to finish.

"Yes, that's correct," Malcolm says. "There's no record whatsoever on Ace Jackson, so I'm going to find out what I can about Ace through his father. It looks like his father's still living in the same home where his wife died and remarried for the third time." A sound of disgust comes from him. "This third wife is the daughter of his second wife. His former stepdaughter. His second wife died in a car accident, and nine months later, he married his eighteen-year-old stepdaughter, and they now have two children."

"Disgusting motherfucker." I shake my head. "Find out whatever else you can and call me back."

"You got it." Malcolm ends the call with a click, just as a knock sounds on my door.

Standing, I walk toward it and open it, spreading my arms out when I see King's tear-stained face.

"Brother." He steps into my arms, wrapping his around my waist. When we break apart, he follows me into the room until I can close the door.

"Oh, Rowen." He grabs me again and cries into my neck, fisting my shirt. On the outside, King looks tough and edgy as fuck, but on the inside, he's a giant fucking teddy bear who's sensitive and has so many emotions that he's not always capable of handling. He's sensitive, something Eli and I are completely aware of and know exactly how to handle.

I stroke his back with one hand and use the other to stroke his shoulder-length dirty blond hair. We remain like that until his sobbing stops, then he pulls away and allows me to wipe his face dry.

With a sigh, he presses his forehead against mine, exhaling slowly, his minty breath fanning against my lips.

"My butterfly kept a secret from me. We shared so much, and she failed to tell me she has a child."

"She gave the baby to someone else to raise. Maybe that's why she didn't say anything. The girl has a mother."

"But we could've helped her raise the girl."

"King, the girl has a mother. What would you have done if she had told you? Take the girl away from the only mother she knows? Make her live with strangers?"

He ponders my words for a moment, then closes his eyes. "You're right. I just hate that there are things I never knew about her."

"Let's relax. We both need to calm down, breathe, and relax."

He lifts his head, his hands on my hips. "You're right. Let's relax." His lips crash against mine, my cock instantly coming to life and pushing against the zipper of my jeans. "Fuck, I need your mouth around me. That should help me feel better," he says with a groan, his hands pulling at my shirt until it's being thrown to the floor.

Our teeth clank together as our kiss becomes heated, both of us working quickly to remove our clothing, desperate to get our hands on each other and our needs met.

"Fuck, brother, I need you," I say, gasping, when his calloused hand wraps around my painfully hard cock that's already leaking with my desire. "Suck me now."

Without hesitation, King drops to his knees, opens his mouth, and slips my cock inside, his warm, velvety tongue circling my engorged tip, sucking me like a fucking lollipop.

"God, your mouth feels so fucking good on my cock." I stroke his hair, knowing how much he loves to be praised when he's on his knees for me. "You're such a good boy. Taking my dick like a champ." He groans his response against my length, and that sound vibrates against my sensitive skin.

"Will you be a good boy and let me fill your mouth with my cum and swallow every single drop?" I ask.

He hollows his cheeks, pulling me out of his mouth with a pop. "Yes, brother, I'll be a good boy and swallow your cum." His tongue pokes out, and he runs it along the visible veins in my rigid length.

One thing about King is that he loves being dominated when it comes to Eli and me. He fucking needs it. I'm glad he trusts me enough to be vulnerable and be with me in this type of way.

We appreciate the human body and the pleasure that humans can bring to each other, no matter what's between a person's legs.

King stands, his lips colliding with mine, and clumsily, we make our way toward the bed. We collapse onto the soft mattress, him on top of me and me on my back.

Pulling away from his lips, I say, "I have lube in my bag. Go grab it." He nods and stands, walking toward the couch where my duffle bag is. "Front zipper." I felt it would come in handy when I was packing, so I brought it with us because you never know.

It's always best to have lube and not need it than to need it and not have it.

King returns to me, and I scoot up on the bed until my back is against the headboard, spreading my legs. "Make me cum, brother."

King climbs on the bed, crawling on his hands and knees to me, his cock heavy and bobbing between his legs, the tip glistening with the leakage of his pre-cum.

Lowering himself between my spread legs, he sets the bottle of lube beside me. Sticking his tongue out, he brings his mouth back to me, sliding my length between his lips until I hit the back of his throat, making him nearly gag.

"Fuuuck," I hiss, my hands tangling in his hair, guiding him up and down my shaft. He sucks me sloppily, his drool sliding down from my dick and between my ass cheeks.

King slides his hands up my hairy legs, lowering them to my ass. I adjust myself, giving him better access to enter me. He uses the wetness of his saliva to slide two fingers inside my ass, pushing his way through my puckered wall of muscle, his fingers curling and massaging against my prostate, causing my cock to twitch.

Countless moans fall from my lips as my brother bobs his head up and down rapidly, choking himself on my cock. He slides another finger inside me, my eyes remaining focused on his movements, watching him closely as he sucks me so fucking good.

Tightening my grip on his hair, I lift my hips to him, giving him deeper access. He moans in pleasure, then his free hand comes up and begins massaging my ball sack, and that's when I lose it.

Without warning, my body tightens and stills, and I empty my load into King's mouth, gasping and panting as the greedy bastard milks my cock for more.

He pulls away, my dick falling from his mouth with a pop. "You taste good, brother." He smiles, licking my release from his lips.

"Fuck, get over here. I need to taste you now." I urge my spent body to climb to my knees. "Get on your hands and knees."

King does as he's told, positioning himself on all fours. Trailing my fingers down his back, I get behind him, grab handfuls of his cheeks, and spread them, exposing his puckered hole to me. Leaning forward, I bury my face in him, circling my tongue over his back entrance, sliding my tongue inside of him.

"Ohhh, fuck," he groans, his body relaxing against my face as I eat his ass. "Please, I need you inside me."

A few seconds later, I pull away from his ass, tug on my dick a few times to get hard again, then take the small bottle of lube and squeeze some on my dick and his ass.

Holding his cheeks apart, I slowly work myself into him, moving from side to side, pushing past the tight muscle, earning a moan from us both.

I push until I bottom out, then I stop, my hands on his hips. Once he loosens around me, I pull out to my tip, then push back inside, setting a quick and punishing pace.

Reaching one hand in front of him between his legs, I grip on to his leaking cock, wrapping my fist around him tightly, using his pre-cum as lube to jerk him off easily.

King leans forward, grabbing fistfuls of the sheets, his body shaking with pleasure.

"Fuck, you feel so good," he says with a moan, his mouth open, moans filling the room. "Harder, Rowen, harder!" I give him what he wants and fuck him harder, moving my hips and hand in perfect sync, working together to bring him as much pleasure as possible.

Seconds later, King roars his release as his warm cum shoots out and covers my hand.

I move my hand up and down his shaft several times, squeezing the tip to force out more cum.

Once he's done coming, I push him back down, grip his hips even tighter, and fuck into him until my second climax takes over. Pulling out of him quickly, thick ropes of cum shoot out of my dick and across his lower back as I mark my brother with my cum.

With a smile, I collapse beside him, my chest heaving and my cock throbbing.

"You're right. I needed to relax," he says with a chuckle.

Fucking King.

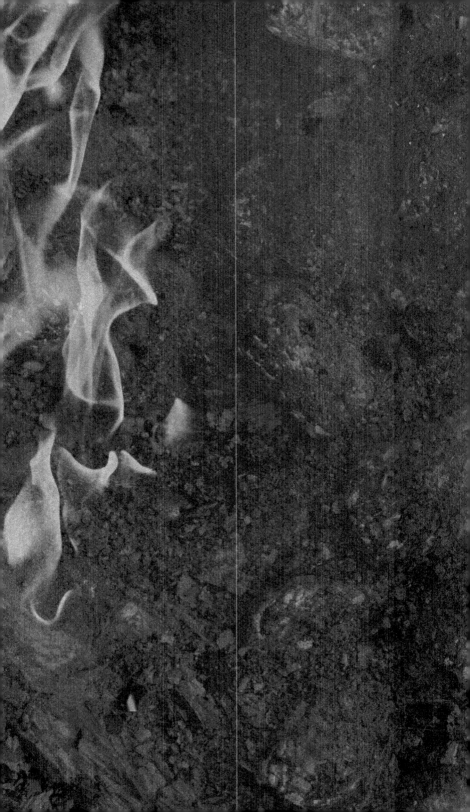

# FOURTEEN
## *Eli*

**M**y brothers have been keeping secrets from me. There's something they're not telling me.

Yesterday, I learned from Maverick that Rowen has had someone discreetly conduct background searches and investigations into things that I have already looked into. There's no reason for him to have someone double check my work. I did what I told him I was going to do, and I told him the honest results that were discovered.

Everything fucking comes back to her. Back to Tate.

Even in death, she's still driving us apart.

Rowen doesn't believe me when I say that I've looked into her past in an attempt to find anything new that might have been missed. The unknown fucker is still out here, and we still need to find him, but my brothers don't trust me.

I can't say I blame them, considering I don't trust *them* either.

We've all lied to each other. I lied when I told them I wasn't having Sebastian investigated any further, and they believed it.

The truth is, I never stopped having him watched. I know

everything about him. Every single step and breath he takes, I know about it.

Three months ago, Delilah Rose was killed in a car accident; it was ruled accidental due to her blood alcohol level. Delilah was Tate's most trusted friend and was also having an affair with her husband. I discovered this when Tate told us that she had documented all of Sebastian's abuse. She'd given a close friend all the evidence to turn over to the police in case of her death. That folder never made it to the police, and I had wondered why, and that's when I decided to have someone dig a little deeper into Tate's life with Sebastian and her friendship with Delilah.

It didn't take long to get photographic proof that she and Sebastian were having an affair, which explains why the folder never made it to the police. Tate's friend was sleeping with the enemy.

I kept tabs on them and learned that a week before Tate's death, Delilah was killed in a crash.

Since money talks, I learned that the police had thought it was suspicious, but the case was closed due to the pull that Sebastian's family has. It was ruled accidental when I knew it was anything but.

I'm willing to bet that he killed her and staged it to look like an accident.

I also know that Sebastian took an extended leave of absence three months ago and came here to the city. To *my* city.

The bastard went straight to the rundown apartment building where his wife used to live. He was searching for her for about a month before he hired a private investigator named Steven and returned home.

The dumbass put too much trust into his PI to dig up dirt for him. All it took was one conversation and the offer to triple the pay for the investigator to agree to work for me and feed Sebastian whatever information I wanted him to have.

He believes Tate's still alive, and he can continue thinking that as far as I'm concerned.

I have plans for him, and when the time is right, he'll receive a phone call from the investigator telling him that he's found Tate and he needs to hurry and come before she returns to hiding. He'll come running, but instead of finding her, he'll find me, and it's not going to end well for him.

He will pay for all the years he's hurt my little hellion. I promised her that he would pay, and I'm not going to break the promise just because she's no longer here to witness the justice I plan to serve.

I had planned to surprise my brothers and let them in on my plan once the time was right, but now I've decided not to, considering they're keeping their own secrets.

I'm not sure what they're up to, but I sure as fuck am going to figure it out.

They left town the other day and gave a bullshit excuse as to why they were leaving. I don't know where they went, but I know it has something to do with Tate. Everything has to do with her.

Perhaps I was wrong in pushing my brothers to get over her and move on, but I was only trying to be helpful. I want them to be by my side again and help me figure out who is setting fire to our businesses.

While my brothers are off doing God knows what, I'm left home doing damage control, trying to prevent anything else from burning, and getting rivals out of our city.

When people hear about the Triad, it no longer places fear in their veins. Instead, they're laughing, thinking they can do whatever they want. They fucking can't. My brothers and I once controlled this city. We own over half the businesses here and used to control the main drug supply.

Now all we control are the legal businesses, which isn't good enough for me.

I'm not giving up control over our drug business to random low-life dealers, which is why I willingly came here to the Westside Disciples territory. I'm willing to form an alliance with the new leader of one of the biggest gangs to team up and eliminate the competition.

Usually, I'd consult my brothers and let them in on my plan, but since they decided to keep secrets from me, I decided to make this decision myself.

A few months ago, the leader of the Westside Disciples was killed in an ambush that also got Rowen shot. They'd been making their way into our city, and we made a deal. For them to stay out of our territory, we'd give them Tate.

That plan blew up in our faces quickly.

We'd thought that with their leader dead, it would take a while for them to restructure their organization, but two months ago, we learned that they're bigger and better than ever.

Leadership was turned over to Malakai's nephew, Jaden, and the little bastard has nearly tripled their profit and supply.

Whatever he's doing, it's working.

He honored his late uncle's deal and agreed to stay out of our city, and they have. They've been keeping their business to their side of town, but they're getting dangerously close to the border of Triad territory.

They've eliminated their competition, and I know if we come together, we'll both be able to get what we want.

Besides, I've got something they need. Something they've been trying to get their hands on but have been unsuccessful.

With a smirk, I enter the dimly bit bar where I was meeting with Malakai only months earlier.

I spot Jaden across the room instantly, surrounded by half-naked women and his right-hand man, Pony.

*What a stupid fucking name.*

"Well, well, well. Look who's here." Pony spots me first, nudging Jaden, whose dark eyes land on mine next. Straightening up, he pushes a few of the women away from him.

When he snaps his fingers, they quickly scurry away. "Eli Hale." He claps his hands together. "What can I do for you?"

I pull out a chair in front of the table he's sitting at and unbutton my suit jacket before I sit down. "I'm here because I have a proposition for you." His eyebrow raises in interest.

"The Triad has something I want? Doubt it. I heard you and your brothers seem to be having trouble keeping your city clean," he says, smirking. I don't argue because he's right. Smaller gangs have been stepping in and setting up shops.

I get to the point. "I know you lost your gun supplier." We may be losing control of drugs, but we still have the main supply of firearms. Thanks to our thriving new business overseas, we now have international suppliers.

"What is it you want?" Jaden asks.

"Let's work together. I'll supply the guns, and the Westside Disciples help to keep Triad territory clean."

He thinks for a moment, then begins laughing. "Basically, what you're saying is that we'd be doing your dirty work. You can't control your city, so you want to give us guns in exchange for us eliminating your competition. Your problem."

"You'd be paying for the guns at a better price than what you've been paying. I have anything you want and any quantity you want." I stare at him with a stoic expression, making it seem as if he's the one who needs me and not the other way around. "In return for discounted guns, you will have some of your men patrolling my city, keeping it free from small-time gangs setting up and any dealers."

"You have the resources to hire your men to do that. Why us?"

"Because the Disciples have become just as big as the Triad. If we come together, we'd both be invincible and could eliminate everyone who dares to step out of line." I lean forward, resting my elbows on my knees. "Truth is, the Triad is getting out of the drug game, which means new potential clients for you. Except, if some low-level dealers get to those potential clients first, you're out of luck."

"Why would you care if you're not dealing drugs anymore?"

"I'd much rather have our clients go to a friend who has pure products rather than some chemical bullshit someone made at home," I explain. "There's a new dealer in the city that began selling last month. Since he's been selling, there's been twenty-one overdoses, all resulting in death. He's lacing his product with some bad shit, and it's not a good look for the city. Especially since we're trying to get away from drugs and focus on firearms."

He thinks for a moment, looking to his left to make eye contact with Pony. "We get rid of the scum, and you give us your drug business and discounted guns. Is that what you're saying?"

"That's exactly what I'm saying."

He seems to think about my offer genuinely, his attention turning back to Pony.

"If you choose not to accept, that's fine, but don't be surprised when you lose clients because they're getting it cheaper in the city."

Pony and Jaden nod to each other. "You've got a deal. We'll clean up your city, take your clients, and take your guns." He laughs. "Sounds like a fool's deal to me."

I stand with a smile, buttoning my jacket. He may think he's coming out on top, but he's not. I was telling the truth when I said I'd rather have our drug clientele go to him and get clean products rather than dirty shit on the street.

To keep my city safe and clean, I have to start by cleaning the streets of dead bodies who've overdosed.

Jaden can take over the drug supply, because little does he know, we'll be supplying guns to those same gangs and dealers that he'll be taking out of my city.

They can bring war among themselves.

"We'll be in touch," I say, then turn to leave, my smile never fading.

One problem down, many fucking more to go.

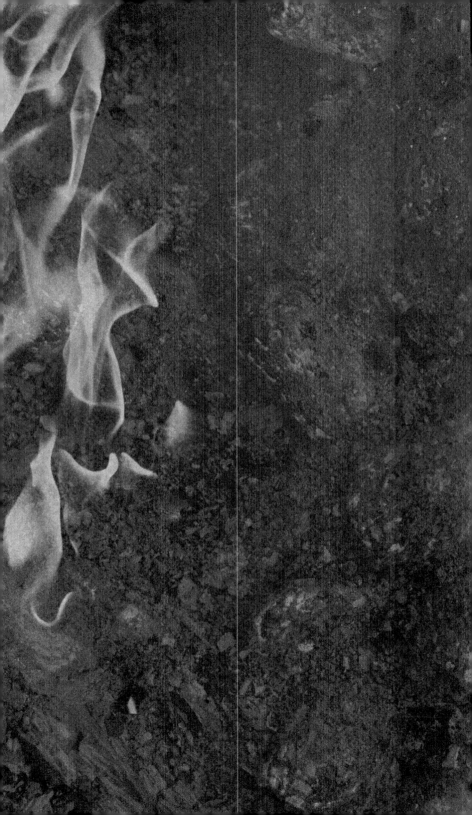

# FIFTEEN

*Lee*

"**N**ope. No fucking way!" Rachel shouts, throwing her hands in the air as she paces the living room of her new house.

"Rach, please. It's so we can help keep her safe in case anything ever happens."

"I said no. You will not stick a tracking chip in her arm and watch over our every move." She shakes her head. "I agreed to the outdoor cameras, and that's already enough of an invasion."

I open my mouth to speak, but Ace chimes in before I have a chance to respond to her. "Let me install the indoor cameras, then."

"No fucking way! This is too much. You guys moved us here because you claimed my house wasn't safe, and now you want to watch our every move and put a tracking chip inside of Olivia like she's an animal."

"We're just trying to keep her safe," I say with a sigh, plopping myself onto the brand-new sofa Ace unwrapped out of the protective plastic. We brought Rachel and Olivia to their new home last night, but since it was late when we got in, they opted to go straight to sleep.

Ace and I came back this morning with bags of breakfast take-out from the diner up the street, and Olivia is currently in the kitchen eating while the three of us talk in the living room. He already had outdoor cameras installed and had wanted to install indoor cameras so he'd be able to keep an eye on them and ensure nothing happened, but when he asked Rachel about it, she declined.

"You're not going to watch me like big brother." She rolls her eyes, sipping coffee from the Styrofoam to-go cup. While Ace set up the furniture, I told Rachel that we wanted to put a tracking chip in Olivia's arm to keep track of her, should anything happen.

"Please, Rachel. Think about Olivia. It'll be best for her." At this point, I'm willing to get on my knees and beg her to say yes and allow us to insert a tracking chip. I'd never be able to live with myself if something were to happen to Olivia when I could've done something to protect her.

"I know what's best for my daughter, and I will protect her." Her words sting. I don't have any room to argue with her, and I don't have the right to choose what happens to Olivia. I have zero say since I gave up that right when she was born. I chose to place her with Rachel and allow her to be Olivia's mother, and as hard as it may be, I have to respect her decisions for her, even when I know she's making a mistake.

Standing from the couch, I leave the living room with a huff, joining Olivia in the kitchen.

From where I stand, I can hear Ace say, "Rachel, she's only trying to keep you and Olivia safe. If anything were to happen to that little girl when there's a chance she could've protected her, she'd never be able to live with herself." Smiling, I turn my attention to the innocent blonde-haired, blue-eyed child sitting at the table, swinging her legs on her chair.

Her face lights up the moment she sees me. "Hi, Aunty Lee." She gives me a wide smile, setting her cup of orange juice on the table.

"Hey, sweet girl. How's your breakfast?" I ask, sitting beside her and stealing a bite of her pancakes.

"You didn't ask, but since you're my favorite aunt, I'll allow you to eat with me," she says, pushing her plate toward me.

Laughing, I pick up her fork again and cut into the soft pancakes covered with maple syrup. She's most definitely my kid and has my sweet tooth. The pancake to syrup ratio is exactly how I eat mine as well—more syrup than anything else.

"I'm your only aunt, but thanks." I lean forward and kiss her forehead, taking another bite of the warm fluffy sweetness before pushing the plate back toward her.

Sometimes, it hurts to look at her. I see so much of myself in her. She's the spitting image of me when I was her age.

By the time I was Olivia's age, I was in my fourth foster home. The parents in those homes liked to slap me around, make me dress in dirty clothes, or refuse to give me a blanket and pillow to sleep on the floor with. I thought things had been bad in those three homes but soon realized how wrong I was once I was placed in my fourth home.

With Rowen.

If I had known the things that would've happened to me inside that home, I would never have complained about the three before that.

"Aunty Lee, did you hear me?" Olivia asks, her small hand shaking my shoulder as she snaps me out of my thoughts.

"Sorry, sweet girl, I was distracted. What did you say?"

"I asked if you could take me to the store to pick out the paint for my room," she asks, eyes full of hope.

"Sure, I can do that. You can go and ask your mommy after you finish your breakfast."

"Ask me what?" Rachel asks, stepping into the kitchen, arms crossed over her chest and Ace behind her.

"Can Aunty Lee take me to pick out the paint color for my room?" she asks, climbing to her knees on her chair.

"Yes, she can take you later, but Ace has to give you a shot right now." Our eyes widen in sync, our attention on Rachel.

"What?" I say that same time Olivia shakes her head and says, "No, Mommy."

Standing, I walk toward Ace who leads me out of the kitchen while Rachel speaks to Olivia.

"She agreed to the chip?" He nods.

"Yes, she did. She doesn't want one, but she'll allow me to insert one in Olivia. She agrees it's for the best and a good safety precaution."

Leave it to Ace to come through for me again. "Thank you for talking her into it. I appreciate it." I lean forward on my tiptoes and press a kiss to his cheek. "You're the best."

"I know I am." He chuckles and wraps his arms around my waist. "You'll have to make it up to me one day."

"What do you have in mind?"

Leaning forward, he presses his lips against my ear. "You, spread out, vanilla ice cream all over, my tongue running the length of your body," he whispers, his warm breath tickling my ear, his words sending chills down my spine.

I gulp. "Well, if you insist, I'm sure I can manage that." I squeeze my thighs together, desperate for him to collect his debt.

"My pretty thing," he rasps in my ear. Stepping away from me, he straightens his posture. "Let's go get her chip implanted before Rachel changes her mind." He takes my hand and leads me back into the kitchen where Rach is sitting beside Olivia, talking her through the process of the shot and trying to ease her worried mind.

"Ace will be very gentle, and after, you can get ice cream. It'll make you feel better," Rachel says, rubbing Olivia's arm soothingly.

Her bright blue eyes, full of worry, look up and connect with mine. "Aunty Lee, will you hold my hand and promise to take me shopping to pick out some paint?" I nod, and she continues speaking. "And buy me ice cream. And buy me a new dress. And buy me a toy."

I laugh, walking toward her. I lift her petite body and sit in her seat, setting her on my lap. No matter how old she gets, she'll never be too big to sit on my lap, and I'll always want to hold her in my arms as much as possible.

"We can do whatever you want, sweet girl."

She seems to think about my answer for a brief moment, surprised that I agreed so quickly to everything she'd like to do in exchange for getting a "shot," but then she nods, blonde locks falling into her face from her messy bun.

"Alright then, let's get it over with." She sticks her right arm toward Ace.

"Come on, my girl. Let's go into the living room." He takes her hand and leads her into the next room.

I stand to follow them, but before I have a chance, Rachel stands and grips my arm, stopping me from leaving. "This is it, Lee. This is our last time moving. Olivia is ten now, and she needs stability. We can't keep moving around anymore. We both need to live a stable life, and she needs the chance to make friends." She sighs, wrapping her arms around herself. "Ten years ago, you trusted me to keep her safe. She's my daughter, and it's time you give me the chance to keep her safe and trust that I know what's best for her. I know you love her, but love her enough to let her live a normal life. That's why you gave her to me in the first place." She walks away, not allowing me a chance to respond to what she'd just said.

Rachel leaves me standing there in the kitchen with a frown on my face and a knot in my stomach. I know she's right. Olivia deserves to have an everyday life and not be forced to leave her friends and house every few years.

It didn't matter much when she was younger since she was too young to have a say or likely remember, but now that she's older and in school, I know that she'll want to create friendships that she won't have to be forced to leave behind.

I hate that Rachel is right. I want to believe that I know what's best for her and that I'm doing what is right, but honestly, I doubt myself.

I know Colton is out there and aware of their names. He revealed that when he sent the photo of them to King and Rowen. If it hadn't been for him sending the picture, Rachel and Olivia would've been able to continue living where they were. They had to be moved for their protection. This time, there wasn't a choice.

Sighing, I walk into the living room just in time to watch Ace preparing the chip to insert into Olivia's arm.

Olivia lies on the couch on her side, her shirt sleeve pulled up to her shoulder, and the back of her arm is wiped clean with an alcohol wipe.

"I can't watch this," Rachel whispers and leaves the room.

I sit on the floor in front of Olivia and hold her hand, tracing small circles on the back of her soft skin. "What color do you want to paint your room? And how do you want to decorate it?" I ask, hoping to keep her calm and her attention diverted.

He kneels beside us, squeezing a part of her arm to gather enough skin to stick the needle in.

Olivia's eyes widen. She squeezes my hand and looks between Ace and me.

"Focus on me, sweet girl. Tell me what we're going to buy for your bedroom." She takes a deep breath and begins telling me about her plans.

"I've already had a purple room, so I think this time I want yellow. Not ugly mustard yellow, but a pretty pale yellow." She smiles. "Do you like yellow? Do you think that will be a good bedroom color?" I keep her talking and focused on me while Ace slides the larger-than-normal needle into her arm, implanting the tracking device.

Tears fill her eyes, and her bottom lip begins to tremble, her hand squeezing mine as tightly as she can. "What else do you want in your room?"

"A-a-a TV." The first tear falls down her face, but my strong girl quickly wipes it away. As she continues talking, Ace cleans the blood away from her arm and sticks a purple Band-Aid on her, rubbing her arm soothingly.

"Am I sick? Is that why I had to get a shot? Am I dying?" she asks dramatically.

"No, not at all. You're not sick, and you're not dying." I climb onto the couch and pull her into my arms. "You have magic inside of you. Ace put magic inside of you so I'll always be able to find you." She seems to like that answer because she sits up and smiles.

"If I ever get lost, or if you ever want to see me, you'll know right where I am so you can find me and see me, right?"

I nod. "Right. I'll always know exactly where you are." She climbs off the couch.

"All right, Aunty Lee, we've got some shopping to do. I'll go get dressed." She takes off running, forgetting all about the brief moment of pain she experienced.

Ace takes her vacated seat beside me on the couch, wrapping me in his arms and pressing a kiss to my head. "You love her so much."

My heart swells as a tear falls down my cheek.

"I do. So much." I look at him. "I have so many regrets." He presses his forehead against mine.

"You're a part of her life now. You have all the time in the world." He presses his lips against mine, and I return his kiss, hoping like hell he's right and I will have much more time to be a part of Olivia's life.

I've missed so much, and I want to make up for it as much as possible.

I've never admitted it before, but I wish I had been able to be her mother.

I wanted to be her mother so badly.

# SIXTEEN

*King*

've been in a funk since discovering that my butterfly has a living child, and I'm having difficulty pulling myself out of it. I'm so fucking angry with her, and I can't stop thinking about it. I know her life was hectic, but how could she not tell me? *Me*, of all people.

Rowen has tried numerous times to cheer me up, trying to give Tate the benefit of the doubt, but I'm having trouble with that. I wish I could ask her why. I have so many regrets, and the only way I've been able to make peace is by finding myself at the bottom of a bottle every night.

I've been torturing myself for two weeks, visiting Sinners and paying for someone to dance for me in VIP room six. In the same room I met my butterfly, and the same room she danced for me for the first time.

Eli fucks his assistant to work through his problems, Rowen fights, and I like to drown my sorrows by drinking and getting a private dance. I'm aware it's not healthy, but my mind is in a dark place right now. I'm thinking things I shouldn't, and I'm afraid that if I don't find an outlet for my feelings, I'll end up doing something I'll regret.

So, I choose to drink and enjoy the show.

None of the women ever impress me the way my blue-eyed butterfly did. None of them make my cock come alive as she did, but it's okay since I'm not looking for anything physical. They're just pretty to look at while I drown myself in booze.

It's been two weeks since we heard from the unknown fucker. There has been radio silence since Rachel and Olivia disappeared from under our noses.

I know the texts will return eventually because the faceless coward is still out there, but for now, I'm taking the time to enjoy the silence.

Well, maybe not too much, considering my mind gets dark when there's not pure chaos around me.

Tonight is no different than the others. I'm at Sinners again, walking in through the private back entrance reserved for our highest VIP members.

We call it the six-figure entrance, meaning only the members who pay the high six-figure VIP membership fee can use it. It offers more privacy, discreet parking, no lines, and quicker service. Plus, it happens to be the same door I dragged my butterfly through months ago when we decided to kidnap her from the club.

That night changed my life forever. With her on my lap in our SUV, feeling her fear and excitement, I recognized something in her and realized right then and there that I was never going to let her go, and she'd be mine forever.

That night, she became mine.

Now here I am, months later, all alone, willing to trade my soul to go back to that night and feel her against me one more time. Just one more fucking time. That's all I want, and I don't believe it's too much to ask for.

As soon as I enter the VIP entrance, I go to the private bar area, and a bottle of my favorite tequila is placed on the counter in front of me. The bartenders know the deal by now. They're all familiar with my nightly routine and know I prefer not to speak. I want as minimal contact with anyone as I can. The only person I want to see is my dancer for the night in room six.

Taking my tequila, I carry the bottle toward the entrance to the private rooms, waving off Cecelia, the floor manager, when she tries to speak to me.

She knows the deal by now. I've made my demands clear. Room six is to be empty at all times, no matter what, and as soon as I get here and get settled, she is to send in a dancer for as long as I want. She also knows I prefer not to socialize, but that doesn't stop her from pulling down her shirt to reveal more cleavage, hoping to entice me.

It's embarrassing, honestly. I'm not interested in her and never will be. There's only one woman and one pair of fake tits that I'm interested in.

"Mr. King! A moment, please!" she yells to make her voice heard over the music, chasing after me as I walk down the hallway.

With a sigh, I stop and turn to face her, my palms twitching with annoyance and the need for a drink as soon as possible. "What?" I snap, causing her to flinch back, taken aback by my aggressive tone.

"Sorry to bother you, sir. I just wanted to let you know there's been a change in dancers tonight."

"Who?" I bark, not okay with the fact they can't do what the fuck I asked. "Is she on my list?" I have a list of acceptable dancers. That may seem a little ridiculous, but I know who I like, and I'm not willing to accept just anyone. When I first became an active patron at Sinners, I began keeping track of everyone's names, and whenever I liked someone and wanted to see them again, I gave their name to

Cecelia, who ensured that only the women on my approved list would dance for me.

She chews her bottom lip nervously. "Yes, sir. I know you were expecting Amber, but someone else from your list became available, and she requested to dance for you tonight." It's not surprising that someone wants to put on a show for me. It wouldn't be the first time, especially considering they all know how well I tip.

Nodding, I dismiss her, not asking any questions, not interested in inquiring who the dancer is that's desperate to give me my own private show. I need to open up my bottle as soon as I can, and I don't have another minute to waste. My palms are sweating with anticipation, and my thirst is so feral that I can practically taste the tequila.

"She's been on vacation for a while and just returned. I'm sure you'll be thrilled to see her."

Rolling my eyes, I dismiss her with a wave of the hand and walk into room six, blinking rapidly until my eyes adjust to the semi-darkness of the room. The only light from the stage is glowing a soft yellow, displaying the stage platform and the pole.

Taking a seat in my usual spot, in the corner of the room on the couch, I open the liquor bottle and take a swig straight from the bottle, not bothering with a glass. A glass would be more work for me anyway.

After a few minutes and a few more gulps of liquor, the lighting changes from yellow to red, and the music begins playing. I instantly recognize the song, and my stomach tightens at the familiarity of the setting.

"Bad Girlfriend" by Theory of a Deadman begins playing as a dark figure walks out of the shadows toward the stage, taking her rightful place. Her back is toward me, and all I can see is her shoulder-length platinum hair since her body is covered by a red silk robe wrapped around her.

Instantly, my interest is piqued for the first time in months. I've never been interested in anyone else, and I'm not sure why I am now, but something about the woman's aura before me demands my attention.

She's familiar, but I can't yet place her without seeing her face or body. As the music plays on, she sways her hips to the beat, her hands slowly untying the robe as she shakes her peachy ass.

My traitorous cock stirs in my pants as I watch her, forgetting all about the bottle I still hold in my right hand. She's holding my attention hostage.

The woman shimmies out of the robe, allowing it to pool around her black stilettos. Seeing her exposed skin causes my breathing to stop.

It's not her creamy skin that captures me or the dimples at the bottom of her spine. It's that fucking blue butterfly tattoo on the back of her left shoulder that makes me throw my bottle across the room, causing it to break against the wall with a loud smash.

I'm instantly on my feet, turning the music off and rushing toward the stage, eager to reach out and touch the woman connected to the butterfly tattoo I know all too well.

This is a dream, I know it, and if I only have limited time with her, I'm going to fucking take it.

With the room now silent, the petite woman turns to face me, bright blue eyes staring at me from behind the black lace masquerade mask.

"Hello, King." Her sweet voice fills the room, choking me and sending chills down my spine.

My eyes widen, and my fingers twitch with the desperate need to touch her before my dream ends and I wake up, losing her again.

"Butterfly," I rasp, reaching a hand out toward her.

Tate takes my hand and steps down from the platform stage. When she's in front of me, I take a moment to appreciate her body and allow my eyes to look her over from head to toe, admiring her petite figure and the sexy red lace lingerie she's wearing, which barely covers her beautiful body.

Reaching behind her head, I untie the mask, letting it float to the floor. I want to look at her face and admire her for as long as I can before I wake up.

My eyes sting with unshed tears, and my vision becomes glossy as I stare at her. With her in front of me, I tangle my hands in her short hair, grabbing fistfuls of her vanilla coconut-scented hair.

Her touch feels so fucking real, and I'd give anything to have her in my arms forever.

"Butterfly." I sigh, pressing my forehead against hers.

Tate wraps her arms around my waist, keeping our bodies pressed together.

"I know I'm dreaming, but fuck. I miss you so much." I can't keep my eyes off her. Seeing her again is something I've been desperate for. When I dream about her, I replay memories we've shared, but I can never feel her. Her touch feels distant, but this time it's warm, and I can feel her and smell her. This is different than any other dream I've had about her.

"You're not dreaming, King. I'm really here." She pulls back, her clear ocean eyes connecting with mine.

"That's not possible. You're dead." My fingers mindlessly play with her new hair, and suddenly it registers. Her hair is different. My butterfly had long black hair with bangs down to her eyebrows.

If her hair is different and I can feel and smell her, that must mean she's here, and I'm not dreaming.

Gasping, I step back, holding her at arm's length. "How is this possible?"

Sighing, she takes my hand and leads me toward the couch. She sits down, pulling me on the sofa cushion next to her. "I'm alive, King. I'm here."

"How is that possible?" I lose the battle with my emotions and allow my tears to be set free and roam down my face freely.

"I'm guessing Rowen didn't say anything to you." At the mention of my brother's name, my skin turns cold.

"What the fuck are you talking about, butterfly? You better tell me everything."

With a sigh, she turns to face me and opens her mouth, telling me how she saw Rowen two weeks ago when he was the first to learn that she was alive. She tells me about her friend, who I know as Travis, and explains how he saved her from the burning house when we thought she was dead.

"Rowen knew you were alive. Did he know that you have a kid, too?" I scoff, quickly standing to my feet, and begin pacing the room.

"No, that part he didn't know."

"Why the fuck would you not come to me? Why did you tell him and not me?" I ask, my eyes pleading with hers. I wonder if she ever loved me as much as I love her.

"I was at Rachel's when you and Rowen showed up. When you left, I followed you both back to the hotel. I didn't know who to tell. But you got off the elevator first, so I told him. I was going to tell you, but to be honest, I didn't trust either of you," she explains calmly. I'm a mess after learning that my love is alive when I've spent three months mourning her.

Meanwhile, the entire time she's been alive and well and has been shacked up with Ace, who I also trusted when I believed that his name was Travis.

"Did you move Rachel Hollis somewhere else?" She nods, confirming what I already assumed when I asked. "Why?"

"Because I know that you guys were sent a photo of them, and I couldn't risk either of you doing something stupid."

My eyes widen, fury flowing through my veins. "What the fuck do you think we would've done to that woman and child?"

"You went to them for a reason. Obviously, you and Rowen had a plan in place, or else you guys never would've visited them." I blink, but she continues, "I didn't know your plan, but I needed to get them away and keep them safe."

"I understand. You have to protect your child." She sighs at the realization that I know her secret. I know about her connection to Rachel and Olivia Hollis. "Yeah, I know. Ro and I know that you have a living child. What I don't understand is why you never told either of us. We shared so much, yet you failed to mention you have a daughter."

She joins me in standing but walks over to the stage and covers herself in her discarded red silk robe. "Rachel is her mother. I'm just the woman that gave birth to her."

"Does she know that she's adopted?"

"No. And she's not technically adopted. Nothing is official or on paper. I was seventeen when I gave birth, and I wasn't in a position to take care of a child. I had her right after I left my last foster home, which burned down."

I arch an eyebrow at her. "The one you set on fire with your foster family inside?"

"Anyway…" She sighs, ignoring me. "I was seventeen, barely had any money, and I was nine months pregnant. I didn't even know who the father was because I'd been raped by two men." I know about her past, minus her pregnancy, but that doesn't make it any easier to hear. What she had to go through at such a young age breaks my heart. I wish I'd known her then so I could've protected her. She looks at me with glossy eyes, a long moment of silence passing between us.

"You went to Rachel Hollis, and she agreed to take care of Olivia?" I assume when it becomes clear that she'll need some motivation in order to continue telling me her story.

"Y-yes," she chokes out. My butterfly has always been so fucking strong, so seeing her choked up and on the verge of tears speaking about her past pains me. It makes me want to wrap my arms around her and protect her from the world. All I want is to take her pain away, even though I know it's impossible.

"She's been taking care of my daughter for ten years. She's the only mother that Olivia knows. She refers to me as Aunty Lee because that's how she sees me. One day, I won't be able to protect her from the truth, and she'll know I'm her birth mother. Olivia's such a smart kid, so I know she'll figure it out eventually." A hint of a smile spreads across her face. The pride she feels for her child is clear as day. She's proud, as she should be.

"Why did you wait all this time to come to me? Why didn't you come to me the second you could've?" I shove my hands in my hair, tugging at the roots. "I don't fucking understand, butterfly! Why wouldn't you come to me?!" I roar, my patience becoming thin as hurt begins to set in. "I thought I meant more to you, but clearly, I didn't. You went to Rowen and not me!" I scream, pulling at my hair until it hurts.

"You don't get to be hurt!" She steps toward me, her hands on my chest as she shoves me back. "Stop acting like you're a fucking victim and didn't leave me!" Her eyes become dark with her anger. "I trusted you of all people. More than Eli and more than Rowen. You were the one I was most excited to see that night in the basement. The second I saw your face, I felt so fucking safe because I knew that my King was there to save me, his special butterfly. You made me feel special and seen, and then I watched you leave. *You* left *me*." She shoves at my chest again with all her strength, nearly knocking me off balance when I wasn't prepared.

"You left me! You left me! You left me!" she screams, her body shaking as sobs rake through her. "You once told me that you'd never leave me, and you promised that I was yours forever. You fucking lied!" One more shove to my chest causes me to fall back onto the couch, my hands slipping from my hair and into my lap.

"Why, King, why?" Tears stream down her angry face. "Why did you leave me? Do you have any idea how it felt watching you and Eli leave? Staring at your backs as you walked away. You could've saved me, but you chose not to. You chose to leave me for dead, even after all the promises you once made to me. You lied to me! You fucking lied!" Her eyes are as wide as saucers, and her usually blue eyes are gray and cloudy like a summer storm. "I laid there and watched you leave me behind, and all the hope I had left with you. I was happy when I first saw you, but that quickly changed when you left me there." Her chest rises and falls rapidly as she falls silent, her heartbreak and anger hanging heavy in the room.

The air feels heavy between us, and the room suddenly feels small.

I don't realize I'm crying until I taste the salt of my tears on my lips.

Wiping my face with the back of my hand, I stand and wrap my arms around her petite body, letting her shake against me with her silent sobs.

Shoving my hands into her hair, I tilt her head back and press my lips against hers, stealing the air from her lungs. "I'm sorry. I'm so fucking sorry, baby. I'm sorry, I'm sorry, I'm fucking sorry, baby," I repeat the words over and over again like a mantra, our bodies shaking together as we cry while holding each other.

"You can hate me, you can hit me, and you can cut my heart out, hell, I'll even give you the knife. You do whatever you need to, baby, but know that I'm so fucking sorry, and if I could go back in time, I would change everything." I hold her so tight against me that I can feel her heartbeat against my chest.

After a pregnant silence, she looks up at me and inhales deeply.

"King, I know who's behind those unknown text messages, and I need your help."

# SEVENTEEN

*King*

"**S**he said what?" Rowen eyes me skeptically. I just told him what Tate told me last night about knowing who's responsible for sending those unknown text messages. When I asked who, she said she'd tell me everything but wanted to tell Rowen at the same time and asked to meet with us.

I go through the story for a second time, telling Ro almost everything about last night when Tate came to Sinners, and I learned that she's alive. I leave out the moment we shared when we cried and held each other. That's between us, and all he needs to know is that I know she's alive and that we're meeting her today.

"Why didn't you tell me that you knew she was alive? You know how much I've been grieving over her, yet you kept that massive fucking bombshell to yourself."

Rowen looks at me, a frown on his face and his shoulders slumped. He looks guilty and ashamed. "I'm sorry, brother. I didn't know how to tell you, and honestly, I didn't want to." His bluntness surprises me.

"You've known since the night at the hotel after we saw Rachel

Hollis. You've known for two weeks and haven't said a single fucking word. I'm supposed to trust you. I can't trust Eli. I thought you were the one I could trust."

He stands. "You can trust me, I swear it. I'm so sorry, but I couldn't. You would've run off trying to find her, and I needed you with a clear head by my side. I knew she'd come to you, and I felt it was best that you hear it from her rather than me."

I sigh, hating that I understand his logic and that he was only looking out for me. "Does Eli know she's alive?"

He shrugs. "I don't know. She never said anything about telling him, but considering Ace has been right under our nose, pretending to be Travis and working for us, I'm sure he's heard enough and told her that we're not on the best of terms with Eli right now." He paces the living room of our cabin. "Did she say anything to you about talking to Eli?"

"No, he never came up. She asked to meet with just the two of us." I check the time on my phone, seeing that there are only a few minutes until Tate is supposed to be here.

"She'll be here any minute. This is so fucking weird. It feels wrong to be sneaking around. We're learning information and keeping Eli out of the loop," Ro says, walking toward the kitchen and returning seconds later with a beer for himself and a bottle of water for me. I'd love a beer, but I've been drinking enough lately, so I think it's time to allow myself to detox.

"Yeah, it feels weird, but that's his fault, not ours. Eli has too many fucking secrets, and secrets are what destroy a relationship. I hate that he acts like he's fucking God and in charge of everything. We have a say in things too." A knock at the door has me grinning like a child.

Rowen opens the cabin door, and in walk my butterfly and Travis, aka Ace, the lying fucker we've employed for over a year.

Tate kisses Ro on the cheek, then skips over to me, jumping in my arms when I hold them out. Her legs wrap around my waist, and her arms drape around my neck. "Hi, butterfly."

"Hi." She kisses my cheek, unwrapping herself from me, and I let her go, setting her on her feet. "King, I want you to meet Ace officially." I glare at the fucker, sizing him up.

I'm looking at him differently now. He's no longer the man who worked for me. Now he's the man responsible for saving my butterfly and keeping her safe when my brothers and I failed her. Knowing that he's the one who saved her from that basement makes me look at him through a new set of eyes and give him a whole lot of fucking respect.

"It's good to officially meet you, Ace. This is a little weird, considering we already know each other. But let's move forward. You saved our girl, and we fucking owe you for that," I say, wrapping my arm around Tate's shoulders.

"Someone had to save her. You guys fucked up, but I wasn't going to allow her to die in that fire. I care too much about her to see anything happen to her." We stand toe-to-toe, Tate to the side of me.

Ace is a tall fucker. He's a few inches taller than me and looks manic. The more I look at him, the more about him I notice. His face is clean shaved, hair dark, and always neatly slicked back. He reminds me of Eli in that way. He, too, always has to have his hair perfectly done.

Unlike my wild eyebrows, Ace's are neatly trimmed, and he's got as many tattoos as my brothers and I, if not more. Several on his face and around his throat.

He's the type of man you take one look at and run the other way, which is exactly why we hired him in the first place. He looks even deadlier when he wears a suit. I would know. I may have asked him to wear one once or twice before just for my own personal pleasure—he looks that damn good in one.

For the first time, I notice his eyes are two different colors. One eye is blue and the other brown. *Heterochromia.* Something I've never noticed about him before.

"Are you done staring at me?" Ace asks, raising his neatly sculpted eyebrow.

"For now." I nod, pulling Tate closer to my side.

"All right, so tell us what you came here to tell us," Rowen says, breaking us up.

"Right." Tate snaps her fingers, stepping away from me. "Okay, so, like I told King, I know who's been sending those unknown messages."

"How do you know who it is?" I ask.

"Because, when I was in that basement, the guy there told me that the man he was working for was waiting for his little bird," she explains, goosebumps visible on her exposed arms. "There's only one person who's ever called me little bird. Colton Adamson," she says, and the name instantly registers in my mind.

The Adamson family. The family died in the house fire she set ten years ago when she was seventeen—her last foster family.

The gears in my head start spinning as I begin putting the pieces into place.

"Oh my God." My eyes widen as Rowen's squint in question.

"What?" he asks, not having yet put the puzzle together.

"The man that could be Olivia's father," I gasp, understanding more of her story.

Tate nods. "Colton used to call me his little bird from the moment I moved into his home. He was a fucking monster." She sits on the coffee table, and Ro and I sit on the couch in front of her, urging her to continue while Ace stands behind her.

"Colton was older than me. He was in college and working for a tech company as an intern. Whenever he was home, he'd bring me white roses to my ballet recital, then sneak into my bedroom after his parents were asleep. He and his father took turns." Bile rises in my throat, and I swallow it down.

"Once, a stray dog had followed me home, and he told me to get rid of him because he didn't like that I showed an animal more attention than him. I refused. His mom said I could keep it. When I got home from school one day, I found the head on the front steps waiting for me, and the rest was cut up and spread over my bedding." She nearly gags, reliving that memory. "He used to torment me so fucking much. He'd never leave me alone. He'd watch me in the shower, watch me when I slept, and follow me anywhere he could. I was never even allowed to have friends because of him." She scoots back on the table and pulls her legs up, wrapping her arms around them.

"I met a girl in my ballet class. Her name was Ria, and she was a better dancer than me. She got the lead instead of me, and a week before the recital, she was attacked while walking home from school. Both of her kneecaps were busted. She said she didn't know who it was, but I did. I know it was Colton. We remained friends even though he told me to end it, then one day, over the summer, she was found gutted in her bedroom with her eyes cut out and her insides ripped out." She shivers, her eyes in a daze as she shares more details about her nightmare of a past. "I know it was Colton. He even confessed to me. He told me that all I needed was him, and if I dared to befriend anyone else, he'd take my eyes just like he took Ria's. I believed him and didn't want anyone else to get hurt, so I stopped talking to all the other dancers. Everyone started hating me because I kept my head down, danced, and refused to speak to anyone. I couldn't have friends because of him. I was completely isolated." She inhales deeply.

"I was even isolated from Ace. Colton's mom, Willa, was Ace's aunt. That's how I ended up there. Rowen, after you killed Greg, I went to be with Ace because I had nowhere else to go. He was trying to get money, and we thought I'd be safe with his aunt. For a while, I was. But after a few weeks of being there, she told me that Ace called and told her he didn't want anything to do with me and was no longer planning on taking me away." She takes a breath, then continues.

"Meanwhile, she told him I didn't want anything to do with him. He thought I was safe with them, and so did I for a while. Until Colton came home, then he and his father started taking turns coming into my bedroom." Ace places his hands on her shoulders, massaging them gently while she continues speaking.

"After I set their house on fire with them inside, I went to Rachel, who I knew from years earlier from volunteering at a center for foster kids. She let me stay with her, and once I went into labor, I had her call Ace, even though I thought he wanted nothing to do with me. He was there when Olivia was born, and afterward, I told him everything." A tear rolls down her cheek that she quickly wipes away. "I stayed with Rachel for six months until I turned eighteen, then moved in with Ace. After that, I kept dancing, then a few years later, I met Sebastian, and you all know what happened after that."

"That's why you moved Rachel and Olivia. It scared you when you discovered Colton sent us their photo, which meant he knew about them," Rowen says, beginning to understand her reasoning.

Tate nods. "Exactly. Up until I was trapped in that basement, I thought Colton died in the fire all those years ago. I never knew he was still alive." She unwraps her arms from her legs and puts them on the floor in front of her. "We moved Rachel and Olivia to a safe house, but I need your help to keep them safe. Please. I don't know what he's planning, but he's already made it clear that he's interested in them. I won't allow him to get his hands on my daughter. I have to protect her."

Rowen and I nod in sync. "Of course. We will do everything we can to ensure they're both protected." He says.

"As much as I hate to say it, we need to fill Eli in on this." Tate says, surprising me.

"Why?" Rowen asks, eyebrows raised in surprise.

"Because we do need all the help and resources we can get. Eli is another set of eyes, and he has men who answer to him only that can help protect Rachel and Olivia." She pleads her case, making valid points.

Ro sighs. "Fine. We'll tell Eli.

"Actually, I'll tell him. I'll pay him a visit at the office tomorrow," Tate says, smiling.

"Poor bastard won't know what hit him," I say, sitting back with a grin on my face.

Rowen stands from the couch. "You both should stay here. We can come up with a plan, and if I'm being honest, angel, I don't want you out of my sight." He holds his hand out toward her, and she takes it, standing from the table.

With his hands on her hips, their bodies pressed together, Rowen leans forward and presses a kiss along her slender neck, grinning against her skin.

Instantly I know what he has in mind for the night, and it doesn't involve talking or sleeping.

My brother wants to play with our new toys.

# EIGHTEEN

*Lee*

R owen's lips on my neck cause my toes to curl in my sandals. I feel like a whore to admit it, but God, have I missed his and King's sexual appetite.

I've missed the way their lips felt on my body. The way their hands felt. And the way all three of them could make me come so fucking fast that I'd nearly forget my name and blackout from the ecstasy.

Separately they're amazing, but together, it's an indescribable experience.

Rowen kisses down my neck, lowering himself until he's on his knees in front of me, eye level with my stomach. With his eyes on mine, he begins to unbutton my jean shorts, slowly working them down my legs, taking my red thong along with them.

While he undresses my bottom half, Ace stands behind me and begins to remove my T-shirt, undressing my top half while King sits back on the couch with his cock in his hands.

I'm not sure when he got naked, but at some point, King also got undressed while I was getting naked.

His large frame takes up half the couch, looking as masculine as ever as he sits there, holding his meaty cock. It reminds me of that night at Sinners when I danced for him, and he made himself come by watching me.

I'd love to watch him pleasure himself and spill his seed while Rowen and Ace play with my body and make me cum.

Perhaps if I'm lucky and a good girl, King will join in on the fun and put his hands on me too.

Rowen and Ace shed their clothing, pressing themselves against me until I'm sandwiched between their warm flesh.

Ace's hard cock is pressed against the small of my back, and I can feel the warmth of his skin and the coldness from his dick piercings.

Rowen's length presses against my stomach, hot and heavy between us.

Warmth floods my core, my thighs becoming slick with my arousal.

My eyes remain on King while Ace trails his fingers up the backs of my arms and around my waist, his fingers gripping onto my nipples and pinching them, earning a low moan from my throat.

My skin is on fire. I feel like a fucking bitch in heat.

Rowen kisses back down my body, kneeling in front of me. He lifts my left leg and places it over his shoulder, giving King the perfect view of my wet pussy.

"So fucking perfect," he rasps. His voice is deep with desire, eyes dark with lust. His fist is tight around his shaft, his hand slowly moving up and down his solid length, squeezing his tip and forcing out white beads of pre-cum.

My jaw aches, and my mouth waters with the need to lick the saltiness from his slit and flick my tongue over the barbell in his cock from his Prince Albert piercing.

"Lick that sweet pussy, brother," King orders, and Rowen obeys. He leans toward me and runs his nose along my slit, inhaling deeply.

"She smells like heaven and sin," he says. King and Ace both groan in response. He presses his nose against my clit, and his tongue sticks out and slides easily inside me, fluttering against my soft walls.

Ace slides his hand down my back, grabs a fistful of each ass cheek, and squeezes, literally spreading them. He's holding me so tightly that it's borderline painful how much he's spreading me open, but Rowen makes up for the sting of pain by wrapping his lips around my clit and flicking his tongue over it, sending waves of euphoria through my body.

Behind me, Ace drops to his knees and trails kisses over my ass, biting into my left cheek. His teeth sink into my peachy flesh, and I yelp in pain as he bites and sucks on me, his teeth breaking the skin.

My hands fly forward, and I tangle them in Rowen's hair, roughly pulling at the roots, gasping and moaning in pain and pleasure.

Without warning, Rowen shoves three thick fingers inside of me, curling them upward to reach that one spot inside of me that'll have me seeing stars in no time. My eyes roll in the back of my head just as Ace removes his mouth from my flesh, runs his tongue along my puckered hole, and then he spits onto my flesh.

I feel the warmth of his saliva around my back entrance, and then his finger is there, replacing his tongue and spreading around the saliva. Slowly, he works a finger inside of me, pushing past the wall of muscle as I allow myself to relax, which is easy to do with Rowen's face buried in my pussy, and my juices squeezing out of me and dripping down his arm.

My pussy makes an embarrassing wet-sucking noise with each trust, but I don't care. I'm too busy floating on cloud nine, enjoying the feeling of both men inside my body.

"Eyes on me, butterfly," King commands. My eyes snap open and connect with his just in time to watch his pace increase. "Fuck. I need your mouth around me, right fucking now," he grunts, his thighs flexing and hips jerking upward.

At King's statement, Ace and Rowen stop instantly, removing themselves from me, leaving me slumped over and throbbing from their loss.

King spreads his legs, and Rowen sits between them, facing me, holding his hand out for me.

"Get on this dick right fucking now, angel," he growls, yanking me toward him. With a smirk spreading across my mouth, I walk toward him, stepping on either side of him, and lower myself on his lap until I'm straddling him, slowly sinking onto his length.

Our lips part, and we groan in unison.

Rowen shifts slightly to the side to allow me access to King, whose angry cock is visibly throbbing, his veins prominent, and his tip a deep shade of pink. I lean forward; Ro helps by gripping my hips and raising me as much as he can while keeping me firmly planted on his cock.

Grinding my hips against his, I open my mouth while keeping my eyes on King and swallow his dick whole, groaning as soon as the saltiness of his pre-cum hits my tongue.

I hear shuffling behind me but pay no mind to it. I can only focus on how King's blond pubes tickle my nose and how masculine he smells. Like spice and pure sex, and the way Rowen bounces me on his cock, stretching me so deeply and hitting the exact spot I need him to.

Suddenly, I feel wet fingers at my back entrance, and slowly one by one, Ace enters three inside of me, scissoring his fingers to help me adjust in preparation for his length.

I've never taken him in the ass before, hell, we've never even had sex before. I've sucked his dick many times, but this will be the first time we've fucked. And I must admit I'm feeling timid. His cock is fucking huge and angry with the metal barbells he has through his shaft.

I love running my tongue along his Jacob's Ladder piercing, but I'm nervous about taking him in my ass.

He must sense my hesitation because he rubs soothing circles along the small of my back, sending chills down my spine while he slides his fingers in and out of me, working me perfectly with Rowen's thrusts.

"God fucking damn, butterfly. You suck this dick like you fucking own it," King groans, fingers tangling in my hair at the back of my head.

"Fuck, this pussy is so good. Brother, you should have a taste when I'm done." Rowen reaches between us and begins playing with my clit, just as Ace lines his cock with my puckered hole and begins pushing himself inside, forcing his way through my tight wall of muscle.

Gasping, King's sopping cock falls out of my mouth, saliva dripping down my chin.

Ace places his hands on my hips, his legs moving to either side of Rowen's.

"I didn't tell you to stop. The only sound we want to hear from you is you gagging on my cock." King forces my head down, shoving himself back into my mouth and down my throat. My eyes water, and I swallow, my throat tightening around him, eliciting even more moans and groans from him.

Ace settles himself inside of me, and once I have a chance to adjust, he pulls out slowly. The barbells from his piercing drag along my insides and send waves of pleasure through me.

Without warning, he slams himself back inside of me, and my body jerks forward at the impact, but this time, I don't let King's length out of my mouth. Not that I could anyway, considering the grip he has on my head.

Rowen strums my clit quicker, my walls tightening around him as my climax begins to cloud my vision.

Ace and Ro work together, thrusting into me at the perfect time. When Rowen pulls out, Ace pushes in. They continue in an ideal rhythm, so I'm never empty.

Every entrance on my body is packed with one of them, and I wouldn't have it any other way. The only thing that would make the moment even better is having Eli join in. I know that Ro and King have their feelings about him, and so do I, but that doesn't mean I miss him any less.

It's actually a little devastating when you think about it. The four of us had grown close, and I loved being with all three men. Things are different now though, and I'm not sure how to cope with the loss of Eli yet.

The loss of the man who cared so much about me and spent countless hours kissing over my body from head to toe, promising that he'd never hurt me, telling me how he wanted to kiss away the traces of Sebastian.

Thinking of Eli and how he betrayed me in the end breaks my heart and causes unwanted tears to leak from my eyes.

Luckily, no one knows the difference between crying from choking on cock and crying because I miss Eli.

Keeping my eyes on King, I reach a hand up and massage his balls while slipping my other hand between his cheeks, using the saliva dripping from my mouth as lube to coat two fingers before pressing them against his back entrance and pushing forward until my knuckles skim his hole.

"Oh, fuck, fuck fuck!" he growls, his hot ass tightening around my fingers. My moans are muffled as they vibrate against his shaft. Drool drips down my neck, wetting my chest.

Ace reaches around me and grabs onto my bouncing tits, pinching my nipples and rolling them between his fingers.

The sensation courses through me like a flame, and without warning, I come with a muffled scream, keeping my mouth connected to King's cock and keeping my fingers massaging against his prostate.

The barbell in his cock tickles the back of my throat, and as I'm submitting to my climax, he chooses that moment to give in to his release with a roar, his unexpected warm salty seed gagging me and nearly causing me to choke.

I suck him dry, milking him of every last drop he has to offer. Once I'm sure he's sucked dry, I pull my mouth and hands away, letting his still semi-erect cock bob out of my mouth and smack against my chin.

His cum mixed with my drool drips from my mouth and down my chin and neck.

"Look at how pretty you are with my cum dripping down your face," King praises, his fingers combing through my hair. "Such a good girl you are for swallowing every last drop."

Before I can comprehend his words and respond, Rowen is gripping my hips, keeping me firmly seated on him as he lets loose. He bursts inside of me, filling me so fucking much that when he pulls out, his cum drips out of my pussy and down my thighs.

My pussy pulses with the loss of him.

Ace is next to reach his release. He pulls himself out of me quickly before pulling me back toward him and turning me around. He shoves me down on Rowen and shoots his warm cum all over my chest, his hand wrapped around his shaft, milking himself of every last drop.

Rowen drags his fingers through the thick white fluid, spreading it around my tits and over my nipples. He takes a cum coated finger and shoves it in my mouth, feeding me Ace's release.

Like a good girl, I wrap my lips around his digit and suck, moaning around it as I clean him.

"Look at how messy you are," Ro says, grinning, his arms wrapped around me, my back against his chest, and my legs spread, giving Ace the perfect view of my dripping pussy.

"Don't spill," Ace says, reaching a hand toward me. He scoops up Rowen's semen with two fingers and pushes it back inside me, repeating the process until he's satisfied that it's all inside.

With his eyes locked on mine, he brings his fingers to his mouth, wraps his tongue around them, and sucks them clean, licking away the traces of Rowen.

A groan leaves his throat at the flavor as it lands on his tongue.

"You're so perfect. My little pretty thing took us so well." Ace presses his lips against mine, shoving his tongue in my mouth to allow me to taste the saltiness lingering on his tongue.

I love how perfectly he fits in.

After he pulls back, the four of us look at each other and instantly burst into laughter.

That was unexpected.

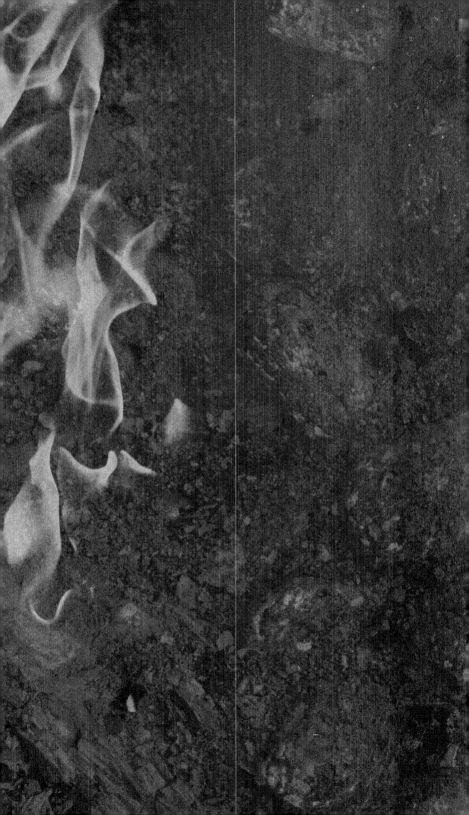

# NINETEEN

*Raven*

"How are you doing, angel?" I ask, walking inside the bedroom Tate had claimed as her own when we brought her to the cabin for the first time against her will.

She's sitting on the edge of the bed, one towel wrapped around her head and another wrapped around her body, her soft skin still damp from the shower.

She turns her head toward me and blinks. "I was just sitting here thinking about my first night here." The left side of her mouth curls in a half smile. "I should've been scared shitless. I'd literally just been kidnapped by three savages, but I wasn't afraid." I rake my fingers through my semi-damp hair from the shower and walk toward her, sitting beside her on the bed.

I place my hand on her thigh as she continues speaking. "Part of me knew I should've been, but the moment King wrapped his arms around me and held me on his lap, I felt safe. I can't exactly explain it, and I know it probably sounds crazy, but I felt like I belonged with the three of you." She removes the towel from her head, stands up, and rubs it against her short hair.

Standing before me, she drops her towel, and my eyes shamelessly roam over her bare body. I catch a smirk on her lips just before she turns and walks toward the closet that is still full of her clothing that hasn't been touched since the last time she was here.

Seconds later, she reappears wearing silky red pajama shorts with a matching top that King bought for her months ago.

"I can't explain it. It sounds crazy, I know, but I was never terrified of you guys." She stands in front of me and places her hands on my shoulders. I trail my fingers up and down her smooth legs, tilting my head back to look up at her.

"You were always meant to be ours. You became mine the moment we met, and once you met King and Eli, you became theirs too."

A faint smile spreads across her lips, and she shoves her fingers into my hair and tugs. "I'm going to see Eli tomorrow, but before I tell him anything, I need to tell you something important."

"You can tell me anything, angel. You know that."

"What I have to say…well, you're not going to like it. You're going to be so angry, but I need you to know that I'm truly sorry." Her words cause unease to set in.

"What did you do?"

"I…" She sighs, looking down at her feet, her shoulders slumping. "I know that two of your businesses burned down." Her words take me by surprise and give me pause.

Slowly, the wheels start turning, and pieces fall into place. "Angel," I warn, standing to my feet and towering over her. "Tell me that you're not going to say what I think you're going to say." She bites her lip, keeping her mouth shut. "No, don't get silent now. What the fuck did you do?"

She steps away from me. "I'm responsible for both fires." My hands ball into fists at my sides.

"What the fuck is wrong with you? Why would you do that?"

"Because I was angry!" she shouts, throwing her hands in the air. "I wanted fucking revenge on you bastards for leaving me. You fucking deserved it."

My eyes narrow. "How poetic. You were left in a fire, so you decided to punish us by burning down our businesses." I pace the room, pinching the bridge of my nose. "What's your plan? Burn down the rest of our shit, or are you done?"

She quickly shakes her head. "I'm done, I swear."

"What you did was fucking stupid. You know that, right? Dumb ass plan."

"Well, I know that now, but I wasn't thinking rationally at the time. I have an entire hit list, but everything is different now that Colton is in the picture and looking for Olivia."

"So, if he weren't trying to find Olivia, would you continue blowing up our shit?"

She thinks for a minute, then shrugs. "I don't think so. Honestly, the second I saw you again, my plan went to shit." Honestly, I should be fuming right now. For weeks, we've been trying to figure out who started the fires at our warehouse and pizza shop, and my not-so-dead angel was responsible for it all along. I know I should be angry, but whatever anger I may feel fades away once I look into her eyes.

"Why's that?"

"Because I..." She pauses. "I feel things for you, and no matter how hurt I was, there's no way I could continue to hurt you."

"What do you feel for me?" I ask, grinning, going to her and wrapping my arms around her waist.

She tries to shove me off, but I don't let her go. "It doesn't matter."

"Yes, it does. I think you love me, but you're too afraid to admit it."

She scoffs. "You fucking wish. You're so full of yourself."

"Admit it, angel. You love me."

"No, I will not admit it."

"Admit it, or I'm going to claim your pussy right now, and I know you're sore." Her eyes widen.

"You're fucked up."

"Maybe," I agree. "But I need to hear you say it. It's easy. Just say, 'Rowen, I love you.'"

"Rowen, I hate you." She pushes at my chest. "You're an asshole."

"We both know you love me. You can't deny it." Her bright shining eyes meet mine as a slow grin spreads across her lips. "You need to go and tell King and then tell Eli when you see him."

She bats her eyelashes at me. "Could you possibly help me out by telling Eli?"

"Fuck no. He's going to be furious, so good luck." I kiss her cheek and pull away, walking toward the door.

"Rowen?" she calls out.

Stopping, I look over my shoulder at her. "Yes, angel?"

"I do love you, even though you're so fucking full of yourself."

"See? Was that so fucking hard?" My heart beats quicker in my chest, warmth and butterflies filling my body.

"Very."

"I love you, but I'm not going to tell Eli for you." I leave the room before she can say anything else.

My angel loves me, whether she likes it or not.

# TWENTY

## Eli

"Is there anything else I can do for you, sir?" Elena asks, a seductive smirk spreading across her overlined pink lips.

I have nothing better to do, and I've been so fucking stressed lately, so instead of coming up with an excuse like I'd usually do, I stand and begin unbuckling my belt. "Close the door and bend over my desk," I demand, pushing my pants and boxers down my ass. I take my flaccid cock in my hand and begin stroking it, as only one face flashes in my mind. She's more than enough to make me hard.

Elena jumps into gear, walking quickly toward me before I have a chance to change my mind and opt for pleasuring myself with my hand instead of her.

She's a warm pussy; what man wouldn't enjoy it?

Unfortunately for me, ever since *her*, I can't seem to enjoy sex as much as I once did. Before her, I never would've complained about Elena walking into my office and spreading her legs. I would've enjoyed it and even wanted to take her multiple times a day.

Since *her*, I can hardly stand myself after fucking someone else.

It's been three months, yet she still haunts my mind daily. She's tainted me. She brightened my life and left her mark on my fucked up black soul, and without her, I feel like I'm drowning.

I hate thinking about her. I hate missing her. I hate how I let her get under my skin.

Most of all, I hate that I allowed myself to be weak and fall in love with her. Now she's gone, and I'm filled with so much remorse that I'll never be able to tell my brothers about it.

They believe I'm the fucking anti-Christ, so fucking heartless that I don't even feel anything about the loss of Tate.

Little do they know, I think about her, and I miss her. I'll just never admit it out loud.

Elena pulls her dress up to her waist, revealing her bare bottom to me. I swear, this girl never fucking wears panties—not that I'm complaining. One less thing to remove.

She leans over my desk, placing her palms on top of it, spreading her legs for me.

After stroking myself a few more times, I reach into my desk drawer and remove a foil packet from the box of condoms I've kept stocked for weeks.

After covering myself in latex, I line myself up with her glistening pussy and fill her with one thrust. A moan spills from her lips.

I know I'm a good lay, but it drives me crazy how much she fucking exaggerates as if it's going to impress me.

Gripping onto her hips firmly, I slam into her, pulling her back by her hips to match me thrust for thrust.

"Oh, Eli!" she cries, reaching a hand between her legs to begin rubbing her clit.

The door creaks open, and in walks the one person I never ever expected to see again.

To keep my jaw from falling to the floor, I clench it closed, grinding my teeth. My cock throbs at the sight of those blue eyes, and poor Elena thinks it's because of her.

Tate holds my gaze and has the fucking audacity to look hurt by the sight in front of her.

*Fuck that. Fuck her.*

She's been alive the entire time, and has been hiding who the fuck knows where.

I lost my brothers because of her.

My eyes are glued to her as she walks further into my office. She goes to the bar to make herself a drink, then takes a seat on the couch. Meanwhile, my eyes never once falter from her gaze.

Groaning, I take a step away from Elena, rubbing my eyes that are playing tricks on me.

My chest aches at the sight of her, guilt instantly consuming me.

*What the fuck is up with that?*

Shaking my head, I press the heels of my hands into my eyes and scrub until I see stars.

"Get out!" Elena gasps in horror when she sees Tate in the room.

I blink the stars away, my eyes once again landing on the little hellion sitting on my couch, sipping my scotch.

"Get out," I rasp, pulling the condom off my dick and tossing it into the trash.

"Yeah, you heard him. Get out!" Elena squeals, pulling her dress down to cover herself.

Looking at Elena, I say, "I was talking to *you*." Her eyes widen in surprise, not expecting that from me. Embarrassed, she hightails it out of my office without looking back, and the door slams shut behind her.

"I see you moved on quickly."

"Tell me I'm fucking dreaming."

Tate rolls her eyes. "Wow, I haven't heard that before." She shakes her head. "Same reaction I've gotten from your brothers."

"What?" I snap, "King and Rowen know you're alive? How?" I demand, buckling my belt.

"Are you really going to pretend like you didn't know?" She leans forward, sets the tumbler of scotch on the coffee table, and stands. "You've always been a great liar." She walks toward me, eyes locked with mine. "All those nights we've shared. All those kisses, all your whispered promises. They were all lies. You fucking turned on me in the blink of an eye."

"No, I didn't know. I don't know if you're aware or not, but my brothers aren't exactly speaking to me lately," I say, earning yet another fucking eye roll from her. I swear to God, next time she rolls her eyes, I hope they get fucking stuck. "And I never lied to you. I simply made a bad call."

"That's what you call turning on me, then leaving me for dead? A bad call?" She keeps walking until we're standing toe-to-toe. "You're unbelievable, Eli."

My hands ball into fists at my sides. "You're not surprised to see me," she points out. "You knew I was alive."

I'm not going to lie. Not to her. "I didn't know for sure, but I had my suspicions recently."

Her chest brushes against mine. "How?" her eyes narrow, "How could you leave me? I loved you, Eli, and you left me. You never even looked back."

My jaw clenches. She doesn't know how much I hate myself for leaving her. How her face haunts my dreams every single fucking night. How I wish I could go back to the night of the fire in the basement and take back what I did.

But I can't. I can't change anything.

Now, I have to stand by my actions.

She lets out a dramatic huff, "Why did you have suspicious that I might still be alive?"

"I felt guilty for leaving you, and I felt responsible for you ending up in that basement in the first place, so I had someone look into the fire," I admit, telling her something my brothers aren't aware of. I did feel bad for keeping this secret from them, but now I'm finding out that they knew she was alive and never came to me to tell me or even ask for help finding her or finding out what happened.

"Why? You didn't believe that I died?"

"I know you, Tate. I know how fucking resilient you are." A hint of a smile spreads across her face for a brief moment. "I wanted to bury you. It's the least that my brothers deserved. It took a while to get information through. According to all the reports, Tate Dawson died."

"Tate Dawson did die."

"So what? You're back to Lee now, or do you have a new name?"

She laughs, surprising us both. "I'm Lee again. I'm no longer hiding from my past, so I'm myself again."

"Okay, then I'll call you Lee. That name suits you better, anyway."

I reach forward and brush a piece of platinum hair behind her ear. "When I was finally able to track down information, my source confirmed that only two bodies had been discovered. Both male. My source also confirmed that a substantial anonymous donation was received to report that three bodies had been found, one of which was Tate Dawson." I wanted to share the news with my brothers, but I couldn't trust them, so I kept it to myself. "That's when I realized that you were still alive. And honestly, I never really felt like you were dead anyway. I had hoped you were out there somewhere, and I'm glad I was right."

"You're an asshole, Eli. Do you know that? You left me." Sadness washes over her flawless features. "How could you do that? How could you believe I'd betrayed you and was out to get you? I don't understand why you'd think that. After all we shared." I take her always cold hands and lead her toward the sofa, making her sit beside me. "And if you believed I was alive, why didn't you look for me?"

"Honestly, I figured you were too angry and thought if you wanted anything to do with us, you'd come to us." My chest aches to touch her again. "Saying *sorry* isn't enough to repair the damage done, but I'd like to try to explain my actions."

"Explain? Don't you mean justify?"

"I'm not trying to justify what I did. I know I turned my brothers against you and hung you out to dry."

"Let's not use cute analogies. Let's say exactly what you did. You turned Ro and King against me, then the three of you left me to die. There's no way to explain that," she says as I grind my teeth.

"You're a piece of shit for doing that. What happened to the guy who built me a ballet studio because I missed dancing? That's the guy I liked. That's the guy I trusted and loved." She waves her hand out in front of her, gesturing toward me. "Whoever the fuck you're becoming isn't anyone that I'll ever like." She walks toward the door but stops with her hand on the doorknob. She looks over her shoulder at me. "By the way, I'm the one responsible for burning your businesses down."

Without another word and without allowing me the chance to speak, she turns on her heel and walks out, leaving me to ponder her words and the fact she's the one responsible for both fires.

I lean back against the couch with wide eyes, and my jaw drops.

*Holy fuck.*

The longer I sit there, the more I have to think about. And then I realize something.

Lee is right. What happened to the guy that built that dance studio?

Where did he go?

I'd like to find him again.

# TWENTY-ONE

*Lee*

"Take a picture. It'll last longer," Ace says, startling me, his concentration never straying from the canvas in front of him.

"How did you know I was here watching you?" I laugh, walking further into the living room until I'm by his side.

He's sitting on a stool with an easel in front of him, a paintbrush in his left hand, and he's adding black paint onto the canvas. He's been sitting here working on this same painting all morning. "I always know when you're near." His dark eyes blink for a brief moment.

"How?" I ask, wrapping my arms around his neck from behind, pressing a kiss to his right earlobe.

"I can smell you." He sets the paintbrush down and turns on the stool to face me, pulling my body between his legs. "I can hear your breathing."

"Am I a heavy breather?" He shakes his head.

"I have a keen sense of awareness, and it's heightened when it comes to you." He reaches up and brushes my short hair behind my ears. "How many times have I told you that you'd never be able to hide or run from me? I'll always find you because I know when you're near." He leans forward and runs his nose along the side of my neck, sending chills down my spine.

Rolling my eyes, I mumble, "I think you were a canine in another life." To my surprise, he bursts out laughing. Ace's laugh is one that I want to record and listen to on an endless loop. It's deep and smooth and does something dangerous to my body. His voice makes me wet, but his laugh, oh God, his laugh...

"Nice to know you think I was a dog in a former life."

I shrug innocently. "What can I say? You have powerful senses."

He nods. "I do. Like now, I know that if I were to stick my hand down your shorts, you'd be wet."

Scoffing, I pull away from him and out of reach. "Whatever. You wouldn't."

He arches a perfectly shaped eyebrow in challenge. "Really? Shall we test that?" I shake my head quickly.

"I can smell your arousal, Lee. It's very musky and sweet, and if I'm being honest, I smell it a lot when you're around. You're wet very often."

"Are you trying to shame me for having a high sex drive?"

"Never." He stands, striding toward me. "So, how'd it go with Eli?" Last night, we stayed at the cabin with King and Rowen, but this morning I got up and left before anyone woke up and went to Eli's office to speak with him.

Now, I'm back home with Ace, and I'm honestly unsure how I feel. I thought I'd feel differently when I looked Eli in the eye and told him I was alive. I feel more confused than ever, though. I wish I could stay angry at them, but I'm not sure why I can't.

They betrayed me, for crying out loud. Still, it's not enough to stop me from running to them and jumping into their arms and onto their cocks. The truth is, I'm deeply in love with all three of them, and nothing they ever do or say will change the way I feel about them.

If anything, I feel regretful for setting fire to their buildings. I knew it was wrong at the time, but I couldn't stop myself. It was too easy to have Ace hack into their camera feed and turn it off, then ignite their buildings in flames.

Of course, I made sure that no one was inside either building. And I set the fires precisely as I had to Colton's house ten years ago.

I walked in, poured gasoline, lit a few matches, and walked out. It was easy, but I regretted it the second I saw the buildings go up in flames. I felt like a fucking fool.

"I don't want to talk about Eli. I don't want to talk about any of them. I just want to take my mind off them, off everything going on."

He nods, holding his hand out to me. "I know we haven't talked about what happened last night. I want to thank you for making me comfortable and not pushing me into anything I wasn't ready for." He's thanked me many times before for not pressuring him into having sex.

Even when he's caught me giving myself an orgasm with the showerhead, he's kissed me and thanked me for finding a release elsewhere rather than pressuring him. I thought it was odd at first, because I'd never push him into doing something he didn't want to do.

When he shared his past with me, I accepted it and understood that sex was off the table. He assured me it was temporary, but I never would've pressured him, even if it weren't.

Before last night, Ace was a virgin. He likes to eat me out, but sometimes that leaves me too feral and wanting more, so he doesn't do it often.

"Can I ask you a question?" I'm hesitant to ask the question that's been on my mind for a while, for years, even, but I've never felt comfortable enough to ask. I don't want him to think I'm judging him because I'm not.

"You can ask me anything."

"Why do you kill women and use their blood to..." I bite my lip, suddenly unsure of myself and not wanting to continue my question.

Thankfully, he finishes for me. "Why do I masturbate with their blood?" I nod.

As I said, I'll never judge, but saying it out loud or even hearing it makes me cringe.

"I'm not sure. I was very young when I first did it, and I liked it."

"When your mom died?" I ask, remembering what he's told me before.

He nods. "I told you that I used her blood to jerk off. It was my very first time, but it felt amazing. Something about seeing the unmoving body, it just made me feel unjudged and free," he explains, walking back toward his canvas and taking a seat on the stool. "The first time I killed someone, I was thirteen. Stabbing her was an accident, but I couldn't stop once I started." His eyes turn black. He's never told me the entire story before.

"I was cutting something in the kitchen, and she kept hitting me, so I tried to wave her off with the knife. She kept coming, and the next thing I knew, she was impaled on the knife. She would've lived if she'd gone to the hospital, but her blood was so beautiful, so I kept going." A smile paints his lips.

"Her wide-open eyes stared at me, her blood covered my hands, and I felt the same way I did when my mother died."

I rest a hand on his shoulder, squeezing it gently to assure him. "Do you miss it?" I ask.

He shakes his head. "Not at all. I realize now that I was filling a void I didn't know I had."

"What's the void you were filling?"

"You. The urges stopped when I met you. You calmed my demons. I didn't hurt anyone for a long time. Not until you went to live with Aunt Willa, and she told me you never wanted to see me again. I started again because I missed you. When I came back into your life, I put all of that behind me and stopped. I haven't done that in a very long time."

"You haven't done any of that in ten years? Do you miss it or even feel bad?" I ask in genuine surprise.

"No, Lee, I haven't. I've had a lot of nights with my left hand and my spit, but never with my victim's blood. And no, I don't miss it or feel any remorse. I probably should, but I didn't care about them." His confession causes a grin to spread across my face.

I'm glad to know he's over his phase of murdering women, but part of me can't help wondering if his urges will return and if I'll be enough for him. He's interested in something particular, and I hope I can one day fill his wants and desires.

"If I accidentally hurt you, I'd never be able to live with myself. I'd be so remorseful. I'd probably kill myself because I'd never be able to live with what I'd done. I could never hurt you." I smile at his words, feeling an odd sense of relief.

What does it say about me that I don't care that he killed innocent women as long as he'd never hurt me? *What type of person does that make me?*

Sometimes, I like feeling pain. I want to bleed; it turns me on to see my blood. It reminds me of the time King chained me in his playroom and carved my skin like butter; it's the hardest I've ever came in my life.

I thought I was weird for liking it because he was hurting me, and

I compared him to Sebastian.

Sebastian hurt me, but I didn't like it. Now I realize that was two different types of hurt. My guys have never hurt me to cause pain, only pleasure, and they'd never do anything to me that I don't consent to and am not entirely okay with. If I ever wanted them to stop, I know they would.

Looking behind Ace and toward the finished canvas, I smile. "Your painting is nice," I say, changing the subject.

He shrugs. "Eh, it's okay. It's missing something, though."

"What's it missing?"

"Your blood." My eyes widen in surprise, and my skin warms with lust and desire at the possibility of bleeding for him.

We all have our kinks, and blood happens to be mine.

"Do you trust me?" he asks. I nod quickly. There's no doubt about it. "Take off your shirt." He stands, knocking the stool to the floor.

My pupils dilate, and desire takes over from the promise of getting to bleed for Ace, something I've never done for him before.

I remove my thin cotton tank top with steady fingers, revealing my bare chest. I haven't worn a bra in days, so I'm bare without my shirt.

Ace's eyes widen as they roam over my exposed flesh. Goosebumps rise on my skin, and a chill shoots down my spine.

He looks at me with a hungry glimmer in his dark eyes as I desperately wait for his next move.

His eyes connect with the butterfly that, months ago, King carved into my skin under my right breast. My heart aches at the memory, wishing I could return to that moment. My panties dampen, my pussy also desperate to return to that moment.

Stepping toward me, Ace drops to his knees in front of me and presses a kiss to my stomach.

He sticks out his warm velvet tongue and runs it along my flesh, then stands as he licks up my body to my chin.

"You taste good." He grins, gripping firmly on my sleep shorts. He balls them in his fists and rips them off with an audible tear, earning a gasp from me at the sting of pain when it rips away from my skin. "Are you certain that you trust me?"

I nod dumbly, too delirious to question anything he'd want to do to me.

Ace steps away long enough to grab something. I'm not sure what, but I'm guessing it's a knife based on the fact I see the silver edge hidden in his palm.

Dropping to his knees again in front of me, he takes my right leg and places it over his shoulder. When he reveals what he has in his hand, I realize I was right. It's a knife.

My heart rate accelerates, beating rapidly in my chest as I watch him, eager to learn what he's going to do next with my favorite little sex toy.

With a smirk, Ace stares directly at my pussy and uses his right thumb and forefinger to spread me open. He turns the knife to the side and runs it along my pussy. The blade's tip connects with my clit and sends a burst of pleasure through my body.

He does it repeatedly, my body jerking when the cold touches my already sensitive bud.

Ace leans closer to me and wraps his lips around my clit and sucks hungrily, his tongue flicking rapidly over the nerve, earning wild gasps and pants from my parted lips.

I tangle my fingers in his hair for support, not feeling strong enough to keep myself standing.

He bites down, adding a sting of pain that he soothes away easily by lapping his tongue along my slit and going back to sucking on my needy little clit.

Carefully, he guides the knife's cold handle inside me and begins moving it back and forth slowly.

My cheeks heat with embarrassment at the sound my pussy makes as he plunges it deeper inside me. I'm so wet, and with each thrust, my pussy swallows it up, creating a wet, squelching noise.

When he moves his mouth away from me, I risk a chance to look down, and instantly I burn with embarrassment when I see the black handle coated with my cream.

"Should I make you cum this way? Or should I use my cock?" His question takes me by surprise, but before I can even answer or wrap my head around his question, he's moving my leg off his shoulder and standing, sliding the handle of the knife into his mouth, sucking it clean of my cream.

"Mmm. God, you taste even better when you're getting fucked with my knife." I gulp. Anticipation and excitement warm my skin. He's already claimed my ass, but he's yet to claim my pussy, and now he's ready to do it. For the very first fucking time.

Standing in front of me, he runs the knife tip along my belly, continuing down between my legs until he presses the blade against my clit.

Chills race through my body and cause me to freeze when the blade touches my sensitive bud, but I trust him and know he won't hurt me.

My fear is all in my head. I just need to make myself relax and fully submit to him.

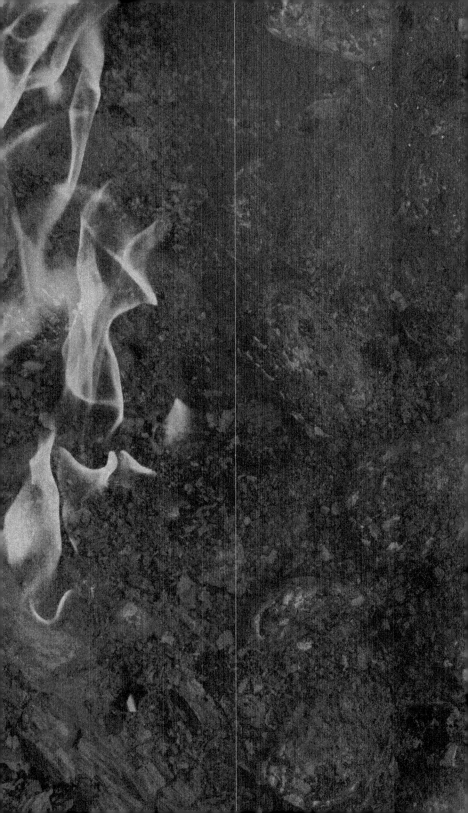

# TWENTY-TWO

*Ace*

"You're so beautiful when you're scared," I rasp into Lee's ear, her platinum hair tickling my nose.

Before taking her ass the other night, I was a virgin.

I'd never been inside of a woman before and hadn't expected it to happen at that moment, but I couldn't help myself once I saw King and Rowen with their hands over my pretty thing. The moment felt so natural, and they made me feel comfortable, so I gave in to my urges and got to feel something new. Now I'm addicted and need more.

Lee always looks so lovely when she's aroused, and I want to feel her wrapped around me.

I've drowned in her pussy juices and choked her with my cock multiple times, but I've never felt her tight walls around me.

Taking her ass was an entirely new experience, and then when she came home today, I couldn't keep my hands off her. All I can think about is being inside of her pussy for the first time.

Her body is fantastic, but I have a desperate need to be closer to her. I want to crawl inside her skin and wear it like a winter coat. I want to feel her touching every part of me, and it's so fucking hard to be gentle with her.

She moans for more, her pupils dilate, and her mouth forms into the perfect O.

God damn, she's breathtaking.

I've murdered countless street whores, felt their blood on my hands, and used it to lubricate my cock so I could jack off, yet none of them could've ever prepared me for this moment. For the moment when I finally get to feel the blood of my pretty thing on my hands. I'm feral with anticipation.

Lee looks at me with so much trust in her blue eyes. My heart swells knowing she wholeheartedly trusts me. She's not afraid I'll go too far and accidentally kill her because she knows I won't. I've never had someone's trust before. I'm not sure how it makes me feel.

Holding the handle in my left hand, I trace the blade up her body, collarbone, and neck until I press the tip against her pulse point.

All it would take is a flick of the wrist to slice her beautiful throat open and drown in her blood. The thought makes me hard as stone.

Her sliced vein would spew blood all over my bare chest, and if I were to lean down, it would cover my face.

God, I wish it were possible to swim in her blood without killing her.

Because I love her, I'll settle with minor cuts that won't threaten her life.

My lips land on hers, and slowly I trail them down her body until I'm back on my knees and her sweet pussy is in front of my face.

I have a front-row seat to paradise.

Raising my knife, I press the blade into the soft flesh of her inner thigh. My mouth connects with her cunt, and I suck her sensitive clit, providing her pleasure as I drag my blade through her flesh, parting her skin like butter. The one-inch cut is deep enough to bleed but not deep enough that she'll need to be stitched up.

She hisses in pain, but her noises quickly turn into moans at the feel of my tongue entering her tight entrance.

Her hands tangle in my hair and pull, her body jerking against me, her hips rising toward me. She needs more—my little dirty thing.

Pulling away from her, I lean back on my heels. "Lie down and spread your legs."

She quickly drops to her knees and lies in front of me, her legs opening to reveal her lightly bleeding thigh and glistening pussy.

My pretty thing likes blood and pain. She fucking loves being cut; the evidence is all over her wet pussy. She's drenched and dripping; I know it's because I made her bleed. My pretty little fucked up creature.

Staring at her center, I slowly lean forward, press my blade against the top of her pussy, and tease her skin until I see the crimson drops I crave.

Lee gasps, writhing in place as her eyes darken with desire. Endless yelps and groans fall free from her perfect lips.

God, she's beautiful and so perfect for me. She's everything I will ever need.

Her pretty crimson blood spills from each cut. The first cut runs down her thigh, and the other flows down the top of her pussy.

My eyes remain fixated on her as I drag the knife down to her thigh to the first cut and press the tip against her sliced flesh, pulling the blade down to make the cut wider. More blood pools out of her skin. Her breathing is ragged and heavy, but it's drowned out by the sound of my heart beating rapidly in my ears.

My cock is so fucking hard that it's painful. I need a release soon, but I must first complete my painting. It's nearly complete, and once I have her blood, I'll be able to paint the final piece and then fuck her.

*It'll be perfect.*

Dipping the blade into her blood, I raise it to my lips and drag my tongue along the sharp edge, licking it clean of the tangy metallic taste. Closing my lips over it, I groan at the taste, my eyes rolling in the back of my head.

So fucking delicious.

I'm not sure what tastes better—her blood or her pussy.

Once I've licked the blade clean, I place the handle back inside her pussy, holding the blade firmly in my hand.

I thrust it inside her, fucking her with the handle, my eyes roaming freely over her body, taking in the way she twitches and jerks. I commit every single movement to memory, wanting to cherish this moment for the rest of my fucked-up life.

The blade digs into my hand, cutting open my palm, but I don't feel the pain. The only thing I feel is the throbbing in my cock and the pre-cum leaking down the side of it. I need to come so fucking badly, but I can't until my painting is complete.

She'll be my reward for finishing.

Blood drips from my hand onto the hardwood floor beneath her and coats her pussy each time I thrust my hand forward.

I place a hand on her pelvis and apply pressure, watching as her pussy sucks the knife in deeper, getting dangerously close to the blade currently lodged inside my numb hand.

With a scream, my pretty thing convulses and lets herself go, her eyes rolling in the back of her head. Her body shakes like she's having a fucking seizure.

A wide smile spreads across my face. "Look how beautiful you are when you come on my knife," I rasp, my voice full of desire. I pull the knife away at the perfect time because her body relaxes, and she squirts out her juices, wetting my arm and the floor beneath her.

She's a beautiful fucking squirter. So fucking perfect that next time I'll have to have her squirt in my mouth so I can drink it before I drown in her.

Pulling the bloody, cum-covered knife out of her pussy, I drop it to the floor with a clank and place my bloodied palm on her chest, slowly dragging it down the length of her body. I smile happily when I see streaks of my blood on her bare body.

Climbing to my knees, I remove the canvas from the easel, set it on the floor beside her, then take my paintbrush.

"Keep quiet and stay there. Let me work in silence," I instruct.

Taking the paintbrush, I dip the soft tip into Lee's bleeding thigh, then apply her fresh blood to the canvas, working quickly to spread it where I want it.

When I'm content with the areas I've placed her blood on the picture, I dip the tip into her pussy, getting her cream, then glide it along the dark canvas, my cock leaking as I get one step closer to finishing and getting to bury myself inside of her sweet cunt.

Once complete, I drop the paintbrush and admire the canvas. "I've always wanted to paint a picture using your blood and cum," I admit, my attention turned to Lee who obeyed me perfectly and stayed silent the entire time.

"Now, are you ready to come on my cock?"

"God, yes," she whines, spreading her legs further open for me.

I adjust between her legs and line up with her entrance. "My name is Ace, not God. Remember that when you're begging me to stop." I slam my hips against hers, bottoming out instantly. My eyes close, and I remain still, allowing myself to savor the feel of her warmth enveloped around me.

"Fuck, fuck, fuck," she pants, her legs wrapping around my waist. Her pussy pulsates around me, matching the rhythm of her heartbeat.

I hadn't expected her to feel this amazing, and at this rate, I know I won't be able to last as long as I want to.

Being inside her pussy is the closest I'll ever get to being in heaven.

"I'm going to fill you with my cum, and you will take it all and say thank you. Do you understand me?"

She nods, eyes shining with lust.

"Answer me," I snap through gritted teeth.

"Yes, Ace," she whimpers.

Pulling out to my tip, I pound back into her and sit back on my heels. Holding her hips tightly, I give in to my inner demons and fuck her wildly. Feral noises fall from my lips as I give her what we both need.

She's so fucking tight, and with each thrust, I can feel the piercings up my shaft drag along her soft tissues.

Placing my bloody hand around her throat, I squeeze, cutting off her oxygen as I quicken my pace, fucking her so deep and hard that our skin slaps and sticks together.

Her body goes lax, her eyes glassy and never leaving mine, her mouth still in the perfect O shape.

With a grunt, I still and roar my release, my cock twitching as I shoot thick, heavy ropes of cum into her pulsating pussy.

I move my hand away before she can pass out, leaving a perfect bloody handprint around her delicate throat.

"I need to feel you come around my cock." I rub her clit with my thumb, still pumping my hips even though my cock is overly sensitive, and it's nearly painful to continue.

Luckily, it doesn't take much, and she falls over the edge quickly, her walls clamping around me as she gives in to yet another climax, allowing me to feel her warm cum around my cock.

Lee looks up at me with a sleepy smile. "Thank you."

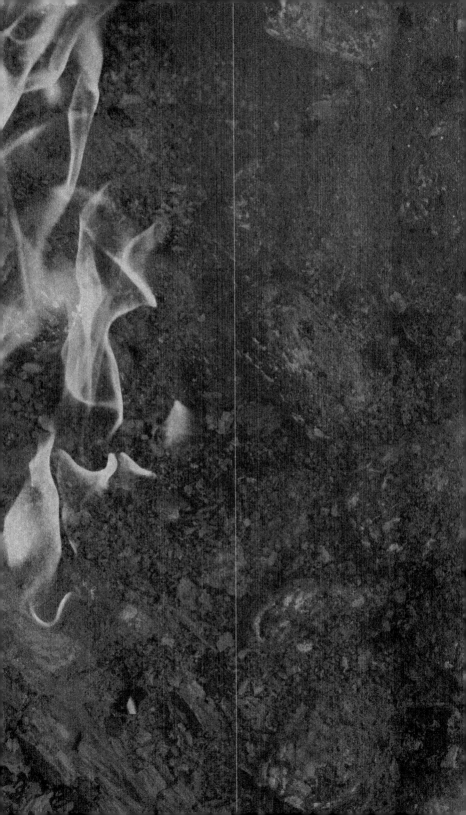

# TWENTY-THREE
## Eli

"Hello, brother." I look up from my computer screen at the sound of Rowen's voice and see him and King standing in the doorway of my office.

Leaning back in my chair, I wave a hand and gesture for them to step inside my office. "What brings you two here?"

"We know that Tate came to see you," King says, taking a seat on the couch in the middle of my office. Of course, they're here for her.

"It would've been nice if my brothers told me she's alive and has been in contact with both of you," I say, turning to face them.

"Yeah, well, it would've been nice if you could've told us that you had suspected she was alive all along. Yeah, she told us that you still had that fire investigated." King rolls his eyes while Rowen looks at me in disgust.

"Why? If I had been wrong, the two of you would've been even more devastated. I didn't want to say anything until I knew for sure, so I wasn't getting your hopes up," I explain, standing.

"Don't pretend you were trying to protect us," Rowen says, joining

King on the couch.

"Brothers, I promise, I was only trying to protect the two of you. If I had proof she was alive and knew where she was, I would've told you both immediately. That was my intention until I learned you both have been keeping secrets of your own." I walk toward the bar cart and pour myself a tumbler of scotch. With my glass in hand, I walk over to them and sit in the chair across from where they are on the sofa.

"I think we can all agree that we've all been keeping our secrets," King says, looking between Rowen and me.

I nod in agreement. "Yes, we have. We know what secrets do to people, and I think it's time we come together and put an end to Colton and Sebastian. Fucking bastards."

"Agreed. Colton Adamson must be stopped before he gets too close to Tate or Olivia," King says with an eager nod.

I bring the glass to my lips and take a long sip. "By the way, Tate prefers 'Lee' now. She said she's done hiding." They nod in understanding. Thinking back to what they said, I raise an eyebrow. "Who's Olivia?"

They give me a deer-in-headlights look, clearly surprised I'm not privy to the knowledge of who Olivia is. "If we're going to be honest with each other from here on out, I need to know who Olivia is," I say.

"Olivia is...Tate's..." He corrects himself. "Lee's daughter," Rowen says. The taste of my scotch turns sour, and suddenly I can't drink it anymore without risking vomiting it all over myself right now at the newest revelation.

Leaning forward, I set the glass on the coffee table. "Excuse me?"

"My butterfly had a baby when she was seventeen. She was pregnant when she set fire to the Adamson family home, and for the past ten years, a woman named Rachel Hollis has been raising Olivia."

My head is spinning with this new revelation. My brothers seem to have much more fucking information than I do.

"Okay, start from the beginning. Tell me every fucking thing that the two of you know," I say, adjusting myself in the chair, preparing to hear exactly how much they have been keeping from me.

Rowen tells me everything they've learned. He tells me about the photograph of Sebastian they received from the unknown fucker, who we now know is Colton Adamson, the son of a bitch who was supposed to have burned in that fire ten years ago.

He continues speaking, telling me about the second photo they received of Rachel and Olivia Hollis that led them to Rachel's house with the plan to take her into their custody to use her to bait out Colton. He shares the details of how Lee went to his hotel room and made it known she was alive and how she had moved Olivia and Rachel to a safe house before he and King could return the next day.

Then King takes over the story, telling me about all the information they've discovered about the lost years we once wondered about. He tells me about Lee and how she went to him at the club and asked for help and how she told them the story of how Olivia came to have Rachel as a mother.

They fill in all the blanks, sharing everything about Lee. Things I never, in my wildest dreams, would've imagined.

Just when I think they're done and couldn't possibly blow my mind even more, Rowen tells me about Travis, who is actually Ace Jackson. He explains Ace faked his identity to work for us once he discovered we had our sights set on Lee.

Once their stories are over, I close my eyes, press my fingers to my temples, and begin massaging, rubbing away the headache I have.

"That's it. That's everything," King says, clapping his hands together. "I know, it's a lot to take in."

"You have no fucking idea," I groan, forcing my eyes to look at the two of them. "Since we're being honest, I guess it's my turn. I never stopped having Sebastian watched," I admit. "You don't need to listen to Colton and use him to get to Sebastian. I can have him brought into the city whenever we want him."

They look at each other with wide eyes. "What the fuck, Eli? You know where the fuck he is? Why the fuck did you lie?" King growls.

"I wanted us to focus on finding the person responsible for setting fire to our businesses. I didn't fucking know that person was Lee." I shake my head, sighing. "He was here for a while looking for her after the fire but, of course, had had no leads. He hired a private investigator, who is now on our payroll." I smile. "Colton sent Sebastian photos of Lee. I'm assuming it's because he wanted him to know that she'd faked her death and framed him for murder. Sebastian is home, waiting for his PI to call him with Lee's location."

"That's it? He's home?" A look of confusion crosses King's face. "Colton made it seem like he was hiding out somewhere."

"Probably because he was trying to get you and Rowen to lead him to Rachel and Olivia. Do we know if he is the father or if his dad fathered Olivia?"

"Actually, yes. Malcolm called me this morning. He was able to find out something. Bill Adamson had a vasectomy after Colton was born because he and his wife, Willa, didn't want any other biological children," Rowen says. "Colton is Olivia's father."

"All right. Well, now that everything is out in the open, let's agree that we won't keep any more secrets," I say, then stand to my feet, ready to make amends and have my brothers by my side again.

King stands. "I agree, brother. No more secrets. We're stronger than this shit, and we need to trust and rely on each other again." He steps forward and hugs me.

"No more secrets from here on out," Rowen agrees, joining in on our hug. A smile spreads across my face as I find myself happy to have my brothers back by my side instead of against me.

I need them more than anything, and I'm happy we can come together and put things behind us so we can be together again. I've fucking missed them, and it hasn't been the same not having them in my corner.

"Have either of you told Lee that Colton is the father?" I question after we break away from our group hug.

"Nope, not yet. We are heading over to their house now," King says. "Do you want to come?"

"I do." I rush to my desk to grab my suit jacket and pull it on, then lock my computer screen and grab my keys and wallet.

"We can take my car," Rowen says once we enter the elevator. "What will we do about Sebastian now that we know where he is?"

"Great question. Let's ask Lee once we see her."

# TWENTY-FOUR

*Lee*

"Lee, your boy toys are here." Ace pokes his head through the shower curtain, giving me a wink. I roll my eyes and splash him with the water, getting a carefree laugh from him.

I turn off the shower and pull the curtain back, stepping out. Glancing in the mirror briefly, I wrap a towel around myself and sigh.

It's been four days since I had Ace inside of me for the first time, and I am so fucking sore and exhausted. Now that he knows what it's like, he wants to fuck twenty-four seven and will not leave me alone.

I started my period this morning and tried to use that as an excuse, but the dirty bastard didn't give a fuck, which is why I had to take a second shower today.

"Tell them I'll be out in a minute, please." I grab a second towel and use it to dry my short hair.

Ace steps behind me, pressing his erection into my ass, his nose against my neck, inhaling my fresh scent. "You smell good. Quickie? We can make them wait."

Wiggling away from him, I put space between us. "You're a dog.

Go away." With a grin, he does. He leaves me alone, his laughter floating down the hallway.

I get dressed, opting for a pair of leggings and a T-shirt. After running a brush through my hair, I quickly pull it back into a small ponytail at the base of my neck.

Stepping into the living room, I find Eli, King, and Rowen squished together on the couch, waiting for me. They look ridiculous here. Their broad shoulders touch each other as they sit squeezed together, and they look even worse when they stand.

The low ceilings are no match for these mammoths. Ace already looks ridiculous when he stands in our tiny house, but now that three more mammoths are joining the party, it's even funnier.

Ace has loads of money, yet he never considered buying a bigger house. We live in a trailer in a rundown trailer park, but according to him, it's better than if we were living in a fancy mansion. He says living like that draws attention, and you're automatically a target.

I've never argued with his logic because living here has kept us safe.

He has cameras everywhere, indoors and out, and no one would ever be able to break in. This trailer park is also the last place anyone would think to look for me, so I'm safe.

Plus, I don't need much.

By the way Eli and Rowen are looking around and peeking out the window every few seconds, I know this is not what they expected, and they're most likely judging the fuck out of the place.

"Butterfly!" King drags me away from my thoughts, rushing toward me. He takes me in his arms, planting a deep kiss on my lips. "I fucking missed you." He smiles, nuzzling his face in my neck.

"I missed you too. What are you guys doing here?" He sets me down, wrapping his arm around my shoulders, keeping me close to him.

"We have some news we wanted to tell you in person," Rowen says. "And maybe you should sit down for this."

I look between their faces, spotting Ace nearby, looking as confused as I am. "What news? What's going on?"

"Butterfly, you should sit." King takes me to the couch and sits down, pulling me onto his lap.

"Colton is Olivia's biological father," Eli shares the news, ripping the Band-Aid right off. That's one thing I've always admired about him. He never beats around the bush or tries to sugarcoat anything. He's always been blunt, whether the truth will hurt or not.

"What?" I blink, taken aback by their announcement. Part of me always knew Colton was the father instead of Bill, but having it confirmed doesn't make me feel any better.

"Bill had a vasectomy. There's no way he's the father," Rowen explains.

"Damn. I'm not even surprised." I sigh, leaning back against King's hard body. "Is that why you guys came here?"

"Yes, butterfly. We couldn't tell you over the phone. Plus, I wanted to see you." King presses a kiss to the side of my neck.

"Don't get me wrong, it sucks, but I had a feeling it was him. Oh well, it doesn't change anything." I look between Eli, King, and Rowen. "So, it seems you three have made up, am I right?"

"Yes, angel, we have. We're back together and good as new," Rowen assures me.

I nod. "Good. You should be together instead of drifting apart." I hated being responsible for coming between their bond and causing them to turn on each other. I never wanted to do that.

"Don't worry, hellion, we're good," Eli chimes in.

"One more thing…" King lifts me and sets me on the cushion

beside him, so he can look me in the eyes. "We know where Sebastian is, and it's your call what we do with him. You said you wanted revenge, right?"

My answer comes easily. I've been thinking about it for a while. "Yes, I want revenge. He hurt me too many times and took the life of my child. He's not going to get away with it. Where is he?"

"His house, your old house. Colton told him you were alive, so he's aware. He has a private investigator looking for you, but Eli is now paying him to say whatever we tell him," King explains, grabbing onto my feet. He lifts them and places them on his lap, one hand holding my feet while the other rubs up and down my leg.

"I want revenge after we do something about Colton. He's the main problem right now since he's trying to get to Olivia. Has he sent any more texts?" I ask.

"He texted me two days ago and said we're running out of time in finding Rachel, but I responded and told him that we know who he is, and there's been nothing since," Rowen says.

My eyebrows pull together in a frown. "Why would you tell him you know who he is?"

"Because, angel, he thinks we're going to do whatever he says, and we're not. Now that he can't use us anymore, he's going to have to find another way to get to Rachel, and Ace said that she and Olivia are safe and secure, and there's no way he'd be able to find them."

"It's true," Ace interjects. "Olivia has a tracking chip in her arm, and I've placed additional outdoor cameras around their house. Rachel's car and cell phone also have a tracker. I'd know if anyone comes or goes." He walks toward me and sits on the coffee table in front of me. "They're safe, I promise." I have to trust him. I have to trust that all four of them know what they're doing and that they will keep Olivia safe. I don't care about myself anymore; I just want my daughter to be safe.

"Okay, I trust you guys. Please tell me as soon as you catch sight of him."

Eli steps forward. "We will. All we need you to do is stay here so we know you're safe. He can't use us to get to Olivia, so he's desperate, and he will be seeking other methods. When he crawls out from under his rock, we'll be waiting." He unlocks his phone and hands it to me. "Is this Colton?" I look at the screen, chills racing down my spine when my eyes land on the blue-eyed devil.

"That's him," I confirm. I never thought I'd see him again. I had hoped I'd never see him again. "Don't tell me your plan. Just find him and tell me once you have him chained in King's playroom." Amusement washes over King's features at the mention of his beloved play shed where I witnessed him kill a man only months ago.

Eli nods. "Give us a couple of days. We're working on a few leads, and this should be over soon. I know it's hard, but I need you to trust us."

Hesitantly, I agree. "Okay."

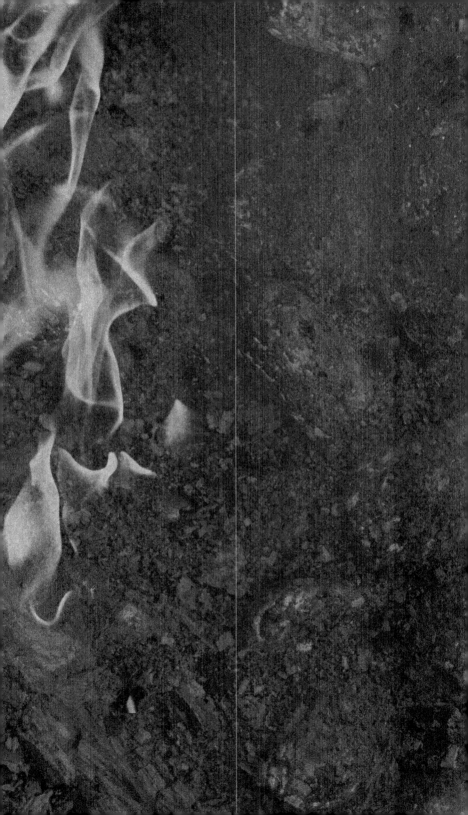

# TWENTY-FIVE

*Ace*

### THREE MONTHS AGO

"Talk to me, Lee. Tell me everything that happened." I take her hands in mine, begging her to speak to me. It's been four days since I took her out of that basement where she was chained up like an animal, but she's yet to open up and give me the exact details as to what led her to end up there.

I'm sure I sound like a broken record as I constantly beg her to open up to me, and I know pushing her isn't the right answer, but I'm desperate to know what the hell happened.

It's been years since I've talked to her, but I watched her as much as I could. I regret that we haven't spoken more throughout the years, but that's not her fault. It's mine.

When she told me she was marrying Sebastian, I begged her not to. I knew he wasn't good enough for her, and I'd been right. She'd been so blindly in love, believing she was finally getting her happily ever after that she turned a blind eye to all the red flags I had seen. She chose to believe he was a fucking prince when I knew he was the devil in disguise.

I lost the fight and had to watch the only girl I've ever loved marry that piece of shit.

For a while, I watched them. I was surprised to learn she'd been right, and he was great. Then, I stopped watching her, and that's when their marriage took a turn for the worse, and he began beating her.

Not a day goes by that I don't punish myself for letting her go and not keeping better tabs on her. I should've known her smiles were fake. I know her genuine smile. I know how deep her dimples are when she's truly happy.

Instead of stepping in, I did nothing while she remained with that monster, living in yet another fucking nightmare.

I'm doing my best to make up for my sins of the past, and I'm trying to make up for all the things I did wrong with her, like leaving her when she truly needed me.

Now, all I can do is ensure that those Triad fuckers pay for what they did to her.

"Ace." She sighs, her eyes connecting with mine for the first time in days. She's been closed off and keeping to herself, and I'm afraid that her dark thoughts will completely consume her if I don't get her out of her head and help her heal—starting with getting her to talk about what happened.

I need to know. I need to know everything, and I need her to tell me rather than me jumping to conclusions and making assumptions.

With tears streaming down her face, she says the one name that I least expected to ever hear again. "Colton. He's alive." Her eyes darken with fear, and her body begins to shake.

Sitting beside her, I pull her trembling body against me, wrapping my arms tightly around her. "It's okay, my pretty thing. I'm here, I've got you, and I will always protect you." I'm the reason that bastard was brought into her life in the first place.

I have so many fucking things to make up for, and I'm willing to spend the rest of my life making up for all my mistakes.

"Tell me what happened, Lee, please." I gently stroke her long black hair, pushing her bangs from her face.

"He put a hit on me or something." She shudders. "He wanted me and hired people to kidnap me. Eli, King, and Rowen." Her bottom lip trembles saying their names. "They took me and planned to trade me, but plans changed, and everything went to shit. Colton turned them against me and convinced them I was working for one of their rivals." She wipes her falling tears. "He threatened my friend, Cassie, and was going to kill her. I had to protect her, so I went to him just as King found me fleeing the club we were at." She pauses to take in a slow and deep breath.

"Meanwhile, he was texting them and telling them lies about me betraying them. King shot me. He was so angry at the thought of me turning on him, but I didn't. I swear I didn't." She sobs into my chest, wetting my light gray T-shirt, turning the material dark. "I went willingly because I was trying to protect my friend, but I think he killed her anyway." She pulls away from me, her eyes wide.

"Please, Ace, please. Look into my friend and see if she's alive or not. See if he actually killed her or if he was just trying to scare and control me."

I rub her shivering arms, nodding. "I will. I'll look into her," I promise.

She sighs in relief. "God, I hope she's okay. I hope he didn't kill her. Cassie didn't deserve that." Her eyes well with tears once again. "I thought he was dead. I thought I had succeeded in killing him. I can't do anything right. I can't even fucking murder someone correctly." Shaking her head, she leans against me again, her face buried in the crook of my neck.

"God, I hope she's okay," she mutters, tears wetting my skin.

I rub her back, not offering any words of encouragement.

Knowing what my cousin is capable of, Cassie is very likely dead, and I don't want to give Lee false hope. There's a high chance her friend is gone.

For her sake, I hope it's not true.

# TWENTY-SIX

*Ace*

Three months ago, Lee asked me to look into her friend Cassie; she believes Colton is responsible for killing her. She was crying and desperate to find out what had happened, so I agreed. I'd do anything for her—anything to put a smile on her face.

When she finally told me about what happened in the basement and told me that Colton was alive, I knew that her friend wouldn't be found alive. Not after everything I've learned about the cousin I once thought was just weird, but realized was an actual fucking psychopath. Though, I don't think I can judge. It's possible that I am too.

If I'd known how fucked up he was, I never would've had her stay in a home with him. That's my regret to live with, and I'll forever be sorry for making such a horrible fucking decision.

I had hoped to find good news about Cassie, but it wasn't easy to find any information at all about her.

There'd been no activity on her social media, and she hadn't been to work. She just vanished one day without a trace.

Vanished into thin air.

I found nothing until three days ago. With the help of Eli, we discovered that a Jane Doe's body had been taken to the morgue six towns over. The woman was missing all her teeth, hair, and fingers, so the small town she'd been dumped in had difficulty identifying her body.

They shoved her away in the freezer and did nothing with her for over three months. One day they finally released a photo of her, seeking the communities' assistance to identify the deceased woman.

I guess they thought she was a washed-up junkie that no one would miss, so they didn't even bother trying to have her identified.

Stupid fucks.

Using the photo from the morgue, I showed it to Lee and asked her to confirm if it was Cassie, and she confirmed it was.

My poor pretty thing has been beating herself up nonstop, blaming herself for the death of her friend.

"I knew she was dead all along, but I had hoped Colton was playing his usual tricks, and it wasn't really her," Lee says with a sigh. We're home, lying in bed, and she's curled up in a ball under my arm, stealing my body heat.

It's been a week since Eli, King, and Rowen were here, telling her they had a plan to find Colton, and it's been a week since she's been able to go outside or see Olivia.

I know she's going crazy and hates not being able to see Rachel and Olivia, but my pretty thing hasn't complained once about the situation. She understands she has to stay inside for everyone's safety.

Colton is unpredictable, and he's out there, and he knows that we're aware of who he is, so now he's desperate. It's only a matter of time before he strikes, and I refuse to have Lee caught in the crossfire.

Eli was able to get Cassie's body and give her a proper burial. Once it's safe, my pretty thing will be able to pay her respects to her friend, but unfortunately, now isn't the time for that.

I've helped Eli, King, and Rowen with whatever they need every day, helping them look into ways to lure Colton out of whatever dark hiding spot he's currently lurking in.

To be honest, it's really fucking difficult. They sent his photo all over the city and even had Jaden with the Westside Disciples distribute the image around their territory in case Colton is hiding outside the city. He also passed it along to the South Lords, a Triad ally gang.

We will find him. It's just a matter of time.

He knows that we're closing in on him, and there's nowhere for him to run, so wherever he is, he's stuck. He's a sitting, scared little duck until we get to him…then he'll wish he were never born.

"I really miss Olivia. I'm anxious to go and see her," she mumbles through a yawn. It's after midnight, but I'm wide awake since I just got home a few minutes ago. I had another long day speaking with people who claimed to have seen Colton and only came forward because they were hoping to get on the Triad's good side.

"I know you are. Soon you can, I promise you. Just be patient a little bit longer." I press a kiss against her forehead. "I'm sorry about Cassie."

"I'm glad you found her and that she's finally buried as she should be. She can rest now, instead of being out there lost." She cuddles closer to me, throwing a leg over my waist. "Promise you'll be safe while you're out there looking for Colton. We both know what he's capable of, and you're his cousin. He could try and kill you for coming after him."

My heart swells in my chest. I love when she's worried about me. It makes me feel loved. "King is going to pick you up tomorrow, and you're going to spend the day with him." Her head pokes up, and her face turns into a huge grin.

"Really?" I knew she'd be happy about that. I know she's tired of being left behind in his trailer alone all the time, which is why I suggested King gives me his workload so he could spend the day with Lee.

"He'll be here in the morning." That seems to be all she needs to hear because now she's wide awake. Lee sits up, throws the blankets off her, and climbs on top of me, straddling my waist.

We're both naked. We've been sleeping this way for months now, so I can feel her wetness against my stomach with how she's sitting on me.

"Have I told you lately that I love you?" She grins, her face lit up by the light from my lamp on my beside table.

Raising her hips, she positions herself over my hardness and slowly sinks down, impaling herself on my cock.

"Show me how much you love me by riding this dick."

# TWENTY-SEVEN

*King*

"King, what are we doing here?" my butterfly asks as I take her hand and lead her away from our parked car and toward the black-painted building with white neon wording above it that reads Skelly's.

"What is this place?" she questions, turning her attention to me.

"Skelly is a friend of mine. This is his shop."

"What kind of shop?" She eyes the outside skeptically. Just looking at the building, you'd never be able to know what type of business it is.

Without answering, I lead Lee to the front door and open it, leading her inside the gothic-style building. Her eyes widen once she realizes where we are. "A tattoo shop?" She steps away from me, dropping my hand, her blue eyes wide as she takes in the décor.

I picked my butterfly up this morning so we could spend the day together. It's been a week since I've held her in my arms. We've FaceTimed every night, but it's not the same, and I've missed her touch. She practically ran into me when she saw me at the door, and her smile hasn't faded.

I wanted to take her someplace special, so I decided to take her to Skelly's.

Skelly and I met years ago; he is the man responsible for giving me my very first tattoo. I loved his work so much that I became faithful to him over the years, and now he's responsible for all of my tattoos—my brothers' too. He's the only one we trust to touch our bodies with ink.

With a little bit of help from us, he was able to open his shop and quit working for the piece of shit he used to work for downtown.

Lee looks at me just as a tall, skinny man dressed in black spandex biker shorts and a white tank top appears, his skin covered in tattoos. His spiked hair is dyed a vibrant fire hydrant red, and he's wearing a bright smile across his pale face.

"King! My man!" He claps his hands together. He's pushing fifty, but you'd never be able to tell by looking at him.

"Hey, Skell, I brought my woman by to get some work done." I wrap my arm around Lee's shoulders as her eyes widen with excitement. "This is my butterfly, and she wants to get her nipples pierced."

"Nice to meet you, King's woman. I'm Skelly, but you can call me Skell." He extends his hand toward her, eyes roaming freely over her body from head to toe.

If I didn't know him and know that he loves cock, I'd be knocking his teeth out for the way he's staring at my butterfly.

Skell loves a nice, fat cock. He's been with his man for nearly thirty years. He's not looking at Lee sexually but merely admiring her beauty. You don't have to be interested in women to admit she's stunning.

They shake hands, and she introduces herself. "I'm Lee. It's nice to meet you."

"So, nipples, yeah?" he asks, taking her by the hand and leading her into the back of the parlor to the private room where he works.

"I wanted my name tattooed on her ass, but she won't agree to it," I say with an eye roll. When Lee told me she wanted to get her nipples pierced, I thought it would be hot for her to get my name tattooed on her ass, but she fucking rejected me.

It's fine for now because I will get what I want, and my new idea is better than tattooing my name on her.

Lee looks at me; her eyebrows are pulled together in suspicion when she sees the giddy look on my face. Of course, she knows me too well and knows something is up with me.

"What?"

I shake my head and press a quick kiss to her lips. "Nothing," I lie. "Just thinking how fucking hot it'll be to see you with your nipples pierced."

Rolling her eyes, she walks toward Skell, but I see the grin on her lips.

"All right, little miss, take your shirt off for me and lie down," he instructs, his back toward us as he gathers the items he'll need to complete the piercing.

Lee removes her tank top, revealing her bare chest, and climbs onto the padded table where she lies down.

I walk toward her and stand between her legs, running my hands up them and loving how smooth they are. I fumble with the buttons on her shorts, unable to help myself.

She wraps her legs around my waist, her head turning to the side. "So, Skell, did you pierce King's cock?" she asks bluntly, earning a chuckle from him.

He turns toward us. "I sure as fuck did. Looks damn good too, huh?" He winks, setting the items in his hands on the metal tray beside the table.

"Sure does," she agrees. "Feels good, too," she mumbles under her breath, but I'm sure the fucker heard her because he's wearing a mighty grin.

"You have very lovely nipples. This will be fun." He rubs his gloved thumb along her pebbled nipples. "Let's get started." He removes a sterile wipe from the packaging and rubs it along her left nipple, cleaning it so he can pierce it.

"King, on the phone you mentioned you were brining your own jewelry?"

"Yup, got it right here." Smiling, I reach inside my pocket and pull out a black velvet bag that contains two nipple rings I ordered specially for my butterfly.

"Can I see it?" Lee asks from where she lies.

"Nope, you'll see it after," I say, giving Skell the bag. He takes it and opens it up, removing both barbells. A chuckle escapes him when he sees the jewelry.

While he sanitizes the barbells, my attention turns to my now pouting butterfly. She rolls her eyes and flips me off, looking so fucking sexy.

Once Skell is ready to start, he picks up the metal clamp and clamps down on her nipple, holding it firmly in place. "Take a deep breath, and count to three," he instructs, picking up the needle from the table and coating the tip in Vaseline.

I slip my hands into the sides of her shorts, reaching toward her warm center. I move her thong easily to the side and run my finger along her slit, spreading her lips and flicking her clit, eliciting a sudden gasp as she tightens her legs around my waist.

With a grin, I turn my attention to Skell, who just gives me a wink.

"All right, here we go," he says, bringing the needle toward her nipple while I slowly slide two fingers into Lee's dampening pussy, my thumb pressing against her clit as I massage against her G-spot.

Skell connects the needle with her skin and begins pushing it through her nipple. She closes her eyes tightly, her lips parting, her face contorting in both pain and pleasure as I apply more pressure and massage her clit simultaneously as I thrust my fingers inside her tight core.

Skell works quickly to remove the needle, insert the jewelry into her newly pierced nipple, and then move on to the next one.

Lee's pussy sucks my fingers in deeper, squeezing them in a vise grip. Her walls are hot and wet against my fingers, and I swear it's the best fucking feeling there is. Being inside her pussy is the most incredible fucking feeling on this planet. She's got magic between her legs.

While he works on the next piercing, I continue rubbing her slowly, letting her climax torture her as it slowly builds.

He repeats the process with the second piercing, pushing the needle through as her walls tighten around me, making it hard to move.

Lee's hands ball into fists, and her climax rakes through her body, causing her legs to shake just as Skelly completes the piercing and places the jewelry inside.

"All done," he says, looking at me with a grin. Taking off his gloves, he picks up the black handheld mirror and hands it to Lee, allowing her to see her newly pierced nipples that are decorated with the jewelry I chose.

On each end of the barbell is a blue butterfly, and they each sit perfectly against her pretty, pink nipples.

Blue butterfly nipple rings for my butterfly.

Pulling my fingers from her pussy, I suck my fingers into my mouth, moaning at her sweet and salty taste.

"Oh my God, I love them." She laughs, handing the mirror back to Skell. Her sparkling eyes connect with mine. "Of course, you'd get these." She laughs, the beautiful sound so carefree and full of life. I love the sound of her laugh.

Leaning over her, I press a kiss to each swollen nipple, admiring the new jewelry.

"Perfect." I press my lips against hers, slipping my tongue into her mouth, allowing her to taste the saltiness from her orgasm.

Lee takes a quick trip to the restroom while I pay and chat with Skell, catching up since it's been a while since I've seen him. Four months ago, I came to him, and he tattooed a blue butterfly on my chest, the same tattoo that Lee has on her shoulder, and that's the last time I saw him.

Once she resurfaces, I see the aftermath of her orgasm all over her flushed face, her cheeks rosy, and her eyes bright with happiness but with a sparkle of desire.

"It was great to meet you, Lee. I hope that you come back to see me again. Perhaps I can ink your skin next time." He takes her hand, pressing a kiss to the back of it.

"Nice to meet you, too. I look forward to seeing you again."

"Later, King. Don't keep your lady hidden away for much longer."

"I promise I won't." I wrap my arm around her shoulder and lead my girl out of the parlor.

We're just approaching the car when she stops and turns to face me.

Staring into my eyes, she wraps her arms around my waist, a slow content smile spreading across her plump red lips.

"Why are you looking at me like that?" I shove my hands into the back pockets of her shorts.

"Because I just realized something."

"What did you just realize?"

"That I love you." My heart swells at her confession.

My butterfly loves many things, and over the time I've known her, she's told me all about the things she loves, but the things she loves have never been a person.

She loves banana French toast drowned in syrup, a ridiculous amount of creamer in her coffee, and she loves reading by the window on rainy days. Now, she loves me, too.

My butterfly loves me, and I'm ready to shout it from the rooftops.

It's one thing to have Lee's attention and to be with her, but it's something else entirely to have her love when it's so rare that she gives it away.

I'm not sure what I did to deserve it, but I'm sure as fuck not going to question the fact that she loves me.

"I love you, butterfly." I press a kiss to her lips, tasting our salty tears.

This is a moment I'll remember for the rest of my fucking life.

# TWENTY-EIGHT

*Lee*

"Hello, my pretty thing. How was your day with King?" Ace wraps his arms around me from behind, pressing a kiss against my jawline.

I ignore his question and ask one of my own. "Have you heard from Rachel?" I've been calling her all day for our daily check-in, but every call has gone unanswered, and none of the texts have been responded to. My anxiety is high, and I'm beginning to worry about her and Olivia. It's not like her to refuse my calls. If she's ever missed my call in the past, she's always called me back within ten minutes. This time, it's been hours that I've been calling and even longer since I have actually spoken to her.

"No, the last I talked to her was when I went to their house last night. I was doing my drive-by when I saw she was playing outside with Olivia, so I stopped until they went inside for the night," he says, locking the multiple locks on the door behind him.

His response does nothing to ease my mind. Rachel and I speak twice a day. Every morning at nine o'clock and every evening at five o'clock. We've had the same call schedule for years; she knows when to expect my calls. "It's after seven, Ace. She's missed both check-ins today." Every night since we've moved them, Ace has been driving by their house at eight o'clock to be on the safe side and see how things are.

His brown eyes widen in surprise, instantly becoming as worried as I am. I watch as he pulls his phone from his pocket and dials her number while sprinting into his computer room. I follow behind him like a lost puppy, hopeful that he'll be able to track their location.

When he gave Rachel her new phone and car, he set up a tracker on both. It may seem extreme, but we need to know where she is twenty-four seven. I would've already been tracking if I knew anything about his computer system or passwords.

I make a mental note to have him show me how to work the systems he's created so I can do it myself whenever he's not around.

Ace claims the seat at his desk and brings his wall of computer screens to life, typing away on his keyboard to enter his multiple passwords. One by one, all twelve screens light up and display different information. He's a fucking genius. The motherfucker can access anything.

Once, just for fun and to be a showoff, he hacked into the FBI database to show me how easy it is for him to access anything and uncover anything.

"All right, give me two seconds. I'm tracking Olivia's chip and Rachel's phone and car to see where they're at right now." He had also offered to place a chip in Rachel's arm, but she refused. I understood, so I didn't push the subject, but now I wish I would've.

Ace points to one of the screens. "It's showing they're at home." I squint, looking at the little red dot on the map he's showing me.

"Then why the fuck aren't they answering?" I redial Rachel, my foot anxiously tapping against the hardwood floor, my patience getting thinner and thinner by the second. The call yet again continues to ring until I hear the automated woman asking me to leave a voicemail.

Catching me by surprise, my phone vibrates in my hand, and Rachel's name lights up the screen. I answer without hesitation. "Oh my God! Why haven't you been answering your phone?"

"I'm so so so sorry, Lee! Olivia and I have had such a busy day. We went to the Farmers' Market you told us about and a home décor store for Olivia's bedroom. We just got home."

"Are you two okay? I've been calling for hours."

"Yes! We're fine. My phone died, and we had some car trouble." She sighs. "I'm so sorry to worry you. Olivia had so much fun today. Is it too late for you to come over? She has been begging me to show you her new sundress for hours."

Laughing to myself, I place a hand on Ace's shoulder, then lean down and press a kiss to his forehead. "I'll be right over." I end the call, shoving my phone into my pocket.

"They're home?" he asks, face full of concern.

I nod. "They've been out shopping for stuff for Olivia's new room. You know how Rachel is when she's shopping." I laugh, feeling foolish that I allowed myself to get so worked up over nothing. "I'm going to head over there. I'll be back in an hour or two."

"I'll drive you. I don't want you going anywhere alone," he says, standing.

"No, I'll be fine. You stay here and think of me. When I get back, we'll do something fun." I smirk, pressing a kiss to his lips.

He shakes his head, towering over me as we stand toe-to-toe. "Don't forget Colton is out there searching for you. You are not going alone."

"Ace, I'm just going to Rachel's. I was out today, and I was fine.

I'm tired of being home locked away and afraid of my own shadow. I've lived this way long enough, and right now, I want to go and visit my daughter." I wrap my arms around his waist. "Please, let me," I beg, fluttering my eyelashes at him and poking out my bottom lip.

His shoulders slump in defeat. "Be safe, pretty thing. Call me as soon as you get there and once you're on your way home."

"I promise." I stretch up on my tiptoes and press my lips against his.

Pulling away, I turn, and he smacks my ass when I begin walking out.

Twenty minutes later, I pull into Rachel's driveway and park beside her car. The door opens when I get out and start walking up the walkway, and a smiling Olivia greets me.

"Aunty Lee! Look at my new party dress!" She spins, the white fabric flying out and spinning around her.

"Wow, it's so pretty." I lean down and kiss her forehead. She takes my hand and leads me into the house.

"Why didn't you wear a party dress? We're having a party."

I raise my eyebrow in question. "A party?"

She nods. "Mommy's boyfriend came to visit and wants to meet you so much." My hand tightens around hers, and instantly I'm on high alert. A knot forms in my stomach. "Your mom's boyfriend is here?"

Olivia nods. "He's in the kitchen with Mommy." She pulls her hand away, skipping into the back of the house where the kitchen is located.

Slowly, I follow behind her, following the sound of Rachel's cheery voice.

Entering the kitchen, I see Rachel's smiling face first. When she spots me, her smile only widens. "Don't be mad, Lee. I know you said no visitors and not to give anyone our address, but I was missing Mike, and we can trust him." My anxiety grows.

I turn the corner, step into the kitchen, and see the man in question. The man Rachel knows as Mike, but I know by a different name. I know his real name.

My heart drops into my stomach. The color drains from my face, and I freeze in place, staring into the sadistic eyes of the man who tormented me for years.

*Colton.* The "unknown" bastard who's been taunting me for long enough.

# TWENTY-NINE

## Lee

"Lee, seeing you again in the flesh is great." A nasty smile spreads across Colton's paper-thin lips. I'm too stunned to speak.

"What do you mean?" Rachel asks, her attention toward the man she believes is Mike.

"Colton." His name leaves my lips in a whisper, causing his nasty smile to widen. Rachel's eyes widen in recognition of the name. She knows everything about Colton because I've told her everything. Including the fact he's Olivia's father. I called her and told her right after I was informed about Bill's vasectomy, leaving him unable to father any more children.

With a quickness, Colton grabs Rachel, her back against his chest, one arm holding her throat while the other hand holds a gun he's pressing against her head.

"Mommy! Mike, stop!" Olivia screams, her voice whimpering in fear. The scene in front of me causes me to jump out of my stupor and step into action. Quickly, I grab the little girl's arm and pull her behind me, keeping her hidden behind my back.

"Glad I have your attention. Now, toss me your phone and keys," Colton demands, moving his finger to the trigger.

Nodding, I do as he says. I remove my phone and keys from my pocket and toss them onto the counter. If I don't, I don't doubt he'll pull the trigger. I've seen what he's done to my dog and Cassie.

"Good. Now, sit down. I've been waiting for this moment for a long time, and it will be perfect."

Right now, he has the upper hand because he has a gun at Rachel's head. For now, I'll do as he says to keep her and Olivia safe, but the moment I get the chance to take control, I will take it. I fucking refuse to let the bastard leave here alive.

I sit at the table with Olivia beside me, holding her hand tightly in mine. "What the fuck do you want, Colton?"

"I want what I've always wanted. I want us to be a family," he says as if it's the most obvious answer. "You killed my parents and tried to kill me too, and you took my baby."

I scoff. "A *family*? How fucked up are you?"

He rolls his eyes, his lip raising in a snarl. "You took my daughter, you fucking bitch." He disgusts me. "Night after night, we'd lie there while I rubbed your swollen belly, and I told you I was so excited to become a family. But you fucking ran!" he screams, his face red with anger.

Regaining his composure, he looks at Olivia with a smile that makes me want to claw his eyes out. "I'm not stupid, Lee. I knew you didn't die in that fire in the basement. I knew one of your boy toys rescued you. It was just a matter of luring you out of hiding. I couldn't find you, but when I found Olivia and Rachel, I knew they were my ticket to finding you. Ten fucking years I've spent looking for your stupid ass." He wasn't searching for Olivia. He knew where she was all along. He wanted me. "I knew if Olivia was threatened, you'd come running. Took me a while, considering I had to get someone to do my dirty work."

Bile rises in the back of my throat, and I swallow it down. "Olivia, did you know that your Aunty Lee is your real mommy? She lied to you." My free hand balls into a fist, my eyes narrowing into slits as I glare at him.

Damn, I wish looks could kill.

"What? That's not true," Olivia says, hiccupping through her tears. Her hands ball in fists as she grips my hand, practically sitting on me with how close she is.

Colton flashes her a smile. "It is true. Lee is your mom, and I'm your dad."

"No! No! No!" she screams, letting go of me and pushing me away when I attempt to reach for her. "Mommy!" she yells, rushing toward Rachel, who is shaking with fear, fresh tears streaming down her face.

Olivia runs to her mother, wraps her arms around her waist, and buries her face into the fabric of her mother's dress as her little body visibly shakes with sobs.

"What the fuck is your plan, Colton? Confuse and scare a little girl?"

"She's my child, so she'll be fine. I know she will be." His grip around Rachel's neck tightens. "Olivia, look at me right now." She obeys instantly, afraid of the harshness in his voice. "You can only have one mom, Olivia. You get to pick which one dies. Do you want Lee to be your mom or Rachel to be your mom?"

"No! Mike, please, don't hurt my mommy and Aunty Lee!"

"You bastard!" Rachel cries.

"Don't fucking do it," I warn.

Smiling, he shoves Rachel away, quickly grabbing Olivia and pressing the gun against her head. One hand wraps around her waist, pinning her arms down as he lifts her, her legs kicking against the air as she screams.

"Rachel, tie Lee to the chair. Now!" he screams, spit flying down his chin. She immediately grabs the rope and duct tape from the drawer.

My eyes never leave his as I sit, allowing Rachel to tie me to the chair, knowing that if I make one wrong move, he'll put a bullet through Olivia's head without hesitation.

Once I'm securely tied to the chair with my arms behind my back, rope and tape secured around my waist, and my ankles tied and taped together, he gestures for Rachel to sit beside me.

"Tie your ankles." She nods, doing as she's told, also knowing that she can't fuck anything up or her daughter will pay for our mistake.

Once her ankles are taped together, Colton walks behind her, sets Olivia on her feet, then finishes typing up Rachel to the chair. When he's done, he stands back, smiling at the sight of us both securely tied to chairs, unable to move an inch.

Colton grabs Olivia's bicep, yanking her back toward him. "It's your choice, little one. Who dies?" He looks at me with a snarl. "I'm genuinely so happy to see you again, little bird. It's truly a shame if I have to kill you."

"Olivia, baby, look at me," Rachel cries out, pleading with her daughter, who's shaking and crying just as much.

"Shut the fuck up!" he roars. Walking over to her, he smacks her across the face with the butt of his gun, leaving a bloody gash on her cheek. "Three seconds to choose, Olivia, or I'll kill both of your moms."

"I can't choose! Please, don't make me choose!" She wipes her eyes and snot, crying so deeply that my own eyes begin to sting.

"Olivia, it's okay. You can choose your mommy," I say, hoping to soothe my frightened little girl.

"I'm sorry, Aunty Lee!" she screams, rushing over to throw her arms around me, hugging me the best she can. She presses her cheek against my face, and I take the chance to whisper in her ear without Colton seeing.

"Run. Run downstairs to the safe room and lock yourself inside. Do not come out for anyone," I whisper, pressing a kiss to her cheek. She pulls away, looking at me with hopeful eyes. My girl is a warrior, and I know she can do it.

When she and Rach moved into this house, the first thing we did was show her how to work the safe room and access it herself if she ever needed to. We made sure she knew the room's importance, and it's fully stocked with enough supplies to keep someone alive for two weeks. When I don't arrive home soon, Ace will know something is wrong, and he'll come looking for me. He'll get Olivia out of the room once it's safe.

Regardless of what happens to Rachel and me, at least our daughter will be safe.

"Last chance, Olivia, who am I killing?"

"Aunty Lee!" she cries, stepping away to the side. Colton closes his eyes, his shoulders rising as he inhales. Smart little Olivia takes that moment to run toward the basement where the saferoom is located.

Luckily, he doesn't chase after her, which allows her enough time to get away from him. I can only hope that she listened to me and is currently locking herself into the safe room.

Colton looks between Rachel and me. "Shame that her choice doesn't matter." He fakes a yawn as if we're the ones who are boring him and taking his time. Bastard. "I have such great plans for us, little bird. There's no way I would ever kill you." He laughs, lowering his gun and placing it back into the waistband of his pants.

He turns toward the counter, grabs the largest knife from the knife block, and walks toward Rachel with a sadistic look. "I have so many decisions to make right now." He presses the knife against Rachel's face, digging the blade into her skin, and moves it quickly downward, earning a painful scream from her as he cuts her skin open, as easy as cutting butter.

"Lee, you're responsible for trying to kill me and taking my daughter away. Rachel, you're responsible for hiding, and lying to my daughter. She's not yours, yet you pretended she was. You knew what Lee had done to my family." He shakes his head, looking at us in disgust. "You both must pay for what you've done." He stands in front of me, presses the tip of the knife against the side of my neck, and slices.

I bite down on my bottom lip so hard I draw blood. I refuse to give him the satisfaction of my screams, which I know he loves. Every time he'd force himself inside of me and hurt me, he'd thrive on my cries and pleas for him to stop. I know what he wants to hear, and I won't allow it. He won't be getting any screams from me.

"Please, please, please, don't kill me!" Rachel begs. Her only response is his manic laughter.

"Will you suck my dick in exchange for your life? You were always too much of a prude to do that for Mike." He chuckles, grabbing a fistful of her brown hair.

"Yes! I will!"

"Will you swallow!"

"Yes! I'll swallow everything." Snot drips down from her nose, tears wetting her yellow cotton sundress, creating a large wet spot.

He makes a tsking sound and shakes his head. "Such a whore, Rachel. That isn't very attractive to me." He takes the tip of the knife and circles it around her face, pressing the blade into a few spots until he draws blood.

Colton grabs her ear and begins cutting while Rachel lets out blood-curdling screams, her eyes rolling into the back of her head as saliva drips down her chin.

He steps away, tossing the piece of flesh to the floor. "Look how hard you'd made me." He points toward his crotch.

"Stop! Colton, you fucking stop!" I scream, thrashing against my restraints. "She did nothing! I'm the one that fucked up!"

"Exactly!" he roars, rushing to me with the knife, pointing it in my face. "This is your fucking fault! You should've never left! You're killing her, not me!" Drops of spit hit me in the face from his screaming.

"Stay away from my mommy!" Olivia screams, running toward him, holding a gun in her small hands that she's pointing toward him.

"Olivia! Run!" I beg of her, my heart racing in my chest. Fuck. She's supposed to be in the safe room, not searching for her mother's gun.

I tug against the restraints, annoyed that Rachel made them so fucking tight. I thrash around, and slowly, I tip over in the chair, yelping, landing with a thud, my head hitting the floor and bouncing.

Colton turns and charges toward Olivia while I'm still screaming for her to run. Her blue eyes widen in fear, and my little warrior pulls the trigger, clicking it repeatedly, her frustration growing at the fact the gun isn't loaded and not going to protect her.

He rips the gun away from her hands, throws it across the room, and grabs a fistful of her hair. He drags her across the kitchen floor, forcing her to sit in the chair beside her mother.

"Three stupid fucking bitches!" He spits, shaking his head as he looks at me on the ground. Leaning down, he grabs a fistful of my hair and yanks, picking me up by his grip on my hair.

My scalp burns as I feel him pull my strands right from the root.

Once I'm sitting up again, I look toward Rachel, who's crying in pain, her head hung between her shoulders, too weak to lift it. Blood rushes from the cut on her face, and down the side of her head from the loss of her ear.

"I'm getting a headache from all this screaming. You bitches can cry all you want. It'll only make me harder." He grabs his crotch, thrusting it in his hand. "Keep crying, and I'll need to find someone to take care of this hard cock of mine." His fingers trail down the side of Olivia's red tear-stained face; the implication clear.

Chills rush down my spine. I bite down on my tongue, refusing to make another fucking sound.

Colton tapes Olivia to the chair and then drags the chair over until she's forced to sit in front of her mother and watch everything.

Tears blur my vision. I want to scream at him, to beg, but I don't want to give him a reason to violate Olivia. I can't take that risk.

"This little bitch needs to fucking learn. She tried to shoot me!" he roars, shaking his head. "If I raised her, she wouldn't be so fucking scared. She needs to toughen up."

"Don't hurt her," Rachel pleads, her head still hanging between her shoulders.

My body shakes, but I will my voice to be calm as I say, "I'm the one who took our baby and ran. Don't hurt them, please, Colton. Hurt me instead." He looks at me, considering my words for two seconds before he shakes his head.

"I am hurting you, little bird. And this is how." His attention turns to Rachel. "I'm tired of hearing you fucking talk." He grabs something from the drawer before walking over to her. He yanks her head back and forces her mouth open. Then, he grabs hold of her tongue with the pliers he grabbed from the drawer and cuts out her tongue. Happiness lights up his disgusting face.

Olivia witnesses it all, her eyes so wide that her eyelids practically disappear. Hanging her head, she vomits all over her lap, staining her white dress. Her cries come out in hiccups.

"You've done enough, Colton. No more! Please!" I beg, fighting against the ropes and tape holding me hostage in the chair.

"You're right. Let's end this now." Standing behind Rachel, he uses one hand to grip her hair firmly at the roots. With the other hand, he raises the knife and plunges it into her stomach.

Rachel gurgles, blood dripping down her mouth and chin, dripping onto her yellow dress. "This is all your fault, Lee. This is because of you." He presses the blade against her exposed throat and drags it along her milky flesh, exposing her tissues.

Blood sprays across Olivia's pale frightened face and white dress, staining it further. The poor girl's head falls between her shoulders as she passes out from what she's just witnessed.

"Rachel, no!" I scream.

"This is your fault. You should've never run away from me, little bird. This is all because of you."

He comes toward me, raises the knife, then I hear it.

*Pop.*

*Pop.*

*Pop.*

Three shots.

Warm liquid splatters on my face.

Colton's eyes widen, he stops moving, the hand holding the knife drops, and his eyes widen.

*Pop.*

One final shot collapses him instantly. With him out of the way, my eyes land on the last person I ever expected to see behind him.

Eli.

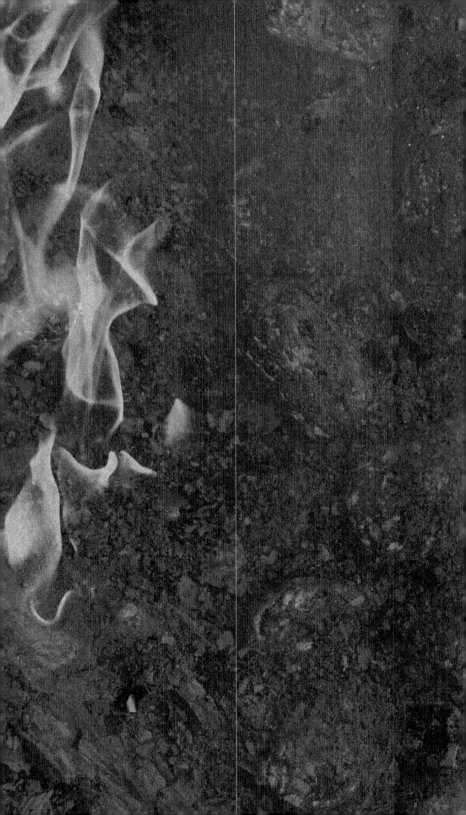

# THIRTY
*Eli*

Since I found out my hellion was still alive, I've kept tabs on her. I've been watching her and waiting for the moment when I knew she'd need me the most. I know she's living with Ace, and he keeps her safe, but I haven't been able to shake the feeling that something was going to happen.

So, I assigned her with her own security detail that's been sitting outside her house every day, ensuring the area is safe. I did tell Ace about it, and we agreed not to tell Lee because we knew she wouldn't want to be watched twenty-four seven.

Maverick called me two hours ago and told me that Lee had left her house and that she'd gone to Rachel Hollis's safe house. At first, I didn't think anything of it since she'd been there plenty of times. But soon an uneasy feeling came over me, so I decided to check on her and make sure she was okay. I hacked into the cameras they have placed outside Rachel's house. I witnessed a familiar man standing in the window and watched as he closed the blinds seconds before Lee got out of the car and Olivia opened the door. The gesture usually wouldn't seem suspicious, but no one is supposed to know where Rachel and Olivia are located, and seeing the man caused an uneasy feeling to come over me.

The man was familiar, but I couldn't figure out where I'd seen him before. That's when I remembered where I'd seen his face before.

Colton Adamson.

Lee's foster brother.

I was already in my car and on my way to the house when I decided to call Ace and get more information, like why the fuck she went over there in the first place. Then I called my security team and yelled at them for not fucking watching her the entire time. Instead of protecting her, they followed her as she drove there, then once she went inside, they left.

Fucking idiots.

Ace told me she went over because Olivia wanted to show her what she had bought from the store today. Of course, she went alone. There was no reason to believe that anything bad was about to happen. He felt secure enough to let her go, knowing she had security that would be tailing her.

I explained to Ace that I saw Colton Adamson at the house, and before I could even finish my sentence, he told me he was on his way and ended the call. I was already on my way over, so I was not surprised that I had arrived before he did.

Knowing Colton was inside the house, there was no way in hell that I would wait outside for Ace to show up, so I took it upon myself to enter the house.

And thank fuck I did.

I made it just in time.

I walked in right as that fucker was heading toward Tate with a knife, and no doubt she would face the same fate that poor Rachel suffered.

I'm standing in the kitchen after just killing the motherfucker who raped and impregnated my little hellion when she was barely seventeen.

"Get Olivia!" she screams, her eyes wide and full of worry for her daughter, whose unconscious body is limp in the chair in front of Rachel's bloody dead body.

Placing my gun into the waistband of my pants, I remove the jacket from my suit, push up my sleeves, and wrap my jacket around the little girl as I carefully remove the tape from her, working her free. I lift her body in my arms, carrying her out of the room just as Ace appears in the living room.

"What the fuck happened?" he asks, holding his arms out for Olivia.

"Careful. She's covered in puke and blood." His eyes widen. "It's not her blood. Rachel is dead." His mouth pops open, but we don't have time to mourn. Carefully taking Olivia's body from me, he carries her upstairs, where I'm sure he will clean her up and change her.

I pull out my pocketknife once I'm back in the kitchen and cut through the rope around Lee. When she's free, she presses a hand against the side of her neck that's actively bleeding and buries her head in my chest, her body shaking with sobs.

"He killed her," she cries against me. I do my best to comfort her by rubbing her back soothingly. It's awkward for me. I've never been good with consoling someone when they're upset. She just lost a friend, the woman she gave her child to, and now their lives will change forever.

"Lee!" I hear Rowen's voice calling.

"Butterfly!" King calls out.

My brothers are here. No doubt that Ace called them on his way over.

They rush into the kitchen, their eyes wide and full of worry when they take in the sight before them.

"Butterfly, come here." King steps to the side, holding his arms out for her. She goes to him willingly, wrapping her arms around his neck and her legs around his waist when he lifts her.

He wipes a hand over her tearful face and carries her out of the room, leaving me behind with Rowen.

"What the fuck happened?" he asks, taking in the sight before him.

"What does it look like?" I snap, turning to face him. "He was seconds away from stabbing Lee, and I didn't have a choice." I'm frustrated. So fucking frustrated. All these months, we've been after the unknown fucker, wanting to get our hands on him to give him a taste of his own medicine and make him pay for all he's done, only to kill him quickly without making him suffer one bit.

I had many plans for him. I had a list of things I wanted to do to him to make him suffer painfully and slowly, and in a moment of weakness, I allowed myself to lose sight of the end goal and killed the bastard quickly.

I'm angry at myself for rushing to the kill shot when there were many other areas I could've shot him to ensure that he remained alive so that I'd be able to torture him slowly.

Fuck me and my desperate need to want to protect Lee. I can never think clearly when she's involved.

Colton wasn't supposed to get off that easily.

It wasn't supposed to end this way.

# THIRTY-ONE

*Ace*

pstairs, I lay Olivia on top of her purple bedspread and carefully remove her vomit- and blood-stained white dress, pulling the blanket over her quickly, so she's not exposed. I should wait for Lee to come and change her, but she's still downstairs with Eli, King, and Rowen, and I'm not sure when she'll be here. She witnessed a close friend's brutal murder tonight, and I know it'll take her some time to recover.

If she ever does.

When Olivia wakes, the last thing I want is for her to see herself covered in her mother's blood, so I'll do my best until she wakes up.

With the dress in hand, I carry it into the bathroom, toss it into the trash can beside the toilet, and take the bag out, tying it up. I'll take it downstairs with me later to throw away, but for now, that'll do to conceal the smell and evidence of the destroyed dress that I'm sure Olivia was thrilled to be wearing. She's always loved dresses and pretty things as much as I do.

My guilt is causing me a stomachache. I should've gone with Lee, and I should've watched the camera footage to ensure that Rachel and Olivia were okay, especially considering Lee hadn't been able to get ahold of them all day.

Instead of taking precautions, I agreed to let my pretty thing go alone, right into a trap where she could've been killed. I'll never forgive myself for not being there for her. I'm so fucking stupid.

I wasn't there to protect Rachel like I promised I'd always do. Nor did I protect Olivia like I vowed the day she was born.

That day my second time meeting Rachel. Lee had asked her to call me, and I rushed right over, surprised that after radio silence, Lee wanted to see me again. She was nine months pregnant and in active labor.

She nearly broke my hand. She was squeezing it so tight. But right there in Rachel's tiny apartment, my pretty thing delivered a beautiful six-pound baby girl with powerful lungs.

Lee has always been beautiful, but at that moment, seeing her holding her daughter, she'd never looked more beautiful. She was sweaty, and her hair was messy, but I couldn't resist capturing the moment. I took Rachel's disposable camera and captured a photo of my pretty thing and her beautiful daughter.

Through the years, I've had a front-row seat watching Olivia grow up. When Lee was unable to be there, I was there. While Rachel worked, I was there babysitting, playing dress-up, buying her first bike, and taking countless pictures of her life to share with Lee.

Olivia is my blood family, after all. Unfortunately, her father is my cousin. Was, considering Colton is now dead, just like his disgusting parents.

"Ace." The child's small, scared voice breaks me away from my thoughts. I rush to her side, sit beside her on the bed and take her small hand in mine. Tears fill her bright blue eyes. "My mommy is dead."

Sitting up, she throws her arms around me. Her heartbreaking sobs fill the air, causing warm tears to slip down my cheeks unexpectedly.

Rubbing her back soothingly, I pull away slightly and brush her blonde hair out of her tearstained, snotty face. "Go take a shower, my girl. It'll help you feel better, then we'll talk it out." Her eyes widen, and her grip on me tightens. She's afraid of letting me go, fearful of being alone.

"It's okay. I'll be right outside the door waiting for you. But you need to get clean first," I say, standing and holding my hand out for her. Thankfully, Rachel had her wear a slip under her dress, so she's still semi-decent.

"Promise you won't leave me?" she asks, holding up her pinky to me.

"I promise, my girl. I'll never leave you." After hooking our pinkies together to seal my promise, she slowly stands up and hurries toward her bathroom, closing the door behind her. A moment later, I hear the shower turn on and the slamming of the glass shower door.

While she's cleaning herself up, I walk into her closet to find some clothing. From my years of babysitting, I know what her favorite pieces of clothing are. For pajamas, she loves her pink and white polka dot long-sleeve pajama set, along with her unicorn slippers.

Five minutes later, I hear the door creak open and see Olivia's pale face peek out. "Ace, I need clothes." Her voice is flat and sad, lacking her usual happiness.

Nodding, I carry her clothes over to her and pass them through the crack in the door. She takes them, shutting the door right after to have privacy while she dresses.

When the door creaks open again, she walks out carrying hair supplies in her hand. Without a word, she empties her hands on the bed and sits down on the floor, pulling on her fluffy pink socks while

I sit on the bed behind her.

Taking the hairbrush, I spray her hair with some strawberry-scented leave-in detangler, carefully brush her hair, and weave her long, silky locks into a braid that goes down her back.

After it's braided and out of her face, she stands up and turns to face me. Her lips part, her big scared eyes fill with tears, and her shoulders begin to shake. "Ace, my mommy is gone." She hiccups.

"Oh, my girl." I reach forward and take her hands in mine. "Your mommy is in heaven watching over you."

"Why would her boyfriend want to hurt us? Mike was always nice to me and loved my mommy." She shakes her head. The poor girl is so confused and trying to make sense of the horrific things she had to witness at the hands of a man she thought she trusted.

"He was a bad man who did an evil thing, and..." Before I can continue speaking, she opens her mouth and cuts me off.

"He said that Aunty Lee is my real mommy and that he was my daddy. Is that true?" Fuck. I'll never lie to her, but I don't think it's the right time to discuss this topic. She's confused and hurting enough right now, and I don't want to further add to her confusion. But seeing the fear in her eyes, I choose not to lie and tell her the truth.

"He's right. Lee is your biological mother. You grew inside of her belly, and she gave birth to you. When you were a baby, she gave you to your mommy, Rachel, so she could raise you."

"Like adoption? Stefan at school is adopted. He has two dads, but a woman birthed him."

I nod. "Yes, like adoption."

"What about my dad? Aunty Lee said his real name is Colton."

"It is. His name was Colton, and he was a very bad man."

"What if he tries to hurt Aunty Lee and me again? Will he kill us?" Her small hands take mine, her eyes pleading with me.

"He will never hurt either of you again. He's dead, and I promise nothing bad will ever happen again." She thinks about my answer for a moment, then nods, accepting my words.

"I'm glad he's dead. Bad people deserve to die." She walks to her closet, takes out her backpack, and begins filling it with clothes.

"What are you doing, Olivia?"

"Packing. I don't have a mommy anymore, so I'll have to be adopted again because my biological mommy didn't want me." Hearing movement across the room, I raise my head to see Lee standing in the doorframe, her sad expression matching Olivia's. Her hair is damp, and her clothes are changed. She must've showered and cleaned up too.

"Hey, sweet girl, can I come in?" Olivia turns and makes eye contact with her. Hesitantly, she nods.

Lee walks over and squats beside her. "You can pack your clothes, but you're not getting adopted."

Olivia pauses, looking at her birth mom with a quivering bottom lip. "Where will I go? I don't have anyone." Heavy tears roll down her soft cheeks.

"You have a lot of people, baby. You'll come and live with Ace and me, only if that's okay with you," she explains, taking her hand.

She thinks for a moment, then pulls her hand away and continues stuffing clothes into her backpack. "No! Because you don't want me."

Hurt flashes across Lee's face. "I've always wanted you, sweet girl. I was too young and couldn't take care of you. Rachel wanted you, too, and she promised to take care of you because I couldn't. But that doesn't mean I didn't want you and didn't love you."

Tears rush down Olivia's face. "I'm really scared. My mommy is gone, and I don't want to call you mommy."

"You don't have to. You can call me Lee." She pulls Olivia in, wrapping her arms protectively around the child. "I am so sorry that happened, my sweet girl, and I'm so sorry that you had to see it. Your mommy loved you so so so much," she says, kissing her head and rubbing her back soothingly while Olivia cries into her neck, her little body shaking with sobs.

After a few minutes, the crying dies down, and there's a brief silence before Olivia breaks it by speaking. "Okay, I'll go with you." She pulls back, and Lee wipes her face, removing any evidence of her tears.

"I'm going to go downstairs for a little bit, and when you're ready, you and Ace can come down and meet my friends. Okay?"

Olivia eyes her skeptically but nods in agreement.

Pressing a kiss on her forehead, Lee stands, gives me a small smile, then exits the room.

After a few minutes, I have everything Oliva needs packed in her backpack and duffel bag. While she carries her stuffed teddy bear, I carry her bags and follow her downstairs and into the living room where Lee and King are waiting.

Olivia grips on to my hand tightly, her eyes bouncing between Lee and King and back to me. She's unsure about the unfamiliar faces, no longer sure who to trust.

"Hey, sweet girl, this is my friend, King," Lee introduces them. Olivia stares at him without speaking.

"Oh, my goodness, why didn't anyone tell me?" He breaks the silence, looking between Lee and me, shaking his head with disappointment.

"Tell you what?" Olivia asks curiously, her grip on my hand tightening.

"That a princess is going to be living with us."

Her eyebrows furrow together in confusion. "I'm not a princess."

"Are you sure? Because you look just like one," King says, taking a step back. He taps his chin with his index finger. "I'm pretty sure that you are a princess. Maybe you're an undercover princess?"

Reluctantly, Olivia's face lights up with a giant smile. "I could be a real princess? Like the kind that wears pretty dresses and a tiara?"

King nods. "Exactly!" He reaches into a shopping bag that wasn't down here before and pulls out a beautiful shiny tiara. "I think you lost this, right?" He winks.

She's hesitant at first, then says, "Right! It's mine because I'm a princess." Based on her behavior, I know she's in shock right now and likely hasn't registered what is happening.

"See, I knew it." He gently sets it on her head, carefully placing the clips into her hair to secure the crown. "There we go. Now you really look like a princess."

"Come on, Your Highness." Lee smiles, holding her hand out for Olivia to take, which she does without hesitation or doubt. She leads her outside, and I turn to King once they're out of earshot.

"What happened with the bodies?"

"Ro and Eli are taking care of them. The kitchen is already cleaned up as if nothing ever happened. You ready to go?" I nod, looking behind him into the kitchen to see several faces I recognize who are cleaning. They brought in their clean-up crew.

Tearing my eyes away, I follow behind him when he begins walking out of the house that is responsible for changing so many lives.

Outside, King climbs into his car and drives away, and then I do the same with Lee and Olivia by my side.

Without looking back, we drive toward our new life.

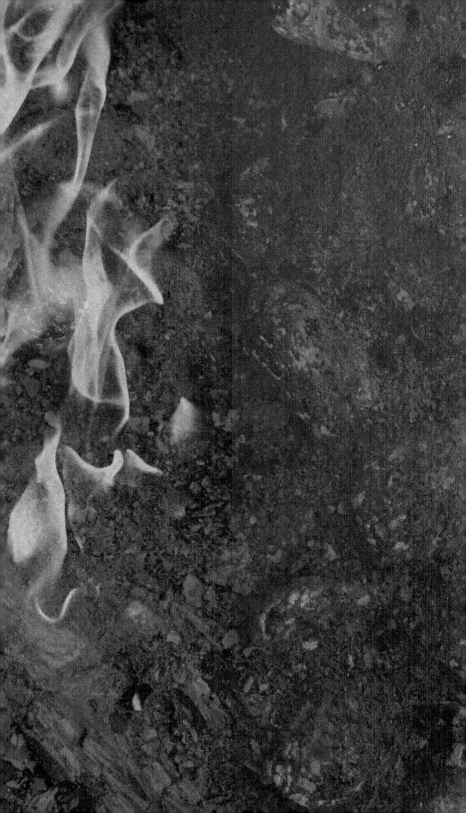

# THIRTY-TWO
*Raven*

"How's the kid doing?" Maverick asks as I pour him a cup of coffee. I'm at the penthouse, where all of us came three nights ago after Colton murdered Rachel. Since we've been here, Eli has been brooding. He's angry at himself for killing Colton quickly. We all wanted him to suffer, but in an attempt to save Lee, he shot him, killing him instantly. The bastard will never have to pay for hurting my angel. He got off easy, but it's not Eli's fault. None of us blame him; we all understand.

"She won't come out of her room," I say, passing the mug of black coffee toward him. Ace and Lee moved in with us here at the penthouse. Lee isn't willing to leave Olivia's side, and Ace isn't willing to leave hers. Eli, King, and I decided it would be best for them to be here with Olivia. But we're only here temporarily, because soon the build of our new house will be finished, and we'll all be moving there.

We're one big, happy, fucked up family.

"Well, she witnessed her mother's brutal murder, so of course she won't. She's fucking traumatized," Maverick says, bringing the steaming mug of black coffee to his mouth and sipping it.

"She wasn't her fucking mother. She has a mother, and she's upstairs," Eli growls, walking into the kitchen. He gets angry when we refer to Rachel as Olivia's mother, but it's true. Lee may have given birth to her, but Rachel raised her. She's the only mother Olivia knows, but Eli doesn't like hearing it.

He yanks the coffee pot from the warmer, dark liquid slipping over and dripping down the sides.

"Anyway," Maverick says with a chuckle, "my boy is her age. Maybe she'd like to have a friend. Someone her age to talk to," he suggests.

"That might be a good idea. What—" My sentence is interrupted by Eli.

"What school does he go to? We need to enroll Olivia so she doesn't fall behind," Eli says, his back facing us as he drinks his coffee.

"I don't think sending her to school right now is the best idea. She's still traumatized," I say. "It's only been three days."

"Well, Rowen, I think Eli is right. She needs a distraction, and enrolling her in school will allow her to be around kids her age and help keep her mind off everything at home," Maverick says, and Eli turns around, looking at me with a wide, shit-eating grin.

*Fucker.*

"Riot goes to Northwest Academy. I'm hoping to get him into Bowler Academy for high school, though." Mav's face always lights up whenever he speaks about his family.

I've heard of Bowler Academy. It's the most prestigious and advanced private high school around. Expensive and complicated as fuck to get into, but considering Olivia will be with us indefinitely, we should look into getting her onto a waitlist for high school.

"How does he like the school?" Eli asks.

"It's a private school, so I automatically like it. He likes his teachers, and yeah, it's a pretty good school," he explains.

"All right, done. I'll handle the enrollment. Olivia will start on Monday," Eli decides before taking his mug of coffee and storming off like the angry asshole he's been lately. He needs to see his hellion and change his fucking mood. Lee seems to be the only one who can ever change our sour moods.

"I'll let Riot know that Olivia is starting in his grade. Perhaps this weekend, all of you can come over, and the kids can play together." Maverick finishes his coffee and then sets the empty cup in the sink. "Mel and I just finished renovating our house, and she's been looking for any excuse to host a party."

Chuckling, I nod in agreement. "That sounds good. Call me with the details."

"All right, man. It's a date." He chuckles, patting me on the back before he leaves.

Once he's gone, I leave to go and find King and Ace to inform them of our plan for Olivia's schooling and that we'll be going to Maverick and Melanie's house this weekend.

When Saturday morning rolls around, we all busy ourselves with getting ready to go over to Mav's house for a barbeque. Lee said she felt terrible about Melanie having to prepare all the food by herself since there were so many of us, so she made a massive tray of potato salad, and she and King went over early to help Melanie cook. Surprisingly, Olivia went along with them to meet Maverick's son, Riot.

Now, it's time for Eli, Ace, and I to join the rest of our family at Mav and Mel's house.

It takes forty minutes to reach the hillside home, and just as I expected, the house is fucking huge. Maverick is our highest-paid employee, and Melanie comes from old money. I remember Mav telling me that she inherited a fuck ton of money when her grandparents died several years ago. Apparently, her great-great-someone invented something which provided a crazy amount of money for her family.

We park in the driveway of their newly renovated hillside home, and the moment we step out of our vehicle, Maverick is out the door to greet us. We've all met his family several times, and we've had a lot of meals together, but this is the first time we've gone to their home and the first time I've seen my head of security dressed so casually.

Maverick wears a white shirt, a pair of swim shorts, and has flip-flops on his feet.

"There they are!" he greets, giving the three of us quick hugs with a slap on the back. Such a dad thing to do. "Our beautiful ladies are inside. Stop and say hello, then meet me out back so you can all help me grill." He chuckles, walking away from us.

One by one, Eli, Ace, and I follow him inside the modern-styled home.

The smell of barbeque fills the air, and as I walk further into the foyer, my angel's voice becomes clearer. Her sweet, throaty laugh flows down the hall, the sound making my cock twitch in my shorts.

Without waiting for Eli and Ace, I follow the sound, my face breaking into a smile when I see my woman in the kitchen. Her back is to me as she stands beside Melanie and cuts up a watermelon.

With a grin, I walk behind her, wrap my arms around her waist, and press a kiss to the side of her neck.

"Hi, Ro." She smiles, looking over her shoulder at me.

"Hi, angel." I press my lips against hers.

"Hi, Rowen. Good to see you again," Melanie greets, carrying a salad bowl around the kitchen island.

"Hey, Melanie. The house looks great."

"Right? I love it. I expect an invite when you guys move into your new house, too." She winks, giving me a playful grin. "So, how's life with a kid? You all went from being childless to having a ten-year-old overnight."

"It's…an adjustment," I tell her honestly. "We all love Olivia so much already. She's going through a difficult time, but I'm hoping that going to school and making friends will help her through it." Lee picks up a piece of watermelon and feeds it to me. I chew it, sucking the sweet juice off her fingers.

"I'm sure making friends will be good for her. My best friend is a children's psychologist, and if you'd like, I can give you her number. Maybe it'll be good for Olivia to talk to someone?" she offers, looking between Lee and me. "Of course, I don't want to overstep at all."

"I think that would be great. Thanks, Mel," Lee answers with a smile.

Olivia chooses that moment to walk into the kitchen, her blue eyes dull and her face sad.

I know it's hard for Lee seeing Olivia this way, and I don't blame her. I'm sure Olivia was perfectly happy and bubbly before she witnessed what happened to Rachel.

"Hey, little warrior." I let go of my angel and walk toward the little girl. Her eyes meet mine, and a forced smile spreads across her pink lips.

"Hi, Rowen," she mumbles. I take her hands and squat down in front of her.

"Are you having fun with Riot?" she nods, looking around.

"He has ice cream, and I was wondering if I could get some, too."

"Of course, you can!" Mel chimes in, walking toward the freezer. "Come here, sweetie. Let's pick out your favorite. I have lots of flavors."

That causes Olivia's frown to turn upside down.

With a broad smile, she skips off toward Melanie.

"She'll be okay, angel. It'll take some time, but she'll be okay," I say when I notice the way Lee stands staring at her.

Until today, Olivia hadn't left Lee's side since Rachel's murder. I know Rachel's death is recent, but I'm hoping that she can start healing and get back to herself soon.

She's too young and sweet to end up jaded by this event, and I know that's Lee's biggest fear for her.

Only time will tell.

# THIRTY-THREE

*King*

"Hi, butterfly," I whisper, poking my head in the doorway of Olivia's room, smiling when I see Lee lying on the bed beside Olivia, one hand stroking her silk strands of blonde hair while the other holds a book. My butterfly is in here every night, reading a story to Olivia, staying with her until she falls asleep.

Olivia started school two weeks ago, and as we all suspected, she's been coming out of her shell more. She also goes to therapy twice a week, and I think having someone else to talk to has been good for her. She's still upset about Rachel's passing, but she's beginning to open up and trust us.

I love it.

She doesn't talk about her death with us. She saves that for therapy, but she talks about the good memories she has.

Lee's eyes meet mine, a smile spreading across her delicious mouth. "Hey."

"Hi, King." Olivia sits up, tucking her hair behind her ears.

"Hi, princess." I walk into the room and sit at the foot of the bed.

"How was school?" I ask.

She gives me a sour look. "I hate Riot. He's really mean to me." She rubs the side of her head. "He pulled my hair today and stole my ribbon."

My eyebrows pull together in a scowl. "He's being mean to you?"

She nods innocently, falling back onto her pillow dramatically. "He said my hair looked stupid, then he pushed me on the ground, pulled my pigtail, and tore out my ribbon."

"I'll talk to his dad and make sure he doesn't bother you again."

"Next time he hits you, I want you to hit him back," Lee says, slapping the book closed and setting it on the nightstand table.

"I don't think hitting is very nice," I say, looking from Olivia to Lee.

"I do. I'm not going to have her stand around and take it. If he wants to be a bully, she must learn to fight back," she says, standing. "The world is full of bullies, and you can either be a victim or fight back." I get the feeling her words have more to do with herself than Olivia getting picked on.

"You know what…" Olivia sits back up. "I think you're right. Can someone teach me to punch?" she asks, balling her small hands into fists.

"Sure, princess. Go practice punching Eli. He's a bully sometimes," I say, winking. She laughs, climbs to her knees, then wraps her arms around my neck, giving me a tight hug.

"Good night, King." She lets go of me and climbs back into her bed, pulling the covers up to her chin. "I love you," she says through a yawn, her eyelids fluttering closed.

My heart stops, and a wave of emotion washes over me. "I love you, too, princess," I whisper, pressing a kiss to the side of her blonde head.

Standing, I reach for Lee, and we exit the room quietly, turning off the light and closing the door behind us.

"She loves you," Lee says, looking up at me. "And I love you. Thank you for taking care of us and for accepting her into your life without hesitation."

I place my hands on her hips and pull her body close to mine, closing the space between us. "She's a part of you, butterfly. How could I not love and accept her? She's a great kid." She presses her lips against mine.

Pulling away, she takes my hand, giving me a devious smirk, and drags me down the stairs, making me follow after her happily.

The second we step into the living room, she jumps on me, wrapping her legs around my waist and arms around my neck. My cock instantly comes alive in my sweatpants. It's been far too long since I buried myself deep inside Lee's tight cunt. We haven't fucked once since Olivia moved in.

"I want to do something to you." I hold her up by her ass.

"I want to do something to you too." She grins, wiggling her eyebrows.

"Come on. We need to go someplace quiet." I carry her down the hallway toward the only soundproof room in the house, which happens to be the gym, and walk inside, seeing a shirtless Eli standing in front of the mirror, lifting. Sweat ripples down his muscular body.

With our intrusion, his eyes connect with mine in the mirror. "I need your help with something," I say.

He exhales a heavy breath, setting his weights back on the weight rack. "What's up?"

"I require the assistance of your dick," I say. He looks between Lee and me with an easy smirk on his lips.

"Say no more. I'm ready to help." He walks toward us, his hand sliding up the sides of Lee's arms before leaning in and pressing a kiss on her cheek.

"My butterfly wouldn't let me tattoo her ass, so I'd like to carve my name into her ass instead." Gripping her hips firmly, I raise mine to her, allowing her to feel my cock. My dick twitches in my pants at the feel of her bottom against me.

"I'd ask if you're joking, but it's you, so I know better." Lee rolls her eyes, unwraps herself from me, and steps down to her feet.

Eli grips her hips and turns her around to face him. "I'll be happy to provide the pleasure while you provide the pain." He presses his lips against hers, wasting no time getting her naked. He strips her out of her sleep shorts and tank top quickly.

"I'll be back." I exit the gym, rushing to my room to get my beloved scalpel that I carved Lee with for the first time months ago. Call me sentimental. I had to keep it.

I carved a butterfly into her soft skin, and her pussy gripped me so fucking tight with the pain that I inflicted.

I became addicted and have been waiting for the chance to cut her again.

She's so beautiful when she bleeds.

Returning to the gym, my attention immediately goes to my brother and butterfly, who are in the middle of the room making use of their time.

Lee is already impaled on Eli's cock, and she's riding him slowly, her head thrown back and eyes closed as Eli wraps his lips around her perfect little nipples that look even more perfect, thanks to her new nipple piercings with the butterfly barbells through them.

Closing and locking the door, I lean against it, watching and admiring how they move together. Lee rides him slowly, saving every second his large cock slides through her soft, warm folds.

I know what Eli's feeling. Being inside of her is the most incredible feeling on earth. It's surreal, unlike anything else I've ever felt before.

Striding toward them, I drop to my knees beside them. "Eli, lie back and hold her down. This is going to hurt." He does as I say and lies flat on his back, pulling Lee with him but keeping her pussy connected to his cock.

I straddle his legs, getting into the perfect position to access her exposed peachy ass.

"Don't move, butterfly. Stay still and let Eli feel how tight your pretty pink pussy will get." I can't see her face from this position, but I can hear the gasping and sucking sounds their kissing makes.

Eli's hands tangle in her hair, keeping her face close to him, and her fingers tangle in his dark locks.

Good. She'll need something to grip on to.

With my scalpel in my right hand, I rub my left hand over her perfect ass cheeks, pressing a finger against her tight back entrance, testing the resistance.

Leaning closer, I press a kiss on each cheek, then slowly begin carving my name into the delicate skin of her ass, my cock twitching in my joggers at the first sight of her beautiful crimson blood.

The blood rises to the surface, dripping down her skin, marking the milky flesh with crimson stains.

Lee writhes on Eli, whimpering and thrashing against him. I know it fucking hurts her because it hurts me too. My cock hurts. I'm so hard that I fucking ache and can feel the tip leaking with pre-cum. I can't wait to fuck her tight little ass while my name makes her bleed.

"Stop moving, baby. You're going to fuck it up." I grip her hips, holding her steady. Eli moves his hands down her back and grabs her hips firmly, his fingernails sinking into her skin as he keeps a firm grip on our girl.

Smiling to myself, I return my focus to her bleeding ass and continue parting her skin, working on the remaining letters of my name.

Lee screams when the blade pierces her skin once I reach the third letter, her body shaking against Eli's grip.

"Fuck, fuck, fuck," he pants out, his legs twitching underneath me. "Oh, my fucking God. She's so fucking tight," he moans, his grip tightening on her hips. Not only will she have a scarred ass, but she'll also have crescent moons on her hips from Eli's grip. He's holding her so tight that he might even break the skin.

*I hope he does.*

"Fuck, baby. Your tight little pussy is choking the fuck out of my cock," he groans, his head tilting back. "King, brother, please tell me you're almost done. I need to move now."

"Almost. Keep her still."

"Hard to do when my dick is being suffocated," he mumbles, pulling her back to him and attacking her lips.

Luckily for me, Eli is able to keep her still until I complete the last letter.

Sitting up straight, I look at the bloody mess and smile, admiring how it looks.

The sight is fucking perfect. Quickly, I drop the scalpel and take my phone from my pocket and snap a photo, setting it as my lock screen so I'll be able to see this image every single fucking day for the rest of my life.

God damn, she's beautiful.

Grabbing a handful of her cheeks, I spread them and spit right on the puckered hole, then use a finger to spread my saliva around, getting her nice and wet for me. I can't wait any longer, I need to be inside her right now, or else I'm going to explode inside of my pants.

Leaning up on my knees, I shove my joggers down my ass, my leaking, aching cock springing free. Spreading her ass with one hand, I push two fingers inside her roughly, forcing my way in and scissoring my fingers, getting her nice and relaxed for me.

When she's ready, I remove my hand and carefully guide my cock into her ass, pushing through the tight wall of muscle that gives resistance.

"Oh fuck!" Lee screams, her back arching. My focus never leaves my bloody name carved into her right ass cheek.

Crimson drops drip down from her cheek, down the back of her thigh, and the side. It's making a fucking bloody mess, and once I'm done with her, I'll need to bandage her up until it heals.

"I'm so fucking full. Please, move, fuck, please," she begs, her ass pulsating against me. Running a hand up her smooth back, I tangle my fingers in her hair and fist it roughly, holding on to her head as I fuck her ass ruthlessly.

Lee climbs to her knees, giving me and Eli better access to her. The elevated position makes it easier for him to thrust into her from underneath and for me to fuck her from behind.

"I'm going to come!" she warms, her body shaking with the promise of an upcoming orgasm.

"Do it, butterfly. Drown Eli's cock that you love so fucking much," I growl, slipping a hand around her sweaty body. I rub her clit in circular motions and place my other hand on her pelvis, applying pressure.

With a scream, Lee removes herself from my brother's cock and squirts her release all over him, whimpering in pleasure.

"Fucking beautiful," Eli admires her. "Good girl," he praises, carefully sliding out from underneath us. On his knees in front of her, he shoves three fingers inside her, finger-fucking her pussy while I continue rubbing her sensitive clit.

"Give me this wetness. King is going to need it." He smirks, placing a final kiss on our girl's lips.

Removing his fingers from her, he comes behind me, his heavy cock bobbing between his muscular thighs that are dripping wet from Lee squirting him.

I know what his intentions are when he gets behind me, so I lean forward, allowing him entrance to my backside.

Eli's warm, wet fingers slip between my cheeks as he circles my bud, lubing me up using Lee's cum.

"Hold on, brother. This might hurt." I hear the humor in the bastard's voice. Eli lines himself up with my hole, grips my hips, and slowly pushes his way forward, forcing through my puckered wall of muscle without bothering to get me ready and loosened for him.

Not that I mind, considering he knows how I like it.

I like it rough and painful, and Eli always delivers exactly what I want and need. His soft lips pepper kisses over my shoulders and up my neck, taking my earlobe between his teeth.

Underneath me, Lee lies on her stomach, sticking her ass backward for me to get better access, and I lean forward, holding myself up with my hands on either side of her body, while Eli grips my hips and fucks me from behind.

With each thrust, my butterfly's blood colors my skin, and the three of our bodies stick together from sweat.

The smell of sex fills the air, and it's only a matter of seconds until I explode and fill Lee's ass with my delicious cum.

We're all three panting and moaning. Eli is hitting the exact spot I need him to, and by the way Lee tightens and twitches around me, I know she's close too.

My fingers move quicker on her clit, applying more pressure.

Until suddenly, she shakes and screams her release, coming for the second time.

She goes lax; her body lying limp on the floor. Gripping her hips, I increase my pace, forcing Eli to follow the same speed as me, his hands on my hips as he fucks me, both of us moving in perfect sync, his cock hitting the spot within me that has me seeing stars and going dizzy.

With a loud groan, I throw my head back onto my brother's shoulder and roar my release into the sweat-scented room, filling my butterfly's tight asshole with my thick cum.

Eli is next. He grips on to my ball sack and massages it, his dick twitching against the walls of my ass as he lets go and comes. His warm fluid fills me, dripping down my thighs once he pulls out.

Moaning, I remove myself from Lee and fall beside her, my chest rising and falling rapidly. My limbs feel heavy. It's like I'm on fucking fire, but holy fuck, that was incredible.

Through tired, hooded eyelids, I watch Eli crawl over to Lee, spread her cheeks, and run his tongue along her seam, licking her from clit to ass.

"Mmmm," he groans, burying his face between her ass cheeks, licking my cum that's dripping out of her. "Holy fuck, you both taste so good." He pulls away, revealing his glistening mouth. Droplets of cum dribble down his chin, and the fucker smiles and licks his lips.

Silence feels the room, and Lee's breathing evens out and becomes slow and shallow, indicating she's fallen asleep.

Eli slips into his shorts, gathers her in his arms, and carries her out of the room, protecting her sleeping figure against his chest.

He walks toward the door, then stops in his tracks. Without turning around to face me, he says, "I'm glad she's alive. Those three months were hell for me, and not a second went by that I didn't think about her, regardless of what I told you and Rowen. I was trying to be strong and put on a strong front. But really, my heart was fucking breaking. I'm not used to loving anyone besides you and Ro. You two were enough for me until she came along. She left her mark on me the minute she walked into my life, and I made a mistake I'll regret forever. I'm sorry I allowed my ego and stubbornness to get in the way." He walks away, leaving me too stunned to speak.

Unlike me, Eli doesn't wear his heart on his sleeve. He has so many fucking layers to him that it's often hard to get close to him and know how he truly feels. Hearing him say that has me fucking stunned.

I love him even more.

# THIRTY-FOUR
*Raven*

"**W**hat's up, buttercup?" A smile forms on my face seeing Olivia enter the house. She truly brightens my days and makes me happy in ways I never would've expected.

The blonde-haired child slams the door behind her, walking to where I'm sitting on the couch in the living room. She sits beside me, throwing her backpack onto the floor.

"Uh-oh, what's wrong?" I question, looking between her and Ace, who just returned from picking her up from school.

"I hate stupid Lucas!" she pouts, crossing her arms over her chest. The movement causes her shirt sleeve to rise, revealing scratches and irritated red skin.

"What the hell happened?" I snap, dropping to my knees in front of her, carefully taking her arm and examining the scrapes.

"That damn kid was pushing her around," Ace explains, anger taking over his features. He sits beside us on the couch.

"I punched him in the gut just like Lee said I could do to bullies. He pushed me down, but I got up and punched him," Olivia says proudly, showing me her fist.

"I don't understand. I thought Riot was the one bullying you? Now it's someone else?" I look at her, confused.

"Riot and I are friends now." Her frown fades away and is replaced by a wide fucking smile. "He likes me, and that's why he was an asshole."

"Olivia, language." Ace tsks, unamused by her words. How can we get angry when she hears so many of us curse?

"Sorry," she mumbles, looking from him to me. "Someone in my class said boys are mean when they like you. So, I went to Riot and asked, and he said he was sorry for being mean to me and said yes, he does like me." She grins proudly. "We've decided to be best friends now."

Which a chuckle, I shake my head and stand to my feet. "All right, little slugger. Come help me make dinner."

She jumps to her feet and leads me into the kitchen

Fuck that damn Lucas kid for putting his hands on my little warrior, but I'm so fucking proud of her for sticking up for herself. I know violence is never the answer, but if he wants to hit her, it's only fair that she defends herself and hits him right back.

"You can have anything you want for dinner." I open the fridge.

Olivia taps her finger against her chin, thinking about it, then says, "French toast."

I nod and pull out a few ingredients from the fridge. "Good choice. I just so happen to make the best French toast ever."

She eyes me skeptically. "Really? Well, I'll be the judge of that." Olivia stands beside me at the counter.

"Really. You just wait and see." Setting the ingredients on the counter, I crack some eggs into a bowl and add the milk, maple syrup, and a cinnamon sugar mixture. Once it's whisked to perfection, I smash some bananas into the bowl, mix in some crumbled bacon bits, and whisk everything together with the egg batter.

"That doesn't look very good," she mutters under her breath, stealing a piece of bacon and shoving it into her mouth.

"When Lee was your age, this was her favorite. In fact, it still is her favorite breakfast food."

Her blue eyes light up. "Really? Did she eat it when I was in her belly, too? Is that why French toast is my favorite?"

I chuckle. Can't argue with that logic. "Oh yeah, that's why. She loves it, so you love it." She thinks about my answer for a moment, then nods in acceptance. She opens the bread bag and pulls out several pieces of the thick Texas toast, setting them beside the bowl for me.

Carefully, I dip the bread into the mixture, then place the coated pieces on the griddle; instantly, they sizzle from the heat.

"What was Lee like when she was my age? I know that you met her a long time ago." As the days pass, Olivia asks more and more questions about her birth mother, and I love the idea that she's beginning to accept that Lee *is* her mother. Therapy has been great for her.

"She looked just like you. Bright blue eyes and silky blonde hair." A smile spreads easily across my mouth at the memory of Lee when I first met her when we were children. "She loved to talk a lot. Even when I tried to ignore her, I couldn't because she made me happy and made me want to listen to her for hours."

"What did she talk about?"

"Random things." I laugh. "One time, she spent two hours talking to me about the main character in a TV show she'd seen once. I didn't say a single word the entire time." She practically had a conversation with herself, but I fell for her easily when I saw how passionate she was.

"She would laugh at her own jokes, and her laugh was always so loud that you could hear it from a mile away."

Olivia giggles, helping me to dip the bread in the batter. "Eli told me you guys met in foster care. I'm sorry you didn't have parents, but I'm glad you had Lee. She's the greatest."

"Yeah, she is pretty great."

Olivia nods. "She was my best friend when I thought she was my aunt. Now, she's my mom, but I don't know if we're still friends or not," she says innocently, unaware of how much sadness her words cause me.

"Do you want her to be your friend still?"

She immediately nods. "Yes, I love Lee. But I don't think she wants to be my friend anymore." I pause, turning my attention toward her.

"What makes you think that?"

"Because now she has to be my mom, and she didn't have to be my mom before."

"Lee loves you so much. I promise you that. And I swear to you that she still wants to be your friend. Your best friend. Whatever you want, she will be there for you." She nods, her eyes focusing on the task of dipping the bread. "Talk to Lee, and tell her how you feel. I promise she'll listen just like I am."

"I'm scared. I don't want her to be mad at me."

"She'll never be mad at you. But, if you don't want to talk to her, that's okay. You can always talk to me."

"Do you think she wants to be my mom?"

"More than anything. One day, when you're older, you'll understand why she couldn't keep you when you were a baby. But I promise that now, she wants you more than anything, and she'll be whatever you need."

She stays silent while we finish the French toast. Once it's complete and I'm removing the final piece from the griddle, she finally speaks.

"Okay, I believe you. One day, I'll ask her. I'd like to have a mom again."

Once again, my heart aches for the innocent little girl who doesn't understand why Rachel was killed or why Lee was unable to raise her.

"Come on, let's go tell everyone that dinner is ready."

# THIRTY-FIVE

*Eli*

I never thought I'd see the day when a child was living in my house.

Hell, I never thought I'd see the day when my brothers and I were reunited and living together again under the same roof. Let alone with three other people, one of which is a child.

Four weeks ago, when Rachel was killed, King and Rowen convinced me to allow Lee, Ace, and Olivia to move into our penthouse. It didn't take much convincing because I was happy to make space for them. I didn't want them going back to Ace's trailer. We all need to stay together.

Last week, we were notified that the construction on our new home had been completed ahead of schedule and was ready for us. It came at the perfect time because our penthouse was getting cramped with three more people.

We began building this house a year ago, and now thinking about it, it's like the universe was aware that one day Olivia, Lee, and Ace would be with us, and we needed the space for them. Funny how that worked out.

Our new home is located in the hills, miles away from the city, hidden away, and secluded. We wanted a private compound to create our perfect oasis. It took months to finalize the plans, but once we did, the build took nearly a year to complete.

Now that it's done and we're moved in, it's even better than I ever imagined. It's everything we could've ever wanted and perfectly represents our three personalities.

Until now, my contact with the kid has been as minimal as possible. I was busy working at the office, and she'd already be asleep by the time I got home.

Plus, she's too fucking nosey and blunt, just like her damn mother, which is crazy, considering Lee isn't the one who raised her. Still, they have the same damn attitude.

I've never been a fan of children; if I'm honest, Olivia terrifies me. I'm not sure how to act or what to say. A few days ago, I mistakenly said "damn" around her, and she took it upon herself to start saying damn too.

Of course, I told her to stop, but she laughed in my face and continued to say it, telling me that, "Princesses can say whatever they want." I have King to thank for that.

Between him, Rowen, Ace, and Lee, they're spoiling the kid.

I get that she lost the only mother she's ever known, but God damn. She's driving me crazy.

Speaking of the miniature devil, I'm in the kitchen pouring myself a cup of coffee when I feel eyes on me. Turning my head to the side, my eyes connect with Olivia, who is sitting on the barstool at the kitchen island eating a bowl of Lucky Charms cereal.

"What are you staring at?" I ask, taking a sip from my steaming mug of dark liquid.

"Can I have coffee, too?" she asks over a mouthful of cereal.

"No."

"Why?"

"Because you're a kid."

"So?"

"So, kids can't have coffee."

"Says who?"

This is partially why I avoid her. She asks too many damn questions. "Says me." She seems to accept my answer and continues to shove a spoonful of cereal into her mouth. In a weird fucking way, she reminds me a lot of myself at her age. It makes my dead heart feel things it shouldn't.

"But you're not the boss of me," she challenges, dropping her spoon into her bowl of milk with a clank.

I roll my eyes. I don't fucking have time for this. "When you're in my house, you follow my rules. If you can't follow the rules, you can find someplace else to live." I regret the words the moment they leave my mouth.

The girl looks at me with her wide blue eyes that are now filling with tears, her bottom lip trembling as she stares at me. The tip of her nose turns red, and if she's anything like her mother, she's willing her tears not to fall. "I didn't ask to live here!" she shouts, shoving the bowl of milk off the island. It crashes to the ground and shatters, milk and glass going everywhere.

I cannot take my eyes off her as I see the sadness and anger fighting on her little face.

Olivia climbs off the seat and runs out of the kitchen, leaving me feeling like the world's biggest piece of shit.

Grabbing the roll of paper towels, I squat down and begin cleaning up the mess. Carefully, I pick up the broken bowl and toss it into the trash, then mop after I've wiped the milk up.

Once I get the mess cleaned up, I walk upstairs to Olivia's bedroom and walk in without knocking.

My eyes widen when I see the young girl beside her bed, shoving her clothes and toys into her backpack.

"What are you doing?" I ask, staying by the door.

"What does it look like?" she deadpans. "I'm leaving." She zips up her backpack and pulls the straps onto her shoulders.

"Why are you leaving?"

"Because I'm not wanted here." The poor girl is trying her fucking hardest not to cry, and I'm still feeling like the world's biggest fucking asshole for putting that sad look on her face. It's a look I never want to see again, and instantly, I'm willing to do anything to put her happy smile back on her face and erase all her sadness.

*She reminds me so damn much of Lee.*

"I'm sorry, Olivia. Will you please stay here with me?"

"Why?"

"Because I want you here. Rowen, King, Ace, and Lee want you here. They all love you and would be sad if you left." She keeps a tight grip on the straps of her backpack, pondering the idea for a moment.

"If you want to leave, I'll give you money. It would be hard for a kid out on the streets, and you'll be hungry, so I'll give you money, but I hope you'll stay instead."

She gives in to her tears and lets them fall down her rosy cheeks.

"I don't know where I belong." She sits on the side of her bed and hangs her head, crying silently.

I sit beside her and place a hand on her back, rubbing it in circles gently.

"You belong here with us, Olivia. I'm very sorry for what I said to you. I should've never been mean to you."

She looks up at me and wipes her tears with the back of her hand.

"Can we be friends? I think I need a friend."

My heart aches for her. This poor little girl's life has changed so much in a matter of weeks. One second, she was living carefree with Rachel, who was the only mother she'd ever known, then she was watching her mother be violently murdered, and now she's having to live with three men she doesn't even know.

King and Rowen took to her quickly, but I'm not surprised. They've always loved children and want to be fathers someday, and now's their chance.

As for Lee, I know this is hard for her, but she's been doing fantastic. It's been challenging, and we're all trying to adjust.

"I really miss my mommy," Olivia says under her breath with a sad sigh.

"I miss mine too." Her head turns to me quickly, her eyes wide.

"Did your mommy die, too?"

I nod. "She did. I was older than you when it happened, but yes, she died."

"Was she killed like mine?"

"No, my mom was sick. She had cancer, and the medicine didn't work for her." She takes me by surprise when she places her small hand on my knee, rubbing it just like I'm rubbing her back. "My father was a mean dad, and he didn't let me say goodbye to my mom before she died."

"Were you sad?"

"Yes, I was very sad. My mom was an amazing person. She was beautiful and loved everybody. She loved me very, very much."

She scrunches her face. "Your dad sounds like an asshole."

I chuckle, looking around me to make sure Lee's not around to hear Olivia curse. She's slipped up a few times and said curse words, and each time Lee scolds Rowen, King, Ace, and me, telling us that we have to watch our mouths around Olivia because she likes to repeat our "colorful" language.

Hypocrite. Her mouth is just as filthy as ours.

I don't care if Olivia says a few bad words; there's worse things she could do. "Yeah, you're right. He was an asshole."

"Did he die too? Did you kill him for being a bad man like you killed the bad man who hurt my mommy?"

Her words give me pause. She was unconscious when I killed Colton, so I'm assuming she heard one of us talking about it, and that's how she knows. The girl loves to eavesdrop.

Her bright eyes are full of curiosity, free of judgment and fear, so I choose not to lie to her. "I didn't, but I wish I did. He killed himself by drinking too much alcohol."

"I've never had a daddy before. Do you think that a daddy would want to have me?"

"Yes, I do. There is someone out there who would love to be your dad." She stares at me for a moment, my heart beating rapidly in my chest.

Olivia opens her mouth to speak, but I'm too afraid to find out what her next question will be, so I cut her off. "Are you going to stay? Or am I going to give you money?"

"I think I should stay. At least until after dinner, and maybe after I shower and brush my teeth too." She grins, standing up from the bed.

With a smile, I stand. "Good choice, kid. Unpack your bag, then go play. Do whatever it is that kids do." I'm walking toward the door, ready to leave, when she calls my name.

"Eli?"

I turn toward her. "Yeah?"

"You'd be a good daddy." My face pales. She hurries off toward her bathroom, leaving me frozen in place with my heart dropping into my stomach.

*Fuck, that was unexpected.*

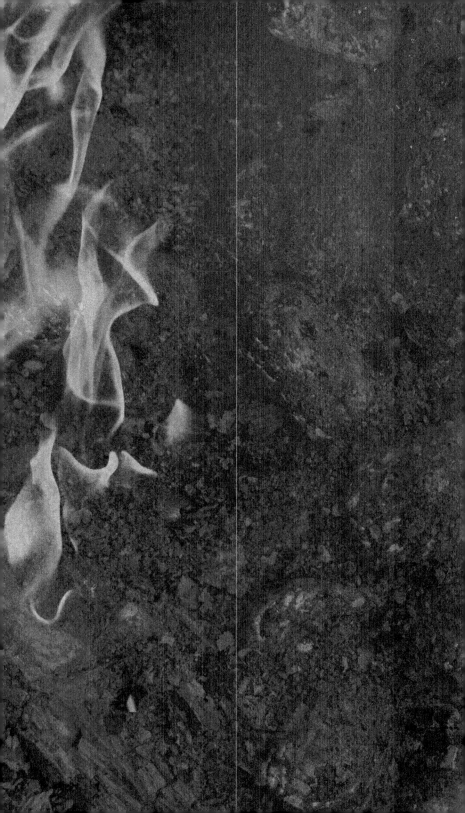

# THIRTY-SIX

*Lee*

E li won't admit it, but he adores Olivia. I know he does, regardless of how much he likes to pretend that she annoys him.

Since the six of us have been living together, I've learned a few things about the not-so-mysterious Eli Hale.

First, despite his cocky egotistical attitude, Eli is shy and unsure of himself.

Second, Eli loves deeply but has a tough time showing it because of his childhood. I know his mother loved him, but he spent his younger years begging for his father's attention after she died.

Third, his love language is physical touch. He needs to be touched to feel loved, and to show his affection, he touches because he has a hard time saying what he feels.

Fourth, Eli Hale is in love with me.

I know he is, even when he doesn't like to admit it.

Fifth, Eli Hale loves my daughter, and fatherhood looks pretty damn good on him.

Sixth, he will do anything for me. If I asked him to reach into the night sky and get me a star, he would. Of course, he'd have a few choice words to say about it, and he would call me a spoiled brat, but he'd do it because he wants me to smile.

It's odd, but having Olivia here has brought us closer together. We're all learning not to be selfish because we have a child to think about. We have each other to think about.

Something always felt like it was missing when it was only Eli, King, Rowen, and me. I now know that it was Ace and Olivia that were missing. I hate to say everything happens for a reason, but part of me has always felt that Olivia being raised by Rachel was only temporary.

I never would've wished death on her. It's tragic, it is, but I can't shake the feeling that she was a necessary sacrifice. I feel like the world's biggest piece of shit for even saying that.

Rachel was my friend, and she died because of me. She died because of my choices, but I can't allow myself to dwell on that. If I spent time thinking of all the people that lost their lives because of me, I'd never be able to get out of bed.

I'm a walking red flag, and everyone should steer clear of me.

Everyone who gets near me dies.

Cassie died.

Delilah died.

Rachel died.

Who's going to die next?

Being my friend comes with a death sentence.

The fucked-up thing is that I wouldn't trade places with any of them. I love my life so much these days that I'm excited to wake up and live. I've spent so many years praying to whatever God would listen and asking him to take me in my sleep. I didn't want to wake up. I wanted to die peacefully in my sleep.

There were days when I hoped Sebastian would snap and kill me. I wanted it and even provoked him on occasion.

I tried to drown myself once, but drowning in a bathtub wasn't very easy, and my instincts to fight kicked in, and that plan failed.

I would even pray to wake up as someone else.

Anyone else.

Anyone besides Lee Spencer, the girl who life loved to kick around.

Now, I wake up every day, grateful that my life didn't end like I wanted it to. I wake up with purpose, and I wake up believing that everything happened for a reason because everything I did in my life led me to this moment.

To this exact moment, lying beside my beautiful daughter, waiting for the four men I love to return home.

Since tomorrow is Saturday, Olivia begged me to let her stay up late to watch a few movies. Being the pushover I am, I agreed. We made popcorn, grabbed some candy, and curled up on one of the oversized beanbag chairs in our home theater room, and watched a movie.

The second movie had just started when I noticed she'd fallen asleep, so I covered her with a blanket and watched the film alone.

Well, I'm attempting it because I can't stop staring at her and memorizing every single one of her features.

The crease between her eyebrows, the way her nostrils flare when she exhales, the way her lips look when they're slightly parted. I memorize everything. She's such a beauty, and I feel like I'm living in a fantasy world. Like I could wake up any second to find it was all a dream.

I've always wanted to be a mother. I had hoped I'd be married and have children one day, but Sebastian quickly destroyed that dream.

Now here I am. Because of an unfortunate situation that was all my fault, that I unknowingly set into motion ten years ago, here I am. Now I'm getting a second chance and getting my daughter back.

I know I shouldn't be happy about it. Someone had to die for this to happen. My friend died for me to have Olivia back, but God damn, I can't stop thanking the Lord for allowing me to have her.

I never realized how empty my heart had been without her.

When I look at her, I don't see Colton or the bad things that have happened to me. I see a young girl who deserves so much happiness, safety, and love. I see a girl that needs to be protected at all costs, and I'm willing to give my life to do that.

I'd do anything for her.

The sound of a door slamming shut catches my attention and pulls me away from my thoughts. Careful not to wake Olivia, I quietly stand up from the beanbag chair and grab my phone from the floor, checking the alert from our security system.

A smile spreads across my face seeing the alert for the open door.

Leaving Olivia to sleep peacefully, I exit the room, walking down the hallway and the stairs until I enter the basement where my guys set up their man cave.

"Hey, sexy." Rowen grabs me from behind when I enter, pressing a kiss to the side of my neck.

"You guys are getting home pretty late," I say, turning in his arms to press a chaste kiss on his delicious lips.

"Sorry, butterfly. We got held up with the shipment," King says, taking a pool stick from the rack and preparing for a game of pool with Ace. The four left hours ago to meet with the South Lords to deliver them a shipment of guns in preparation for a turf war with the Westside Disciples. Since I learned that Eli had promised guns to both sides, I've been begging him to end his deal with one or both of them. He's pouring gasoline on a dangerous fire that could eat him alive at any second.

He's supplying guns to rival gangs, and they're using those guns to kill each other. It's not going to end well.

Of course, Eli waves me off, kisses me, and tells me he has everything under control.

"Well, while you guys were away, I've decided something," I announce, walking toward the pool table and sitting on the edge of it.

"What did you decide, pretty thing?" Ace asks.

Smiling, I say, "I'm ready." I've put a lot of thought into what I'm about to say, and it finally feels right. For months I've been thinking about it, wondering if or when it would happen, but when Steven called me this morning and told me his latest update, my decision became clear; the timing is perfect. Now that my life is finally falling into place twenty-seven years later, I know it's the ideal time for Sebastian to pay. He's the only one who's gotten off easy. Everyone else who has ever hurt me has since paid the price.

*Except him.*

He owes me, and I'm ready to collect the debt, only in blood.

Eli looks toward me. "Ready for what?"

"To kill Sebastian." They exchange a look among them.

Clearing his throat, Rowen asks, "You want to kill Sebastian?" It's been weeks since his name has been mentioned. None of us have forgotten about him, but we've been occupied with finding a new normal in our lives, taking care of Olivia, and getting her the needed therapy.

"Why now?" Eli asks.

"Steven called me today." I pull my phone from my pocket, pull up the link to the online article he sent me earlier, and read it aloud, "*Two years after his wife's disappearance, Doctor Sebastian Riley will be marrying his fiancée Courtney Piedmont on September 14th.*" I show them the headline.

"The bastard is trying to get remarried. He knows I'm alive, and he's increased my life insurance policy. We're still legally married, so I think it's safe to assume he plans to do something about the fact that I'm alive." I put my phone back into my pocket. "Steven told me that Sebastian has been desperate. It's not a good look for him to marry someone else when his wife is still missing."

"It will not be a good look if your body suddenly appears. He would be a suspect, then," Rowen says.

"Probably not. The police would assume I ran off somewhere with a guy because that's what he's been telling them. It's been two years, and if I suddenly appeared dead, they'd think it was the guy I ran off with. They'd know my death was faked," I explain, brushing my hair behind my ears.

"He's marrying one of the women he cheated on me with. She has seen the bruises he left on me, she even witnessed him slap me before, yet she continued to fuck him. If he marries her, I know he will beat her, just like he beat me." I shake my head. "I will not allow it to happen to another woman. He doesn't get to have a happy fucking ending after abusing me for so long. I lost so much because of him. Now, it's time he pays."

"You can have anything you want, butterfly." King all but skips over to me with a wide fucking grin on his mouth.

"I've been waiting for this moment," Rowen replies.

"I'll get a babysitter for Olivia," Eli says, taking his cell phone from his pants pocket. "I'll have Maverick get one of our unmarked cars ready, and tomorrow night, we can put this sorry fucker down."

"Is this really what you want?" Ace asks, cupping my face.

"Yes. This is what I want."

A grin spreads across his lips. "Looks like you're about to become a widow."

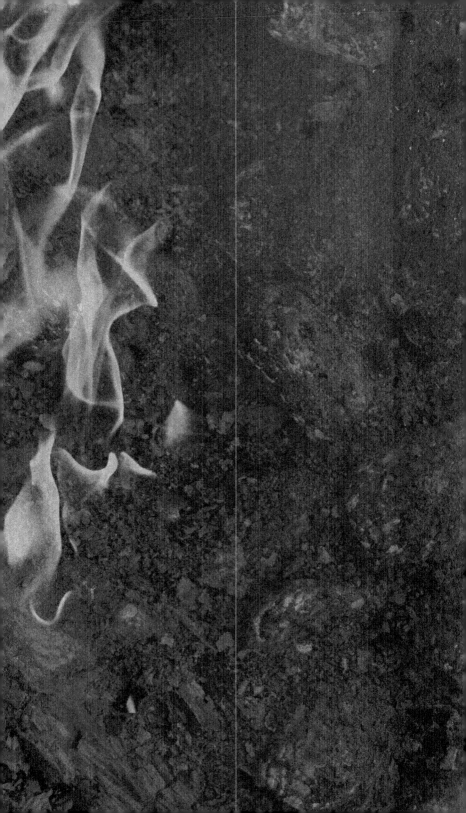

# THIRTY-SEVEN

*Eli*

"Thanks again for agreeing to babysit Olivia this weekend, Melanie." I thank her again for the twentieth time since she and Maverick agreed to watch Olivia while me, my brothers, and our girl take a weekend trip to the town Lee left behind two years ago.

I was so fucking proud of my little hellion when she decided she wanted to make Sebastian pay for all the shit he's done to her. She wants to torture him the same way he did to her. If he dies in the process, well, I'm not going to mourn his loss.

The bastard deserves every single thing that he has coming to him.

His fate was sealed the day he decided to lay a finger on Lee's pretty little head.

"We're happy to have her." Mel smiles, taking the pink and white polka dot backpack from my hands with Olivia's clothes for the weekend packed inside.

When Olivia's eyes land on Riot, who's currently walking down the stairs, she takes off, running toward him. They had a rocky start when they first met, but now they're begging to see each other as often as possible.

I'm glad she's found a friend. She needs someone her age she can talk to and to help keep her mind off the tragedy she witnessed.

"Bye, Eli!" she yells from the top of the stairs without looking back, right before she takes off running, golden-blonde hair flowing behind her. Ever since that day in the kitchen when I lost my cool and snapped at her, I've been doing my best to be better for her.

To have patience, listen, and learn. It's an adjustment because I'm not used to having a child around, but she's starting to grow on me. Now I look forward to hearing her voice and her ridiculous questions every day.

"Tell Maverick I'll call him later, please," I say, taking my car keys from my pocket.

Melanie nods, walking me outside to my car. "I will. And don't worry about Olivia. We'll take great care of her, and you can pick her up tomorrow night." After giving her one final thanks, I leave, speeding my way home because I'm so fucking eager to pick my family up so we can go and take care of Sebastian by tonight.

Tonight is our only chance.

His new fiancée has moved into his house, and she's currently away at a spa, thanks to me. The dumb bitch thought she won a spa package for one and happily accepted and went away.

Obviously, she had no idea that I'm the one that booked the trip and had Elena call and tell her she'd won and deliver all the details. Lee was surprised when she learned that Sebastian allowed her to go, considering he never let her have any freedom. But she also mentioned that he had been the perfect gentleman while they were dating and engaged. She said his true self and anger didn't show until after they were married, so she never had any idea what she would be getting herself into.

With Courtney out of the way, we'll have access to Sebastian without any witnesses or interruptions. He has no neighbors, and his house is miles outside of town, so I'm thrilled.

Everything will be perfect tonight.

My little hellion will get exactly what she deserves. And so will Sebastian.

I've just pulled into my driveway when my phone rings, and Jaden's name flashes on the screen. With the roll of my eyes, I answer the call. "What do you want, Jaden?" The needy fucker has been testing my patience lately. As the Westside Disciples prepare to go against the South Lords to gain control over territory, he seems to be blowing up my phone more than ever.

"Eli, we need more. Those dumb South Lord fuckers have some serious fucking power," he growls into the phone. "They have some military-grade shit, and I want you to get what they have."

"What makes you think I can get what they have?" He doesn't need to know that I'm the one supplying guns to the South Lords.

"Did you or did you not tell me that you can get anything I need? I held up my end of the deal, and now you need to hold up yours." His tone darkens, and I can tell his anger is about to get the best of him.

"Fine." My eyes roll. "I'll call Maverick, and he'll be in touch."

"Good. I swear to fucking God I'm going to find out where they're getting their guns, then I will fucking kill the bastard supplying them," he vows, bringing a smile to my face. I'd like to see him try.

"All right, good luck with that. Maverick will call you." I end the call, not needing to wait for his response. One thing about Jaden is… he's a little bitch. Since he's taken over leadership, there's been zero gang wars between WD and anyone else. He wouldn't even know what the fuck to do in a real fight.

As for his threats about killing the supplier, I'm not worried. I stay behind the scenes, and no one knows I'm the supplier for the South Lords. Apart from my family, no one has a single fucking clue.

Maverick knows because he's the one who arranges for a third party to drop off to the South Lords, but I consider him family, and I'm not worried he'd break our confidentiality agreement.

Besides, Jaden would never bite the hand that feeds him. He needs me too much to ever do something stupid.

The passenger side door opens, and Lee sticks her platinum head inside. "Hey, are we going or sitting out here all day?"

A smirk spreads across my lips. "I was just coming in to get you."

"Lucky for you, we're all ready." She climbs into the seat, buckling up.

My attention turns toward the front door, and I watch as King, Rowen, and Ace walk out, each carrying a duffle bag.

Rowen ups the trunk of the SUV and throws the bags inside while King and Ace climb inside the backseat.

"God damn, how many fucking bags do you all need?"

"Well, we'll need a change of clothes and whatnot, and King wanted to bring some of his…toys," Lee explains with a shrug as if it were completely fucking normal for us to be on our way to kill someone without a single care in the world.

King's big ass squeezes between our seats in the front, leaning over the middle console. "Group selfie, guys. We have to document this moment."

"Document what? Premeditated murder?" Lee deadpans, her voice full of amusement.

"Butterfly, shut up, and let's all say my cock is the biggest while we smile." He opens the camera app to the front camera and tilts the phone to the side to allow us to all get into the phone, Ace and Rowen squeezing in the best they can.

With a laugh, we all shout, "My cock is the biggest!"

King snaps several pictures, and after he's had his photo fun, he sits back and whines, "Guys, you were supposed to say 'King's cock is the biggest.'"

"Next time, clarify that." Rowen chuckles. I look up into the review window, grinning, watching as King pouts like a big-ass baby.

Turning my eyes to the front window, I begin driving us away from our home, ready to start this journey.

Lee twists in her seat, looking at the three burly men in the backseat squashed together, saying, "You guys look ridiculous. One of you should sit in the very back."

"How about you sit here in the middle, angel? I'll sit in the front," Rowen suggests.

"Nah, I'm good. I like it up here."

"My pretty thing, if you come back here, I promise to make it fun," Ace says, voice full of innuendo.

Instead of replying, Lee reaches forward and turns the radio on, turning it up loud enough it drowns out the laughter and sexual comments from the three in the backseat. I watch her from the side of my eye, making herself comfortable. Her feet are on the dash, and her hand is on my thigh.

The organ in my chest that I always thought was useless beats rapidly, swelling in size. Placing my hand on hers, I smile to myself, realizing that I have everything I could ever want for the first time.

I've got my girl by my side and my brothers in the back as we drive to serve justice.

This is what happiness feels like.

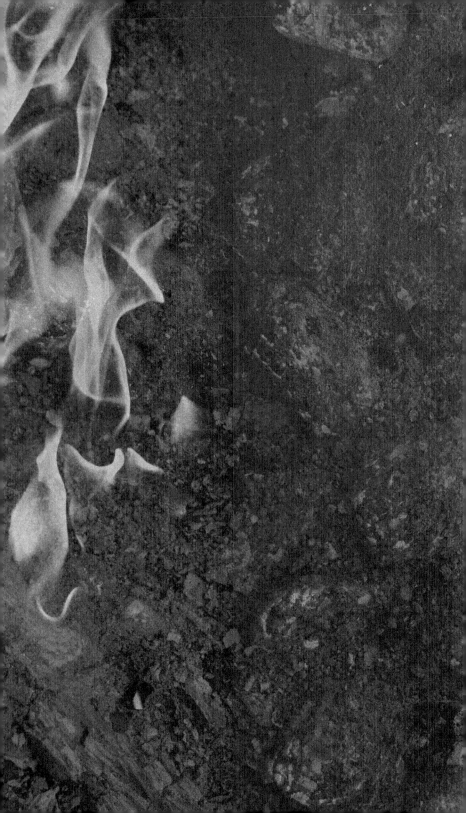

# THIRTY-EIGHT

*Lee*

Ten hours later, Eli turns off the headlights and brings the car to a stop, parking down the hill that leads to the driveway of the house of horrors that I lived in for so long. I've been so excited to do this since I told them I wanted to kill Sebastian, and I've been mentally preparing myself during the drive.

Now that we're here and I'm seconds away from coming face-to-face with the man who hurt me for years, I'm not sure how I feel.

Eli turns toward me. "Baby, you okay?" He takes my hand, noticing the vacant look on my face.

Slowly, I force myself to nod, and without a word, I unbuckle my seat belt, open the door, and climb out of the car.

Rocks crunch under my shoes as I walk up the hill and toward the driveway. I hear my guys following behind me, but I don't pay them any attention and walk ahead, anxious to get closer to the house where I spent so many years.

Standing in the driveway, I stare at the glass house I once had been so excited to live in with my new husband. I had fantasized about all the moments we'd share and the memories we'd make. I pictured us bringing our children home and raising them in this house and putting a treehouse in the backyard for them. I imagined us standing in the doorway, greeting our grandchildren when they'd come to visit us.

I pictured our entire lives in this house. But that fantasy ended when Sebastian decided to lay his hands on me. He ruined everything good about this place and set fire to every dream I had.

He destroyed the house I once loved so much, and staring at it now, I feel the same hatred I did two years ago when I stood in this exact spot after faking my death.

In a fucked up way, this house made me stronger. I'm no longer a victim; I'm a survivor. A survivor who will do anything to continue surviving.

My first tormentor, Greg, is dead, thanks to Rowen when we were children.

My second tormentor, Colton, is dead, thanks to Eli.

Now it's time for my third and final tormentor to die. But this time, justice is all mine.

Staring at the house, I quietly walk around to the side where I can see inside. Sebastian has the glass clear instead of frosted, allowing me to see directly inside the main floor.

Everything is the same. Not a single fucking thing has changed décor-wise. The only difference I can see is that instead of photos of us that once hung on the walls, I now see pictures of him and Courtney.

"I can pick the lock and open the door," King says, the strap of his black duffle bag in his right hand.

"No need. I'm willing to bet the code to the gate in the backyard is the same, and the backdoor will probably be unlocked." I wipe my sweaty palms on my leggings, blowing out a few puffs of air to calm my nerves.

Sebastian can't hurt me anymore, but still, that doesn't stop me from being nervous about walking into the house that holds so many bad memories.

"Stay here," I finally say, walking along the side of the house that leads toward the kitchen that is enclosed by four walls. The main living room and upstairs living room are the only rooms that are made of floor-to-ceiling windows, and everything else is covered.

I walk along the side until I reach the seven-foot-high white gate that conceals the backyard from view. Standing in front of it, I stare at the lock that requires a passcode, and with shaky fingers, I punch in the code, 051460, his mother's birthday. Sebastian is as predictable as always.

The light flickers from red to green, and I twist the handle, push the gate open, and slip inside the backyard. Walking toward the back door, I stay hidden in the shadows of the night, tiptoeing my way to the sliding glass back door.

Looking in, I don't see any movement or anyone on the first floor, but better safe than sorry. Quietly, sliding the door open, I slip inside, quickly drawing the blinds and locking the door.

Knowing I made it in without getting caught brings a smirk to my lips and a sense of pride.

Upstairs, the floor creaks with movement, but I know this house well enough to know which room the noise is coming from. He's in the bedroom, and I assume he has the door wide open as he always did.

Inhaling, I hold my breath as I run across the living room and unlock the front door, allowing my four guys access to the house that once meant everything to me.

It was my first real home. The first house I ever truly felt safe in until Seb ruined it for me. Destroyed my fantasy and sense of security.

This is the house where he killed me.

One by one, my guys easily fit through the door, smirks on their silent faces. When they're all inside, I close the door with a silent click and lock it, then push the buttons on the touch screen panel beside the door to allow the windows to frost, shielding the outside from viewing inside.

We're going to need privacy for what's in store tonight.

The floor creaks above me again, then I hear footsteps, adrenaline shooting through my veins at the voice that follows. "Courtney, babe, is that you?" Sebastian calls from upstairs.

Pressing my finger to my lips, I shush my guys, urging them to keep quiet. Luckily, they do as I say, and all four take a seat in the living room, making themselves comfortable in my former home.

I hold my breath and stand at the bottom of the stairs, exhaling slowly as I say, "Honey, I'm home." I can't keep the amusement from my voice.

The footsteps falter. I clearly caught the bastard off guard. A few heartbeats later, the footsteps quicken until Seb's face comes into view, standing at the top of the stairs.

He stands only a few feet away, looking the same as always. Soulless blue eyes, a nasty snarl, his mouth ready to spit pure venom. Looking at him now, I can't believe I ever once thought he was the most handsome man I'd ever met.

He's so different from Eli, King, Rowen, and Ace, and it's hilarious.

Sebastian was the man who swept me off my feet the second I noticed his clean-cut Hollister boy country club look. As for my four savage men, they're covered from head to toe in tattoos, and their appearance screams danger and would make anyone want to turn in the opposite direction and take off running. They hunt their prey and take whatever they want, and I'm the lucky one that got caught in their trap.

My men are stunning, and compared to them, everyone else is fucking basic.

Especially Hollister boy Sebastian. He's nothing compared to them.

"You little fucking bitch," Sebastian barks, shaking his head as his eyes roam over me. "I knew you'd come crawling back, begging for me to take you back. I never believed you were dead." He laughs. "I never would've been that lucky. You never knew how to die, but I wonder if you'll finally stay dead this time." He takes the stairs slowly, getting closer to me.

"I don't recall begging to come back and be your wife again."

"You are still my wife, Lee. My dead wife, whom no one is looking for." For the first time, I'm not afraid as I stand before him because I'm not the same person I was two years ago. I'm no longer that weak woman, plus I know that if he were to try anything, my men would get to him first.

They're only standing down now because of respect for me. They know that I need this. That I deserve this.

God, I love them.

"I might be willing to take you back. Perhaps if you were to get down on your knees and beg, I might leave Courtney and allow you to come back." The bastard smiles. He believes his words, and he's actually considering it.

"The only begging she's doing is begging for me to fuck her harder!" King calls out from the living room, followed by Ace's laughter.

Sebastian's trimmed eyebrows pull together in a scowl at the voices. Taking the final step down, he pushes me aside, turning into the living room, his face visibly paling at the sight of his unwelcome house guests making themselves comfortable.

Rowen is sitting on the arm of the couch while Ace is lying back on the cushions with his dirty boots on the material. King is standing close to me, while Eli is standing in front of the built-in shelves, looking over the hideous décor and crystal vases that Seb spent a fortune on when he went house shopping with his mother.

Who the hell does that? When you're a newlywed, you'd typically go home shopping with your new spouse, but instead of taking me, Seb took his mommy, and they picked out everything in this house.

Fuck them both.

"Who the fuck are you?" Seb snaps, eyes bugging out of his head as he looks between all four men, taking in their appearance, all dressed head to toe in black pants and hoodies, their tattoos visible on their hands and necks, and Ace's facial tattoos visible. "Get the fuck out!" he yells, his voice becoming high-pitched.

This is the first time I've seen Sebastian afraid, and I love it. Fear is a good look on him.

"I'm willing to bet twenty bucks that he'll piss himself," Ace says, adjusting his position, so he's sitting up.

"Make it fifty. He will most definitely piss himself." Rowen slaps Ace on the knee, agreeing to his bet.

"A hundred says he cries!" Eli chimes in, throwing the crystal vase into the air, stepping aside when it begins to fall. The glass connects with the floor and shatters, shards of pricy glass near his feet being crushed under his boot when he steps through it.

Sebastian's eyes are ready to pop out of his head at the sight of his precious vase that Mommy picked being destroyed. "Stop! Get out!"

Eyes on Seb, Eli stalks toward him, face stoic. "Say please. Get down and beg," he says, standing behind him, his posture straight and confident, his hands in his pockets.

From where I stand, I can see the goosebumps that form on Sebastian's arms, the hair on the back of his neck rising. The fucker is scared but trying to play it cool.

Without his money and the influence of his family, he's nothing. He's only strong enough to hit a woman, which is why he's abused me for so long. I was afraid to fight back, but looking at him now, I realize that he isn't as scary as he once seemed.

In fact, he's nothing.

Sebastian is nothing to me anymore.

Squaring his shoulders, Seb straightens his posture, attempting to appear unaffected by the four strangers in his house. "I'll say it one more time." He holds his breath. "Get the fuck out, or I'm calling the police," he hisses, a smirk spreading across his face when Eli steps back and surrenders, holding his hands in the air.

"Uh-oh. He's going to call the cops, so we should probably go," Eli teases, walking toward Rowen, King, and Ace, who are now standing.

"Yeah, that's what I thought." Seb smiles. "Don't let the door hit you on the way out." His attention leaves them and turns toward me. "Lee, honey, I forgive you. Let's start over. I'll take you back."

His words fade into the background as I walk away from him and find myself rushing upstairs, suddenly feeling the need to see the rest of the house.

I'm not sure why, but I feel compelled to walk through the house that holds all my secrets. The walls of his house have seen everything.

Every cruel word, every punch, slap, kick, everything. The walls were my witness to every violent thing my husband did to me.

"Get off me!" Sebastian yells from downstairs. "I'm calling the cops!" he vows, his voice fading farther away as I hear shuffling. I'm not sure what they're doing to him, but I don't care right now.

My mind isn't on him; it's on the house. For my sanity, I need to walk down the memory lane and remember everything that happened to me. I need my anger and rage to fuel me to ensure that I follow through with what I need to do instead of chickening out at the last minute.

I may no longer care about Seb, but I still deserve justice. There's no turning back now, no matter what.

Finding myself in my former bedroom, I stand in front of the massive walk-in closet, pull open the double doors, and take slow steps inside. My fingertips run along the soft material of the women's clothing that hangs where my clothes once hung.

Two years ago, my shoes were the ones displayed on these shoe racks. My clothes were neatly hanging, clothes that Sebastian had to pick out because I couldn't wear anything he disapproved of. Nothing too short or revealing, and nothing too bright that would attract attention.

I wore the exact shades that are currently hung on my former shelves. Nudes and pinks.

Seb's taste hasn't changed. I'm sure he's also controlling Courtney's clothing choices, but I bet she's so in love with him, just like I was, that she doesn't even notice that he's controlling her.

Looking back, the signs were there, but he made me feel special, and I wanted to be everything he wanted me to be. I would've given anything for him to continue wanting me. I was young and had hearts in my eyes and clouded vision.

My fingers grab hold of the white fluffy dress bag hidden away in the back of the closet. I remove it from the hanger, pull it out, and place it on the floor. Carefully, I unzip the bag, revealing a fluffy, white princess-style strapless wedding dress.

Holding the dress in my hands, my breathing nearly stops, my heart aching in my chest for a reason I don't quite understand.

Courtney's wedding dress is nearly identical to mine, except Seb didn't allow me to wear strapless.

With a smile, I strip out of my clothing and climb into the dress, zipping myself into it the best I can. I'm not surprised that we're the same size; Seb does have a specific type, after all.

Holding the skirt in my hands, so I don't trip, I carefully walk barefoot down the stairs, following the voices. I find Seb and my guys in the kitchen. He's tied to a chair with his hands behind his back while Rowen sits on the counter, King and Ace search through the fridge, and Eli sits at the table with a bored expression, scrolling through his phone.

"Take that off! That isn't yours!" Seb hisses, fighting against his restraints that aren't budging.

All four heads pause to look at me, curiosity and humor filling their eyes.

King is the first to speak up. "What are you doing, butterfly?" he asks, shoving half his peanut butter and jelly sandwich into his mouth. I spin around, enjoying the feel of the heavy dress skirt flying around me.

When I finish spinning, my eyes land on King. "I'm just admiring this pretty dress." My hands run over the material.

"Take it off! Courtney had that dress custom-made. You're going to ruin it!" Seb yells, rocking back and forth in the chair, attempting to free himself.

Ignoring him, I say, "I wore a dress like this on my wedding day. Except I wasn't allowed to have strapless because Seb thought it was too revealing. It's funny that his new fiancée can wear strapless."

Eli sets his phone down and stands, placing his hand on Seb's shoulder, keeping him steady so he can no longer continue fighting against his restraints.

"She's not a fucking whore like you are. I was right about you all along," Seb spits venom, his eyes darkening with hatred as he looks me up and down. "Just another dirty whore. You left me to be with these thugs. I bet you're fucking them all, too."

Rushing toward him, King cocks his fist back and crushes it into the side of Seb's face with an audible snap. "Don't fucking speak to her that way!" he roars.

Stepping behind him, I place a hand on his shoulder. "King, it's okay." I grip his arm and pull him toward me. "He doesn't have the power to hurt me anymore." I pull him away, standing in front of Sebastian.

"You hurt me because you're a coward. The only way to get what you wanted was by inflicting pain on me. You can't do that anymore because you're nothing to me and no longer have the power," I tell him, a weight suddenly being lifted from my chest. "By the way, you are right about one thing. They are fucking me, and they're so much better than you."

A smirk spreads on Eli's face. "Baby, tell me, did he ever make you come?"

My eyes remain locked with Sebastian as I answer, "No. Never."

"Did he ever eat your pussy and make your toes curl?" Eli asks, stalking toward me, lust in his eyes.

"Never," I answer.

"You fucking bitch! I fucked you so good that you'd scream for more!" Seb's face is as red as a fucking tomato from his anger. "You were such a greedy whore that you always wanted it!"

"You're wrong." I shake my head, leaning back against Eli's hard body when he stands behind me. "I hated having sex with you. You forced yourself on me, and for it to end sooner or cause less pain, I'd lie there and go along with it. I hated every single time you touched me."

"You weren't good anyway. You could never satisfy me." His words no longer affect me. Before, I would hope to please him, hope that I was fulfilling his needs and was enough that he'd stay with me. I used to be so afraid that he'd leave me, and that I would have nothing. All I knew was him, and he made me dependent on him so that he could control me.

"What's your plan, Lee? Tie me up, punch me, try and scare me? Destroy my home? You can do whatever you want, but I promise you, you will fucking regret it."

"Me? No. I'm not going to do anything to you. You'll get a taste of your own medicine, and I'll laugh while you're bleeding and crying. Just like you did to me." I turn away from him and look at Eli, King, Rowen, and Ace, giving them a sincere smile.

"Do your worst, boys," I say, walking toward where Rowen sits on the counter. He hops off, kisses my forehead, then joins Eli, who is currently standing before Seb.

"You better let me go right fucking now, or you'll all be sorry!"

"Wow, I'm so scared. I'm shaking in my boots," Eli taunts, reaching a long hand forward and firmly gripping Seb's jaw, applying pressure. "Did you show any mercy to Lee while you were beating the fuck out of her?"

I hadn't noticed it before, but King has his duffle bag open on the counter to reveal all of his favorite toys. Reaching inside the bag, I pull out a curling iron, a grin spreading across my lips. He brought it just for me. How special.

Taking the curler, I plug it in the outlet near the island where Sebastian's sitting and set it on the counter, waiting for it to heat.

"Do you remember that time you burned me?" I ask, running my fingers along the curling iron burn at the back of my neck. Years ago, I was getting ready for a charity gala, and I was taking too long curling my hair. His solution was to press the hot iron to my neck until I was screaming in pain as my skin sizzled. I could smell my skin burn.

Seb sits silent, refusing to answer me. But it's okay; I know he remembers it. He doesn't need to respond.

Finally, his eyes connect with mine.

"Is this your plan, Lee? Do to me what I did to you? Teach me a lesson?" He sighs, shoulders slumping in defeat. "Okay, fine. Do it, then. Get your little revenge with your thugs because at the end of the day, I'm going to marry Courtney. She's the love of my life, and I'll never need to lay a hand on her. She wants to make me happy, and she's everything you're not. Do whatever you need to make yourself feel better, then get the fuck out of my life. For good," he growls, his eyes narrowing into slits as he glares at me.

"Great. Let's have some fun, then." I don't bother mentioning that he won't be making it to his wedding day. Come morning, I'll be a widow.

I'll finally be free from him once and for all.

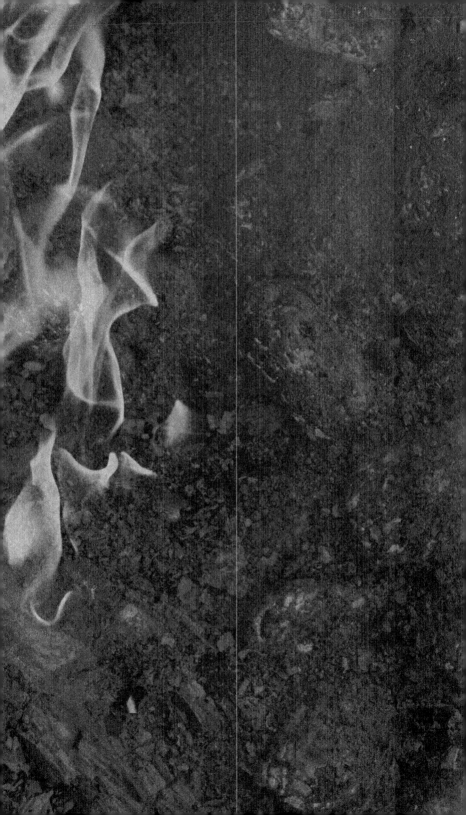

# THIRTY-NINE

*King*

**M**y butterfly looks so fucking sexy wearing that pretty white wedding dress that will soon be stained red. The thought causes my cock to thicken in my pants.

We're upstairs in the master bedroom now. After we had stripped Sebastian and began burning him all over his naked body with the hot curling iron, Lee's phone started blowing up with calls and texts from Melanie, so she went to the backyard to answer the call. While she was talking, the four of us decided to take our fun upstairs.

My brothers have taken their shirts off, and I've stripped down to my boxers, eager for the blood splatter I know I'll get before the night is over.

They're doing something to make the deserving bastard squeal, but my attention is on the beautiful woman dressed in white standing in the doorway.

"Everything okay, butterfly?" I ask, walking toward her. Her bright blue eyes meet mine, a smile forming on her lips.

"It was Olivia who called. We need to hurry. She's homesick and wants to come home," she says, walking into the room and setting her phone on the dresser.

Nodding, I press a kiss to her pink lips. "You got it, baby. We'll hurry here and get home to our little girl." I knew she was anxious about leaving Olivia behind, and even though Olivia was excited about getting to play with Riot, I knew she was going to have a hard time being away from her mother. Away from all of us. My little princess is a strong kid, but she's not ready to be away from us for very long.

Eli turns his head to look at me, his eyebrows raised in question. "We need to hurry this along. Olivia needs us. She's homesick," I explain. He nods in understanding.

Turning his attention back to Sebastian, a manic grin spreads across his lips. "Sucks that we're not going to have more time together. But we've got a kid waiting for us." He grabs the golf club from the set in the closet, swinging it around in his hands.

"Turn him over," Eli demands, and Ace nods, rolling Sebastian's naked body onto his back. His ankles are taped together, and his arms are taped together behind his back.

I watch in awe as Eli runs the cold club along Sebastian's pale skin, hitting him with it in several places and leaving angry red marks.

The bastard whimpers, begging Eli to stop.

"Did you stop when she asked you to stop?" he asks, slapping his ass cheeks with the club, sliding it between them.

"Fine! Okay! Fuck, Lee, I'm sorry!" he whines, his muscles tightening, his ass cheeks flexing as he clenches, refusing to allow Eli access.

"It's too late for apologies. You should've listened to her when she begged you to stop." Tightening his grip on the handle, he thrusts it forward, forcing it between Sebastian's tight ass and inside of him. He screams, thrashing against the bed. Ace climbs onto the mattress, holding him down while Eli works it in further. "Is this the same set that you used to violate her?" he hisses, venom in his words.

Despite Eli's cold exterior, I know he cares deeply for every single one of us. Especially Lee. If he didn't care about her, he wouldn't be so angry that her bastard of a husband abused her for many years. If he didn't care, he wouldn't be doing the same things to Sebastian that he did to Lee. Everything that she told us that he did to her, Eli is now doing to him in return.

I call that justice.

"Please! Lee, stop them! Please, I love you! I'm so sorry!" His words fall on deaf ears because none of us give him the attention or pity he's looking for. The five of us are solely focused on Eli shoving the golf club up his ass.

Once he's worked the curved handle in, Ace rolls him over, allowing him to lie on his back. His body is clenched tightly and shaking with his silent sobs.

I knew the bitch was going to fucking cry. Pussy ass.

My butterfly stands at the foot of the bed, watching the scene play out in front of her, her face stoic as she stands tall, witnessing everything.

With a smirk, I walk toward the bed and climb onto it, standing on my knees. Pulling my boxers down, I pull out my cock and give it a couple of tugs. "I need to take a piss," I say, earning a roar of laughter from Rowen and Ace. Rowen steps toward the bed and forces Sebastian's mouth open by shoving in a bite block, preventing him from being able to close his mouth.

Scooting closer, I keep hold of my cock and release my bladder, warm piss spraying directly into Sebastian's open mouth. He thrashes around, coughing and gagging, but cannot spit it out due to the bite blocks. Ace grips his head firmly, preventing him from being able to turn it to the side and let my urine fall out. The bitch has no choice but to swallow.

Once I'm done, I give my cock a few shakes, then pull my boxers up, climbing off the bed.

"Drink it, bitch," Ace growls, keeping his head steady. "Swallow. Now!" I hear a gulp, followed by loud cries, and more pleading for us to let him go.

"Fuck you! Fuck all of you disgusting fucks!" Snot and tears spread down Sebastian's face, and it's the most beautiful fucking sight. I have waited so fucking long for this moment.

Laughing, Rowen flips him back over. Using his boot, he steps on the end of the golf club, then extends his leg, shoving it deeper inside Sebastian's body until he's screaming bloody murder. The club moves inside his body, causing blood to leak from his ass.

My own ass clenches at the sight. Holy fuck. I know that shit hurts. While he was screaming, I hadn't noticed Eli leaving the room and returning with another golf club. He stands above the useless body and begins swinging the club, connecting with Sebastian's skin every time.

Karma's a bitch. Had he not abused his wife, none of this would've been happening right now. His fate was sealed when he decided to be an abusive bastard.

Ace turns him onto his back again. "You beat Lee so badly that she bled and wished she were dead." He climbs onto the bed. "Now it's your turn." I stand back, watching with hearts in my eyes as my two shirtless brothers beat the crying fucker who caused so much pain to our girl.

I know he's in pain, yet somehow it doesn't seem like it's enough. He deserves more, but I also know we need to make this as short as possible so we can hurry home to our little girl. Olivia needs us, and we'll return to her once justice has been served.

"Stop!" Lee shouts, eyes wide as she stands in the white dress, staring at her bleeding husband. He's a worthless, bloody, crying, useless lump of flesh.

Eli and Ace turn toward her, dropping the golf clubs on the bed. Their chests are lined with drops of blood that have splattered on them.

"Pretty thing," Ace says, jumping to his feet. "What's wrong?" He towers over her as they stand toe-to-toe.

"Fuck me while you kill him and make him watch," she says, pupils blown with lust.

"My dirty fucking butterfly." I smile proudly, standing behind her, slowly unzipping the fluffy white dress and sliding it down her creamy body. My cock stands at full salute of the sight of her milky skin covered in only a little red thong.

"Are you getting wet at the sight of watching us?" Ace asks, helping her to step out of the dress.

"Answer him, angel. Would you be wet if I were to touch your pussy right now?" Rowen asks, attention entirely on our little vixen.

Standing behind her, I wrap a hand around her body and slide my calloused palm down her stomach, slipping under the waistband of her thong, and diving toward her pussy that's wet and ready for us.

"She's fucking dripping." I run my finger along her slit, gathering her moisture before pulling my hand out and offering it to Ace, who sucks my finger into his mouth, his tongue running along the length of my digit.

"Mmm. Wet and fucking delicious." He smirks, sliding her panties down her legs. Lee steps out of them, and Ace reaches down and gathers the damp fabric in his hand. "Open," he orders.

Lee's mouth pops open, and Ace shoves the wet material into her little mouth, gagging her with her panties. "Keep them in, and keep quiet. You'll stand there and watch while King fucks you, and you're not allowed to come," he says, walking back toward the bed where Eli remains.

Feeling giddy as fuck, I shed my boxers and push her toward the bed. "Hands on the bed, and spread your legs." She does as I say, getting into the perfect position.

Eli and Ace turn Sebastian's body, so he's facing us and forced to watch me fuck his wife through his one eye that isn't yet swollen.

Hands on her hips, I line myself up and jerk my hips forward, burying myself in her tight, warm center with ease. She sighs in relief, her body melting with sudden pleasure.

My eyes remain fixated on Eli and Ace while I fuck our girl, and Rowen stands to her side, kissing along her body, dropping to his knees and placing his head in front of her pussy.

Lee's moans and Sebastian's cries of pain fill the air, each sound making my dick painfully hard.

When the familiar tingling in the bottom of my spine begins, I pull out of her, spread her ass cheeks, and spit down her crack, spreading my saliva around before lining myself up and slowly sinking into her ass.

Rowen sits on the edge of the bed and guides Lee over his now naked lap, impaling her on his cock while I fuck her ass.

Ace and Eli drag Sebastian's limp body toward us, forcing him to stand, though it's difficult with the golf club that's sticking out of his ass, but they make him stand anyway. He's unrecognizable.

His face is swollen and red, both eyes are now shut, bruises are forming all over his body, and blood is pouring from his ass. He's never looked better. He's getting exactly what he deserves.

Ace holds him up from behind as Eli extends a knife toward Lee with a smirk on his face. "Hellion, would you like to do the honors?"

Without hesitation, my butterfly takes the knife and presses it against Sebastian's throat. Rowen pulls the panties out of her mouth, wiping away the strands of saliva.

With a content smile, Lee stares at her husband. "Goodbye, Seb. You're getting exactly what you deserve. I hope you rot in hell," she says with a smile, pressing the blade deeper. She then slices open his neck, blood immediately squirting out, spraying her chest and the side of both Rowen and me.

The knife drops to the ground with a clank, then Ace lets go of his body, and he collapses at our feet with a loud thud.

Her bloody hand rests on Rowen's shoulder as she continues riding him, and I quicken my pace, my climax building even fucking quicker after witnessing my perfect girl kill her husband while riding my brother's cock.

I'm so fucking proud of her.

As soon as I pull out of her tight body, Ace is right there to take my place and fucks her violently, her screams filling the air.

My cock weeps, and the metallic scent of the room has me needing an immediate release.

Leaning over the bed, Eli takes my cock in his hand, works his way into my backside, then fucks me until the room is filled with screams and cries of pleasure and until we're all coming together simultaneously.

It's a family fucking orgy.

# FORTY

*King*

Thinking back on all the moments in my life before meeting her, I can't remember a time when I felt happy, loved, and safe. Of course, I love my brothers, and I know they love me, but that's different. The love we share is different than the love I share with Lee.

She's the oxygen I need in my lungs to survive. She's my rib.

If God really took Adam's rib to create Eve, then I know that Lee was formed from my rib and made just for me. In every possible way, mind, body, and soul, she's mine.

I can't put into words how much I fucking love her, how much I fucking need her. My skin crawls when I'm not around her, my palms get sweaty, and I start to panic whenever she's not within a walking distance. For a while, I wondered if it was love or obsession, but I've realized it's both.

I'm both in love and obsessed with my little butterfly, which is unfortunate for her because that makes her the subject of my attention in every possible way. We spent three months apart, but I'm vowing never again to spend a single minute away from her.

I'd rather die than be apart from her.

If she were ever to leave me, I'd be willing to kill us both so she'd have no choice but to be with me forever. She's it for me, and I'm not giving her a choice. I've decided for her.

The only people I enjoy sharing her attention with are my brothers and Olivia. Every time she's near the golden-haired child, her entire aura sparkles and shines so fucking bright. Since learning she's a mother, I love her even more.

I've always wanted a family of my own but knew that would never happen because I hadn't met a woman I liked enough to impregnate, but thanks to Lee, I have a family.

Sometimes, I wish she could get pregnant so I could pump her tight pussy full of my sperm and force her legs in the air until every one of my swimmers can get to where they need to be. If I could, I'd knock her up one right after another. The thought of seeing her barefoot and pregnant makes my cock painfully hard.

Any one of my brothers, Eli, Rowen, or Ace, could get her pregnant; that doesn't matter to me. All I want is to witness her belly grow with life inside.

I want to experience everything with her for the rest of my life.

"What do you think about when you stare at me like that?" My butterfly's voice cuts through my train of thought.

Blinking, I turn my attention to her. "Like what?"

"Like you want to wear me as a body suit." She's fresh out of the shower and stands at the foot of the bed, smothering herself in lotion that wafts through the air, leaving her sweet scent everywhere.

"Maybe that's what I want." An easy grin curls the side of my mouth. "Come here," I say, leaning up, so my back rests against the headboard.

Setting her lotion on the dresser, she climbs onto the bed on her knees and crawls to me, her blue eyes never leaving mine, her peachy ass swaying with her movements.

Lee kisses up the length of my body, starting with my thighs, and works her way up to my chest, kissing the blue butterfly tattoo.

She presses her lips against mine, kissing me slowly and stealing the oxygen from my lungs. "I've never been more in love with you than I am right now," she whispers, her lips trailing from mine, then along my jawline and to my left earlobe.

We got home early this morning, and exhaustion consumed us all. The second we walked in the front door, we all went to our rooms and passed out, and I was the lucky one because my butterfly came with me.

We have to go and pick up Olivia soon, but until then, I'm enjoying the moment I have with my girl.

Lee lies beside me, her naked body curling up under my arm.

"I love you, Lee. More than I ever thought would be possible to love another human being." I turn my head to look down at her. "You killed a man last night. How are you holding up?"

"Is it weird if I say I'm fine? I'm not in shock or feeling sad. I feel so fucking free, and I know that's probably not okay to say, but I'm not sad." I look into her eyes, searching them for lies, but I only find the truth. Of course my butterfly is handling it well. She's a lot stronger than she gives herself credit for.

"Okay, baby, that's all I need to know." I press a kiss to her lips, my cock throbbing with the need for her pussy, but for now, I ignore it. Right now, I want to hold her in my arms and enjoy the moment.

"We left DNA there. What's going to happen when the police investigate?"

"Eli has it handled. Courtney will find his body when she gets home today, call the police to investigate, and the detective handling it will be someone on our payroll."

"But Seb's family is well connected. They're going to call in favors. They won't allow it to become a cold case. And what about me? They all think I'm dead, and I can't resurface now. It would look suspicious." Worry fills her eyes.

"That is where Ace comes in." I begin explaining the plan my brothers and I devised. "Lee Spencer-Riley was never missing. You're very much alive and have been living and working here for two years under your maiden name. After a fight with Sebastian that left you almost dead, you went to a hospital while fighting for your life. Once you were released, you moved here, where you had friends from when you were a child, Ace and Rowen, and you've been here ever since." She sits up, holding the sheets against her bare chest.

"You didn't know what had happened with Sebastian because you never looked into him, but he only filed a missing person's report because he was trying to lure you out of hiding. The police will also be finding years' worth of documented abuse, so he will not be the victim. You will be," I explain, reaching a hand up and brushing her silky hair behind her ears.

"Okay, that explains me. But that doesn't excuse his murder," she says, trying to figure the plan all out. Ace has already falsified hospital reports and everything else to align perfectly with our story.

"Sebastian was involved with some pretty dangerous people, and the police will find evidence of that too. They'll suspect one of them killed him."

"Was he really?"

A smirk spreads across my lips. "Maybe. Maybe not. Maybe they'll find a real person, or maybe they'll spend years chasing a ghost. Either way, you're clear, and you can live freely. No one will ever doubt you. Within a few days, everyone will know the beloved Doctor Sebastian

Riley abused his wife." Her lips press against mine, her body shaking with laughter.

"What will we do now that there's no one after me? Now that I no longer have to look over my shoulder and can be myself without fear for the very first time in my life."

"Whatever you want, butterfly. The world is yours. *I* am yours until my dying breath." I seal the promise with a kiss, slowly laying her on her back and climbing on top of her. Her legs spread and wrap around my waist, and within seconds, I'm sliding into her wet center, right where I belong.

If I were to die right now, I'd die a very happy man.

In love, and balls deep in my girl.

Life doesn't get better than this.

# FORTY-ONE

*King*

"King! King! King!" the bubbly blonde-haired child yells my name the second she steps into the house. "Look at my math test!" Olivia smiles widely, running toward me when she spots me in the kitchen.

I bend down and open my arms, catching her as she runs right into me, tightly gripping a piece of paper in her hands. I spin her around, and laughter flows freely from her, causing a broad smile to spread across my face.

Setting her on her feet, I take the paper from her hands. "Look at my math test! I got an A!" she cheers, pointing to the bright circled 'A' at the top of the paper.

"Wow! Look at you, smarty pants." Picking her up, I place her on the counter, helping her to pull her backpack off her shoulders. "Good grades get rewards. How about an ice cream sundae?"

She claps her hands together. "Oh yeah, that's what I need."

"It has to be our secret, though, or else Lee will be mad that I ruined your dinner." I chuckle, walk toward the freezer, and open it to take out the carton of vanilla ice cream.

"Don't worry. I can keep a secret. She'll never know," she says, putting her fingers together and moving them across her lips as if she were zipping them.

"Who'll never know what?" Lee asks, walking into the kitchen with an eyebrow raised. She looks at the ice cream in my hand and shakes her head.

"Really, King? I was just coming to start dinner."

Olivia saves me from having to respond by saying, "Look at my math test. A's get ice cream." She holds the paper out toward Lee, who takes it proudly.

A smile spreads across my butterfly's lips that are still swollen from being wrapped around my cock only moments ago. "Better get another bowl then, because I'd like a sundae, too." She sets the paper on the counter and pulls Olivia into her arms. "I'm so proud of you, sweet girl." She's an intelligent kid but has struggled with her schoolwork.

When we first enrolled her in school, she refused to participate in class, complete her homework, or even do the work she was given during class.

It was a struggle to get her to come out of her shell and be interested in school, but now she loves it. This is the first test she's aced, and I'm fucking thrilled for my little princess.

While I begin scooping ice cream into three bowls, Lee grabs the fudge and caramel from the fridge and warms them up.

Olivia hops down from the counter and asks, "Is everyone else home? I want everyone to see."

"Rowen and Ace should be home soon, and Eli is downstairs in the gym," I say, handing Lee the bowls of vanilla ice cream so she can scoop spoonfuls of fudge and caramel on top of them.

As if on cue, Eli walks into the kitchen wearing basketball shorts, using his shirt to wipe the sweat from his forehead.

"Hey, kid." He smiles, seeing Olivia. His relationship with her took me by surprise. He's never liked children, and it's interesting to see how much they adore each other. He probably wouldn't admit it, but she's grown on him, and he loves her.

"Eli, look." She happily shows him the grade on her test.

Eli looks at the paper and nods, a faint smile spreading across his lips. I watch silently as he walks to the fridge, removes the butterfly magnet I gave Lee as a joke, then uses the magnet to hang the paper on the refrigerator. "I'm proud of you, kid."

"Hey, baby." He kisses Lee's cheek, then opens the fridge and grabs a bottle of water before walking toward the table and sitting down, Olivia running after him.

While they chat, I help my butterfly finish the ice cream. I laugh when I see how extreme she made the sundaes. They're loaded with fudge, caramel, whipped cream, and sprinkles.

"Don't want to ruin dinner, right?" I tease, placing a spoon in each bowl.

She shrugs. "My girl got an A. Look how happy she is." She picks up two bowls and carries them to the table, placing one in front of Olivia, then sits beside her and begins eating her ice cream.

We've just finished our ice cream when Rowen and Ace join us in the kitchen. Ace carries boxes of wings and a salad, while Rowen carries pizza boxes.

I'm sure that Lee texted them and told them to bring dinner home since, instead of cooking, she decided to join Olivia and me for ice cream.

They set the food in the middle of the table and wash their hands before rejoining us.

Excited, Olivia wastes no time telling them all about her day at school and the grade she received that Eli proudly hung on the fridge door.

For years, our family dinners have consisted of just Eli, Rowen, and me. And now, our family has grown by three, and I couldn't be happier.

Ace, Lee, and Olivia complete our family.

We're one big, unconventional, happy family, and I wouldn't trade it for anything.

I've always dreamed of having a big family. Having a woman to share my bed with and hearing a child's laughter in my home. I wanted it, but I never believed that it would ever happen to me.

Little did I know that one day it would.

I don't know how the fuck a guy like me got so God damn lucky, but I'm counting my blessings every single day.

After dinner, we're all sitting at the table talking about our day when Olivia takes us all by surprise and says, "Lee, I don't want to call you mommy."

It's entirely out of the blue, and silence washes over us.

Lee reaches for her hand. "I didn't ask you to, Olivia. What brought this up?"

"I already have a mommy, but I was wondering..." She pauses, looking around at us shyly.

"It's okay, sweet girl. You can tell me anything."

She takes a deep breath. "I was wondering if I can call you mom. I want you to be my mom and me to be your daughter." My jaw drops, my eyes quickly looking toward my butterfly, who sits there silently, her eyes welling with tears.

Unable to speak, she nods her head. "Y-yes. You can call me mom," she chokes out, wiping away the tears that dared to fall.

Happily, Olivia wraps her arms around her mother and hugs her with a huge smile.

Pulling away, she looks toward Eli, Rowen, Ace, and me.

"I've never had a daddy before. Everyone at school has one, but I think it would be best if I have four." My heart stops beating.

Olivia looks at me. "Every King has a princess, right?" she asks, her eyes full of hope. "My mom is your queen, so can I be your princess?"

Unlike my butterfly, I don't try to hide the tears that fill my eyes and roll down my cheeks.

Today is the best day of my fucking life.

"Yes, you can be my princess." She smiles widely at my answer, looking toward my brothers, who have matching tearful expressions as I do, Eli included.

"Will you all be my dads?"

I've never seen the bastard cry, but I can see the sparkling tears in his eyes.

"Fuck yes, I'll be your dad!" Ace shouts, jumping up from his seat.

"Hell yeah." Rowen stands, walking toward Olivia.

Eli stands and reaches her first. Kneeling in front of her, he takes her in his arms and hugs her lovingly. "We're your family, kid. We'll all four be your dads."

"Group hug!" Lee says with a giggle, all of us quickly squeezing together to join in on hugging our girl.

*Our daughter.*

I knew the day my butterfly entered my life, I'd never be the same.

I found my purpose in life.

My heart is bigger than ever. It's full of love for my family.

# FORTY-TWO
## *Eli*

t's been six months since the day in the kitchen when Olivia asked my brothers and me to be her dads and asked to call Lee her mom.

Immediately after, Ace filed whatever paperwork online to change Olivia's last name, and Lee even asked to change hers as well.

They both took our last name, officially becoming a Hale.

Ace didn't want to feel left out, so he even took on our last name, not wanting any ties to his family and wanting to be forever a part of ours. And just like that, our family of six was complete.

My girls became mine forever.

Olivia Elizabeth Hale.

Lee Spencer Hale.

My woman, and my daughter.

*Daughter.* I have a daughter. Sometimes it feels odd saying that, but I'm filled with more gratitude than I've ever felt in all my life. For the first time, I'm genuinely happy.

The Triad officially ended all drug dealings a few months ago, and we allowed the Westside Disciples to take over the trade. They kept up their end of our deal and cleaned up our city while my brothers and I got our London office of Hale Enterprises up and running. We've been testing it for months by supplying firearms to the Westside Disciple and the South Lords, but now we're officially supplying everyone within a six-state radius.

We receive firearms from overseas and distribute them here. We've nearly tripled our income, earning more than ever when we were involved with drugs.

I don't miss my ruthless days when all I cared about was bloodshed. I'm not that person anymore, and I like my life. I love it.

I never thought the domesticated life was for me, but it sure as fuck is.

I even do school drop-offs and stay up late helping Olivia with her homework.

King, the poor bastard, somehow always gets roped into baking treats for Olivia's class or whatever fucking PTA meeting he's attending.

Yeah, you heard that right.

My brother King, who once skinned a man alive, shoved a hammer up a man's ass right side up, and once forced someone to eat their own eyeball, is a proud PTA parent.

He looks funny as fuck being the only man in a room full of women, covered in tattoos and carrying trays of homemade cupcakes that he carefully frosts himself in the shape of a rose.

Yeah, King loves this life just as much as me.

We're both fucking suckers for our little girl, both our girls, and they sure as fuck know it.

Olivia is starting to take after her mother. One bat of her eyelashes, and we're all putty in her hands—like mother, like daughter.

Lee is just as spoiled. Neither one understands the word *no*, and if you tell them no, they'll stand and stare at you until you say yes. But how can you not give in?

I'd cut off my left nut if Lee were to ask. I'd do anything for her.

For the first fucking time in my sorry-ass life, I'm in love. I never thought I'd be someone or have someone worth waking up for, but look at me now.

I'm a man in love.

"I can literally hear you thinking," my hellion mumbles, turning over in bed so she's facing me, her bright blue eyes staring up at me.

"You can read minds now?" She shoves me away. "How can you hear me thinking?" I laugh, pulling her body against mine.

"Because when you're deep in thought, you part your lips and breathe through your mouth, and I can hear it." I trail my fingers along her silky bare skin.

This morning was Ace's turn to take Olivia to school, so Lee and I got to sleep in. Thank fuck. Parenting is great and all, but it does slow your sex life, that's for sure.

We have to get creative when we only have five minutes to spare, and if we want to fuck at night, it's always slow, sweet, and quiet.

No more all-day screaming fuck fests like we used to have.

Our sex has been restricted to only during the hours Olivia is at school, and during those hours, we're usually all busy and don't have a chance to be together.

Despite those roadblocks, I wouldn't change anything. I'd never trade my girls.

"What are you thinking about?" Lee asks, her body moving on top of mine, her legs falling to either side of me.

Looking up at her, I rub my hands up and down her creamy thighs. "I was thinking about how much I love you." She smiles down at me. "About how much I love Olivia. How much I love our life."

"I know that your life has done a complete one-eighty. Things are very different now, but you're amazing with Olivia. I hope you know that. She loves you so much." She sits up, straddling me, her fingers tracing circles over my bare chest.

"I was thinking how I've never been happier. That may be odd considering how our life used to be but look at us now. We're thriving, and we're safe. We're all happy." I reach up and brush her silky strands of hair behind her ears. "Are you happy, Lee?"

She nods, her hips moving against mine, waking my cock from its slumber. "I'm very happy." She raises herself on her knees and lines up with my erection. "I've never been happier." She exhales, sliding her wet pussy down my shaft inch by inch.

Groaning, I place my hands on her hips, holding them firmly as I help her bounce on me, taking my cock like the champ she is.

My hands are on her breasts when the door opens, and King walks in, a smirk curling his lips at the sight of his butterfly impaled on my cock.

The bastard never fucking knocks.

"Good morning, you two. I see someone is already up." He laughs at himself, thinking he's the funniest fucking guy ever. "Rowen! Ace! Mom and Dad wanna have some fun!" he yells from where he stands in the doorway.

The thought of having my brothers join us excites me. It's been far too long since we've all been together in this way. I miss everyone's body and how they all feel as we come together.

Seconds later, Rowen and Ace join us in my bedroom, and the three of them are quick to shed their clothing; meanwhile, Lee remains seated on my dick. She stopped moving but hasn't disconnected us. I'm still deep inside of her, able to feel her heartbeat.

Rowen pulls the covers back and climbs onto the bed, the mattress dipping with his weight. He climbs behind Lee, right between my parted legs, and begins massaging her breasts, pinching her nipples as he kisses over her skin.

"God, you're so beautiful," I say, admiring the view. Loving the way her eyes darken with lust, and her pussy squeezes me with need.

King and Ace join us on the bed, but they quickly have their hands all over each other. When I look over, I see King on his back, and Ace is between his legs with his mouth full of King's cock while his finger plays with Lee's clit.

"Get on all fours," Rowen instructs, helping Lee to remove herself from my dick. She does as he says and gets on her hands and knees once Ace and King move out of the way and stand beside the bed.

With her glistening pussy exposed to him, Ace lines up his cock that's dripping with King's saliva and shoves into her roughly, jerking her body forward.

King lies underneath her body, his mouth latching onto her clit. Climbing onto the bed beside them, Rowen grabs a fistful of her hair, bringing her closer to him as he feeds his cock into her little mouth.

Soon the room is filled with grunts, moans, heavy breathing, and squeaks of the bed.

Ace fucks her until he fills her pussy with his cum, then pulls away and slaps her ass, allowing me to fill her tight hole next. She's slippery with Ace's cum, and it feels fucking fantastic getting to feel her warmth and his cum around my throbbing, aching cock.

"Don't fucking cum," I growl in her ear. Gripping her hips firmly, I watch as she lowers herself toward King and takes his cock inside her mouth, sucking him while he eats her pussy like a fucking caveman.

I watch as Ace climbs on the bed, lies beside us, and Rowen goes between his legs and swallows his cock, moaning at the taste of Ace's cum and Lee's cream.

God, I fucking love my family.

# FORTY-THREE
*Eli*

"I love you. Please hurry. You can't be late for Olivia's recital tonight," Lee says, pressing a lingering kiss on my lips.

Today was a rare day where we all got to be lazy and lounge around the house, enjoying a day off and exploring each other's bodies.

After our two-hour long group fuck, we showered and cuddled together in our home theater, watching the ridiculous movies that Lee picked. It was the perfect day spent inside our ideal bubble, but now our perfect bubble has popped, and it's time to get back to reality.

Rowen left to pick up Olivia from school, and I received a call from Jaden saying he wanted to meet. He probably needs more guns, but we never discuss it over the phone, so I agreed to meet him in town at a Triad-owned diner.

Olivia has her first ballet recital tonight, so I don't have time to drive out to Jaden's territory. He has to come to me.

"I promise, love, I'll be there on time with flowers in hand." I take her hands in mine and kiss each of her knuckles. "I'll meet you there, so save me a seat." Kissing her goodbye, I leave, knowing I'll have to keep my meeting short, so I don't miss out on seeing my daughter's first performance as the lead ballerina. She's so proud of herself for getting the lead position, and Lee has been helping her practice for weeks.

She's a perfect little ballerina, just like her mother once was.

Getting in my car, I stare at Lee in the review mirror, smiling as I see her waving me on, knowing that I can't wait to return home to her. To my family.

We've had the perfect day.

It takes twenty minutes to get to the diner where I'm meeting Jaden, and just my luck, the bitch is fucking late. He doesn't show up until I'm standing to leave thirty minutes later.

"Eli, sit down. We need to talk," he says without properly greeting me.

Rolling my eyes, I reclaim my seat. "You're wasting my time. You're half an hour late, and I have somewhere I need to be."

Jaden nods, and I notice he came alone. His usual group isn't with him. "Yes, your daughter's ballet recital, I know all about that." He smiles, tapping his fingers on the table.

"What do you want, Jaden?"

"I found out who has been selling to the South Lords." He stares at me, his left eye twitching. I'm curious to see where he plans on going with this. I've been selling to them for months, and I'm not sure how he found out, but I don't care either.

"Good for you. I don't have time for this." Before I can stand, he speaks again.

"I want you to stop selling to those motherfuckers. You've been going behind my fucking back!" I wait for him to tell me he's joking, but he doesn't.

Laughter comes from me, breaking our silence. "You don't have any place to tell me who I can and cannot do business with." Standing, I shake my head, looking down at him. "Make that mistake again, and you'll need to find a new supplier." I turn and walk away, not giving a fuck what else he has to say.

I know about the longtime rivalry between the Westside Disciples and the South Lords, but their rivalry isn't my concern. I'm the middleman selling guns to them both, not caring if they use those guns to kill each other.

They will shoot each other and solve my problem if I'm lucky.

Rushing to my car, I get in and drive to the nearest flower shop, picking up a dozen pink roses for my daughter and a single red rose for my woman.

I'm just walking out of the flower shop and getting into my car when my phone rings, Lee's face lighting up the screen. "I'm on my way now, love. I'll be there in about twenty minutes."

"I need you to pick me up first. My fucking tire is flat." She huffs into the phone.

"Are you home alone?"

"Yes, I had to come back to grab part of Olivia's costume that she forgot. I went to leave again, but I have a flat tire."

"Okay, I'm on my way. Go inside, don't stand outside waiting."

Her throaty laugh comes through the phone, causing me to smile. "I'm already inside. I'm throwing the laundry into the dryer. Hashtag mom life."

Laughter rips through me. "Fuck, baby, don't ever say that again."

"I love you, Eli. Hurry home to me. We can't miss our girl's performance."

"I love you, baby. I'm on my way." I end the call, driving in the direction of our home.

Seconds later, my phone rings again, and Lee's voice comes

through the speaker before I have a chance to say anything. "Never mind, one of the guys just came to get me. I'll meet you at the school," she says. In the background, I can hear the dryer slamming shut as she starts it.

"Which one is it?"

"I'm not sure. I'm going to check right now." Unease begins to set in as silence flows through the phone line.

"Lee?"

"Come on, asshole. We don't have time to play!" I hear her yell in the distance.

"Lee? Which one came to get you?"

As if she had just remembered that she was on the phone, she brings it back to her ear, her voice clear. "Ace. He's playing his stupid games." She laughs. "We'll meet you there." She ends the call, but it does nothing to ease the knot growing in the pit of my stomach.

Ace does love to play games with her. He's like a fucking child who plays hide and seek because he likes when Lee runs from him. But he'd never play with her when she's home alone because he knows she scares easily when she's alone.

Quickly, I pull up the app on my phone for the cameras and I'm met with nothing. The house looks empty. No cars are in the driveway, and there's no sign of Lee in any of the rooms. I'm sure it's nothing, but I'm unable to shake off the feeling I have. Tossing my phone into the passenger seat beside the roses, I continue driving home, speeding my way through the city. I'm desperate to get to my girl and ease the feeling I have.

Once home, I park in the driveway and run inside. "Lee! Baby! Are you home?" I yell, running up the stairs to check all of our bedrooms.

I'm met with silence. Lots and lots of silence.

Rushing downstairs, I begin turning on the lights, lighting up the house that's encased in darkness.

"Lee! Baby!" I check the laundry room. Empty.

I run toward the open front door, needing to get my phone from the car to call my brothers and see if one of them did in fact come to pick up Lee.

I'm in the foyer, ready to step outside, when a tall, broad figure steps in front of me, blocking my view. I instantly recognize the man as one of the members of Westside Disciples; he's one of their security guards.

"What the fuck are you doing here?"

"I gave you a chance, Eli." A familiar voice behind me comes. "I gave you the chance to stop selling to the South Lords, and you laughed in my face," Jaden says.

My skin turns cold as I spin around to face him and find myself staring down the barrel of his gun.

"Where the fuck is Lee?" I ask through clenched teeth. I don't give a fuck about myself. It's her I care about.

"Anton!" he yells, and another big and tall fucker walks in. Anton has one arm around my girl's mouth, and the other holds her hands behind her back. The fucker is so big that he's easily carrying her, her feet dangling above the ground.

"Get the fuck off of her!" I yell. I attempt to rush toward her, but a gun pointed at the back of my head stops me from moving. I don't have to look back to know it's the giant fuck from the front door holding the gun.

"It didn't have to end this way, Eli. I gave you a chance. You chose wrong."

*Pop.*

It happens in an instant.

One second, I'm standing, and the next, my knees buckle

underneath me, and I'm falling to the ground. I place my hands on the bleeding bullet hole in my thigh, roaring out in pain.

"You son of a bitch! I will fucking kill you!" My eyes connect with Lee, and I can see the fear and worry in her bright blue eyes. "Let her go!" Adrenaline courses through me, and I urge myself to stand on my good leg, limping toward Anton and my girl that's kicking and trying to fight against him.

"Okay, fine." Jaden laughs. He nods to Anton, and the fat fuck releases Lee. She nearly falls to the floor but regains her balance. She rushes toward me, wraps an arm around my waist, and helps me wrap mine around her shoulder. I apply some of my weight on her, needing to stay off my leg that is throbbing. Warm blood seeps out of me, staining my pants and dripping onto our white floor.

"Get the fuck out of my house!" I yell, hissing in pain when Lee tries to move us.

Placing my head against hers, I whisper, "Get the gun from the lockbox in the kitchen." Like a fucking idiot, I left everything in the car. My gun is in the glovebox, my phone is on the seat, and I didn't bother calling my brothers to tell them anything, either.

No one knows that we're here and what's going on.

*Fucking great.*

Lee steps away from me, waiting until I get my balance before she slowly and cautiously starts walking away, only to stop in her tracks when the sound of a gun clicks.

"Don't fucking move, bitch!" Jaden yells.

Lee looks from him to me, wide eyed, and I know she won't be able to make it into the kitchen without him shooting her. It's a chance I'm not willing to take.

"Say goodbye, Eli," Jaden says, giving me a look of boredom.

"Fuck you! You want me to stop selling to the South Lords? Fine,"

I say through gritted teeth.

With a smile, he lowers his gun. "See, now, was that so hard?" He chuckles. "Too late, but it wasn't that hard. Now, say goodbye to your pretty girlfriend. I won't tell you again."

"He said he'll stop! He'll do whatever you want! Please!" Lee begs, tears running down her beautiful, scared face. She rushes to my side with trembling hands, but I'm busy staring at Jaden.

I see the look in his eyes. It's the same look I've had in my eyes right before I've taken a life. He's not bluffing. He's going to kill me, but at least he's allowing me the chance to say goodbye before he does, which is more than I've ever done.

"Last time, I'll say it. Say goodbye to your girl, and apologize for making the wrong decision. Let her know this is all your fault." With shaking hands, I turn toward the woman responsible for unthawing my cold, dead heart.

"Don't you fucking dare say goodbye to me, Eli Hale. You're not fucking dying." I admire her so much, but we both know how this will end.

Even if she runs to try to get a gun, he'll shoot me, and possibly even her.

Cupping her face, I press my forehead against hers. "I love you, Lee Hale, so fucking much. With every fiber of my being, with every ounce of my soul. You are my heart, my breath, and the air in my lungs."

Tears cloud my vision.

"Don't, Eli, please. Don't say these things. You can't leave me."

"I need you to take care of our family. Take care of my brothers, and tell them I love them. Tell our daughter I love her."

"Shut the fuck up, Eli. You're not leaving us."

"You have two minutes, Eli. Be grateful I'm allowing you to say goodbye." I block out Jaden's words and the pain radiating through my body, causing my vision to blur. I want to be able to see my beautiful girl.

I press my lips against hers, relishing the way she feels against me, savoring her kiss and the way she tastes in my mouth. One last time.

"You're everything to me, baby. You're my home, my heart, my soul." I kiss her again. "Just know, hellion, that you will always have my heart. I'm forever yours." I let her go, limping away to put space between us.

I wipe my tears with the back of my hand, my eyes never leaving hers. She attempts to run toward me, but Anton stops her by wrapping his arms around her waist.

"Please! Stop! Please! I'll do anything! Please," she screams, and her face turns red. Her screams are like knives to my ears.

"You, baby, you will always be right here." I press my hand against my heart.

"Get on your knees," Jaden orders, staring me down.

I shake my head. "I will not." He rolls his eyes in annoyance.

"You can never fucking listen," he complains.

"Lee, baby, close your eyes."

"Eli, no!"

"I need you to close your eyes! Close them for me and keep them closed!" She's heaving and choking over her tears, but she submits and closes her eyes.

"Listen to the sound of my voice." The third man forces me to my knees. I hiss in pain when I have to bend the leg that's been shot. "Keep your eyes closed, and picture us lying in bed, tangled in the sheets. Your head is on my chest, listening to my heartbeat. Can you hear my heart beating, baby?" Pony stands behind me, gripping my hands behind my back to prevent me from doing something stupid.

I'm not afraid to die, and I'm not going to do anything stupid anyway. Not when I can see the man standing in the corner pointing the gun at Lee, trying to remain hidden.

"Y-y-yes. I can hear it." She chokes on her sobs.

"Pretend we're in your studio, and I'm watching you dance. Can you feel my eyes on you? Can you see me watching you dance?"

"Eli, please, don't leave me."

"It's not possible to leave you, baby. Answer me. Do you see me watching you dance?"

She nods, her lips trembling, her body shaking.

"Pretend we're in the kitchen with the guys eating banana French toast and laughing over King's stupid jokes. Can you taste the food, baby? Can you hear the jokes?" She nods again.

"Remember me, baby. Remember how much I loved you, and know that I'm always with you, and I'll always be watching." My voice clogs with emotion, but I force the tears away, willing myself to be strong. "I love you, hellion."

"I love you, Eli."

Jaden stares me down as he places his gun against my forehead and pulls the trigger.

# FORTY-FOUR

*Raven*

"Have you heard from Lee or Eli? They were supposed to be here by now," I say, anxiously tapping my foot.

"I'll try calling them again," Ace says, scrolling through his phone and then placing it to his ear.

Lee went back home to get a part of Olivia's costume that she forgot, and Eli had a business meeting and was supposed to meet us here at Olivia's recital. We've all been calling their phones, and neither of them are answering.

Olivia will be devastated when she finds out her mom and Eli aren't here, so instead of rushing home to find out what the fuck is keeping them, I stay put because I know Olivia will be searching the audience for us, and if she doesn't see us, she'll be upset. She's worked so hard to get this part.

We claimed the seats in the front row, so she'll notice if we're not here.

"No answer," Ace says. *Fuck.*

"Eli probably got back early, and they're fucking," King says, wiggling his eyebrows. Eli and Lee have been sneaking off to steal five minutes to fuck every chance they can get. You'd think one of them would be tired, but nope, they're always ready to go.

Rolling my eyes, I settle into my seat, realizing he's probably right. This wouldn't be the first time they were late to something because they were too busy fucking and lost track of time.

I'm positive that's what happened, and I will claim both of their asses when I get home and discover they were late because they were fucking.

An hour later, the recital is over, and my bright-eyed daughter is running toward us. "Did you guys see me?" She smiles, looking around us.

"Where's my mom and Daddy Eli?" She started adding "daddy" to our names when she asked if we'd be her dads. There are four of us, so she calls us daddy and our name to make it easy.

"You did amazing, my girl," Ace jumps in, scooping her up in his arms and letting her climb onto his back. "They had something they had to do at home, but they are so proud of you."

"Can we get ice cream?" she asks, her voice full of hope, quickly forgetting about the absence of her mom and Eli.

"Of course, anything for you. We'll stop at home to pick up your mom and Eli, and then we'll go," King assures her as we walk toward the parking lot.

When we get home, the first thing I notice is the open gate leading toward our driveway. Then, I realize Eli's car in the driveway is still turned on with the driver's door wide open.

Ace must notice the eerie setting because instead of stopping in the driveway, he speeds up, and exits. He drove with Olivia while

King and I took my car. Better safe than sorry.

We never leave the gates open, and if something is happening inside, we can't risk our daughter by having her involved, so thankfully, he removes her by driving away.

I stop the car quickly, and King is at my side, our guns drawn.

We're running toward the house when we hear it.

Blood-curdling screams.

We run inside our house, guns pointed in front of us, and the second we enter, we pause in our tracks.

Lee is on her knees, holding Eli against her chest, his blood covering her hands and chest. She's rocking back and forth, screaming so fucking loudly I'm surprised she hasn't ripped her vocal cords.

It takes me a moment to register what the fuck is happening in front of my eyes.

King processes the scene first and jumps into action, running to Lee's side.

In shock, I look away from Eli's bloody corpse and rush through the house, checking it to make sure it's clear.

It doesn't hit me until I'm coming down the stairs and see the back of Eli's head with the visible hole—his hair matted with blood and chunks of his brain.

King tries to get Lee's attention, but she won't stop rocking Eli and screaming and crying. Her grip isn't loosening.

I walk toward them, but my knees give out, and I collapse. I have to drag my body by my hands to reach their side.

"Lee, butterfly, please, talk to us." King is trying to soothe her, tears already falling down his face as he refuses to look at our fallen brother.

Carefully, Lee lays Eli down, and his dull, cloudy, lifeless eyes stare at the ceiling. With her shaking, blood-covered hands, she presses on his chest and begins CPR, placing her mouth against his parted lips.

"Come on, Eli, baby, wake up. Come back to me!" she screams, pushing on his chest, heaving as she repeats the motions. "Wake up, baby. Wake up!" She doesn't stop. She's in a trance. Even as King and I try and stop her, she doesn't budge.

We're not much help to her right now. We're both crying beside her, refusing to accept what's happening in front of our own eyes.

I don't know how long we stay like this, but eventually, Ace comes rushing in. I think I hear him say that Olivia is with Maverick, but I'm not positive that's what he said.

Ace wraps his arms around Lee from behind and forces her off Eli's cold body. "He's gone, Lee, he's gone!" She thrashes against him.

"Liar! Get the fuck off of me!" He holds her even tighter.

"He's dead!" That seems to get her attention because her body goes still. She sags against him, and the color drains from her face.

"Kill me," she whispers. "I don't want to live without him. Kill me," she begs, scratching at his arms, trying to pry herself free from his grip.

"No, baby, you're not dying. We can't lose you too," Ace says, holding back his tears and doing his best to keep calm for her. He carries her out of the room, and King and I quickly look at our brother.

I met Eli when I was sixteen years old. We met at a grocery store where I was stealing food, and without even knowing me, he distracted the clerk so I could get away. We'd both been living on the streets but had never met before. I waited outside for him, and once he came out, I shared my food with him; we instantly became best friends. He was the brother I never had. Every single day with him was exciting and new.

We were homeless, but Eli ensured we always had food—and he

kept me entertained. He always told me that being homeless was just a phase, and he would see to it that one day we'd have everything we ever wanted.

He was right.

We may have had our moments when we disagreed, but in the end, Eli always had everyone's best interest in mind. He'd been trying to take care of King and me since the day he met us.

Closing my eyes, I lean forward and kiss his cold cheek. "I love you, brother. I'll take care of our girls."

# FORTY-FIVE

*Lee*

It was a Saturday when we buried Eli Michael Hale, the man who was often as cold as stone and hardly ever let anyone close to him. He loved his brothers fiercely, and he loved me.

It's been two weeks since Eli was placed in his final resting place, six feet below ground.

It's been three weeks since I held his hand, felt his lips on mine, felt his warmth against me, or heard him tell me that he loves me.

Three weeks since my heart broke.

I've never experienced a loss like this before—this soul-crushing loss when you lose someone you love.

The only actual family I've lost was my parents, but I was young when they died, and losing them feels nothing like what I've been feeling.

We had a small funeral for Eli, and it was beautiful. We didn't wear black; instead, we all wore blue. He once told me blue was his favorite color because it's the color of my eyes.

Only close friends attended. Those who knew Eli best came to pay their respects, and I wanted to scream the entire time they were coming to me, apologizing for my loss.

Everyone looked at me with pity and kept saying that Eli was in a better place, and I wanted to tell them to stop looking at me and tell them they were wrong.

Eli's "better place" is here with me.

He should be here with me.

With his brothers and our daughter.

He should be here.

He should fucking be here.

"Has she moved from that spot?" I hear Rowen ask King. I know King has been behind me, watching me, for a while now. I can always tell which one is near me. I can sense it.

"No. She still won't eat and hasn't even blinked," King responds. They speak as if I'm not in the room. They walk on eggshells around me, and I hate it. They talk to me in gentle voices, and I want to scream and tell them to shut up, but I can't bring myself to open my mouth and speak.

I can't bring myself to do anything besides sit.

I sit day after day in Eli's bedroom, dressed in his clothing.

Today I'm wearing a pair of sweatpants and a T-shirt I found in his hamper. I wanted the smell of him on me.

I haven't moved from my current spot in Eli's room, curled up in his La-Z-Boy recliner, staring out the window since the day we came home from the funeral. This is my daily routine.

I watch the sunset, and I watch the sunrise again.

I'm always watching and waiting.

Waiting to wake up from the nightmare I'm going through. There's no way this can be real. It can't be.

There's no way that a world can exist without Eli in it. I don't want to live in that type of world.

My love is gone. My heart is broken. I'll never be the same.

"The doctor should be here soon to examine her. I think we should ask about medication to help her sleep. She hasn't slept in days," Rowen says, voice full of concern.

They're bringing their doctor to check on me, but I don't need to be examined. I'm heartbroken, and there's nothing they can do to cure me.

King sighs, and I hear him stand up from the bed and walk toward Rowen. The two quietly leave the room, leaving me be.

"Can I see my mom?" I hear Olivia ask from outside the door. She's frightened and having a hard time understanding everything. I'm sure she feels I've abandoned her, and I guess I have.

That breaks my heart even more. She asks her dads every single day if she can see me, and every day they make her feel more and more defeated by telling her no. I can hear it in her voice when they deny her.

I wish she knew how sorry I was. How fucking sorry I am that I can't be there for her and be the mother she needs me to be.

She'd be better off without me. They all would.

I don't know how much time passes, but eventually, the door creaks open, and the bald-headed doctor comes into view.

"Hi, Lee, I'm Doctor Williams. Is it okay if I touch you?" he asks, coming into my line of sight. I don't respond or even look at him. Instead, I look through him, looking out the window that gives me a view of the trampoline in the backyard where Eli and I once spent time jumping and kissing in the rain after he told me he loved me for the first time months ago.

*"I've never been in love before. I've never had anyone to love, and I probably won't be any good at it, but you make me want to try."* He

*wiped the raindrops from my eyelids.* "You came crashing into my life like a thunderstorm. You were unexpected and made my heart beat for the first time." *He pressed his lips against mine and kissed me.*

"I'm sorry for what I did to you. Forgive me, hellion."

*I had smiled at his words and returned his kiss.* "I've already forgiven you, Eli."

"I will love you until the end of time."

I can still hear his whispered words in my ears. That day was perfect.

Dr. Baldie with cold hands doesn't wait for consent, probably because he knows I won't answer him.

He shines his stupid fucking light in my eyes, probably to see if anyone is home.

He examines me, and I want to tell him to get fucked because I'm not physically sick or wounded, but I can't. How can I explain that it's my soul that aches? My heart that aches? No medication or exam can cure me.

"What's wrong with her?" Ace asks. Yet again, they speak as if I'm not there.

"She's experienced something traumatic…she's traumatized. We can't expect her to get back to normal right away."

"It's been three weeks, doc. She won't eat, sleep, or speak. She sits there staring. Please. How can we help her?" Dr. Williams ushers him outside the room, but I hear their hushed whispers through the open door.

"I brought some sleeping pills. If she won't take them, crush them and mix them with tea. She desperately needs to sleep. Try and get her to eat something, even if it's only a few bites." I hear him open his bag and hand something to Ace. "If it's okay, I'd like to draw some blood to see how her body is doing. Especially if she's not eating or sleeping, she could be damaging vital organs."

"Do whatever you need to do."

Dr. Bald Head returns and sets up a tray of needles and vials to collect my blood. I don't know what he thinks he's going to find. Hopefully, he'll learn that I'm lifeless and bury me next to Eli.

He takes my arm and sticks me with a needle, but I don't feel it. I'd rather feel the pain of a thousand needles than the pain I'm currently feeling.

After Dr. Baldie leaves, Rowen brings me a cup of tea and a piece of toast. Fucking idiot. I'm not going to let them drug me.

They can all get fucked.

He tries to force me to drink but fails and eventually leaves.

They sleep in the room with me every night, babysitting me, probably to make sure I don't take one of their guns and blow my brains out.

As much as I want to do it, I won't. I refuse to do that to Olivia, even though I'm sure that would be better than the zombie mother she has currently.

When night comes, King climbs onto the bed behind my chair and makes himself comfortable. He tried to get me to sleep with him, but I don't want to be touched, and thankfully he knows that.

Eventually, King's breathing deepens, and his soft snores fill the room. With stiff limbs, I quietly stand from the chair, my bones cracking as I stretch for the first time in days. Forcing myself to blink, my eyes burn with the sudden moisture.

It feels weird standing after so long. Quietly, I leave the room, walk down the stairs, walk out to the backyard, and find myself standing at the pool ledge.

With a deep breath, I jump into the clear water lit up by the pool lights, sinking to the bottom.

Closing my eyes, I exhale and scream. I scream so fucking much that the water around me bubbles and gurgles around my mouth.

I'm still screaming when arms wrap around me and pull me up from the bottom. King swims us to the edge, sets my body on the ledge, and pulls himself out. Quickly he grabs a clean towel from the towel rack we keep outside and wraps it around me, holding me tightly to him.

"Are you trying to kill yourself, butterfly?" He scowls at me. "I can't fucking lose you too, do you understand me?" He shakes my shoulders as if he's trying to shake some sense into me.

For the first time in a long time, I look at him. I look at him and notice the dark bags under his eyes, unkempt facial hair, and blood-red eyes.

King is just as heartbroken as I am, and I've been too blind and focused on my grief that I haven't noticed what he and Rowen must be going through. What everyone must be going through.

I wasn't trying to kill myself by jumping into the pool. I just want to feel.

"I miss him." I speak for the first time in days. "I miss him so fucking much, and it hurts." He pulls me against him and wraps his arms around me, hugging me tightly.

"I know you do, butterfly. I do, too. I fucking miss him." Our bodies shake together as uncontrollable sobs rake through us.

"It hurts so much that sometimes I can't even breathe. My heart fucking hurts." I dig my nails into the skin of his back, clawing him closer to me.

"You can't leave me, butterfly. You have to stay. You have to stay for our family and yourself because Eli would want you to." I pull back and look at him, my bottom lip trembling, my body shivering from the cold.

"I'm so sorry. I'm so fucking sorry." Suddenly I feel embarrassed to look at him because of all I've put everyone through. I look away, too ashamed to make eye contact.

King places a hand under my chin and tilts my head back. "You have nothing to be sorry for. Promise me you will not shut down and shut me out again. I need you too much for you to block me out."

"I promise I won't ever again." He presses his lips against mine and breathes life back into me.

# FORTY-SIX

*Lee*

"Hello, Lee. How are you feeling today?" Dr. Williams asks with a smile. This is his second visit this week, and I'm not sure why he's here again. I didn't need anything from him the first time he was here, and I don't need anything from him now.

Since seeing him, I've been eating, and I've showered, changed my clothes, and slept. There's no reason for another visit from him.

"Thanks for showing me in, Rowen, but if you don't mind, I'd like to speak to Lee privately."

Ro shakes his head quickly. "No can do, doc. I'd like to stay." He looks to me, expecting me to ask him to stay.

"It's fine," I whisper, pushing the half-eaten cup of yogurt away from me. Since it's been so long since I've eaten, my body has decided to reject food. Anything I eat makes me sick, and I'm lucky if I can keep liquids down. Guess that's what I get for neglecting my body.

Hesitantly, Rowen exits the kitchen, leaving Doctor Baldie and me alone. He pulls out the chair next to me and sits down, opening the folder he is carrying in his hands.

"I got your test results back. Lee, you're pregnant," he announces with a smile.

Staring at him, I blink once, waiting for him to tell me he's joking. Surely, I didn't hear him correctly, so I say, "Excuse me?"

"Based on your levels, I'd guess about eight weeks along."

"That's impossible. I cannot get pregnant since I had an…accident a few years ago." I didn't have an accident, but that sounds better than saying my husband beat me so severely that it caused me to miscarry and caused infertility. I gave up the dream of ever raising a child a long time ago.

"Well, based on your bloodwork, you are, without a doubt, pregnant. I've taken it upon myself to schedule you an appointment." He hands me another piece of paper with the information for one of the best OB/GYNs in the state.

Looking from the paper to him, I suddenly burst out in laughter. "You're joking. There's no possible way." He shrugs, smiling at me, as he stands.

"I'm positive, Lee. It looks like you got a miracle. Now, take care of yourself." I walk him out, waving him goodbye.

On unsteady legs, I walk to the living room, where Rowen is patiently waiting. When he sees me, he stands. "What did he say?"

With trembling fingers, I place a hand on my flat stomach, an easy smile spreading across my lips for the first time in three weeks. "I'm pregnant," I whisper, a single fat tear rolling down my face.

For once, I'm not crying because I'm sad. I'm crying because I'm happy; this baby is a miracle, and I feel that in my heart. This baby was given to me for a reason, and for the first time since losing Eli, my heart is whole.

"W-w-what?" He blinks, giving me a blank deer-in-headlights look.

"Dr. Williams says my blood test came back, and I'm having a baby."

King appears from around the corner with wide eyes. "You're having a baby?" He rubs his eyes, looking from my face to my hand on my stomach. "We're having a baby?" I nod quickly.

Walking toward me, King drops to his knees in front of me. He raises my T-shirt, sticks his head inside, and peppers my stomach with warm kisses.

"We're having a baby!" Rowen shouts, rushing toward me; he wraps his arms around me from behind, kissing over my jawline and neck.

At that moment, Ace walks inside with Olivia at his side. He left about an hour ago to pick her up from school.

"What's going on?" he questions, helping Olivia out of her backpack.

Removing himself from my shirt, King stands. "We're having a baby. Lee's pregnant."

"I'm getting a baby sister?!" Olivia spins around happily, skipping toward us.

"Or a baby brother," I say with a laugh, leaning down to press a kiss on her forehead.

Ace joins by my side, wrapping an arm around Rowen and King's shoulders. "Guys, we're going to be dads again."

Looking at my family, excited by my news, my heart and soul come back to life, and suddenly I'm filled with nothing but warmth and love.

"So, who had the magic baby juice that knocked our girl up?" King asks with a wide fucking grin.

They take guesses, but they're all wrong because I already know.

I already know who's responsible for giving me this gift.

"Eli," I say with a smile. I know that, without a doubt, he's the father. They can take a paternity test, but I know they'll all turn out negative. This baby truly is a miracle, and I feel that in some twisted way, God knew Eli was going to die, so he chose to give me a piece of him that I'll have forever.

"Eli is the father," I repeat. They all nod in agreement, knowing exactly where I'm coming from and how I feel.

Eli gave us a piece of himself.

# FORTY-SEVEN

*Lee*

t was a cold Wednesday in October when Oliver Eli Hale was born. He was a perfect six pounds and four ounces and came into the world screaming at the top of his perfectly healthy lungs. He was born with a full head of black hair and eyes as dark as his father's.

My little Ollie is a spitting image of his father.

I knew from the moment I found out I was pregnant that Eli was the father, and I'd been correct. We didn't bother with paternity tests because the four of us knew who the biological father was.

There's no denying it. All it takes is one look at the beautiful little boy, and you can tell. He's Eli's twin, and the older he gets, the more he looks like him.

My baby boy is absolutely perfect.

As my belly grew and my days became filled with doctor appointments and nursery shopping, I'd been worried about how Olivia would react to not being the only child in the house, but she was the perfect little helper and the best big sister right from the start. She adores her little brother, and thankfully, she's never felt left out.

Sometimes it's hard with two kids, especially with such a large age gap.

Olivia turned twelve after Oliver was born, and sometimes I still can't believe I have such a stunning and well-mannered daughter.

She is perfect. Ollie is perfect. My life is perfect.

"Butterfly, come to bed," King whispers in my ear, pressing a kiss beneath my earlobe.

"Not yet. I want to stare at him a little bit longer." He wraps his arms around my waist from behind, and I relax against his chest. "I can't believe our baby boy is going to be one tomorrow."

"I know. He's growing up so fast. He and Olivia both."

I reach down into the crib and run my finger along Ollie's soft chubby cheek.

"I never imagined this is how my life would turn out. If you would've told me five years ago that I'd be a mother of two beautiful children and a wife to three men, I would've laughed in your face," I whisper into the stillness of the room, my focus on my sleeping baby.

King, Ace, Rowen, and I got married a month after Ollie was born. It was a small ceremony that took place in the backyard of our cabin. It felt fitting, considering the cabin is what brought Eli, King, Rowen, and me together in the beginning.

It was a bittersweet day. Bitter because Eli wasn't there, but sweet because I got to marry the loves of my life with my children by my side.

It was an amazing day, and as a tribute to Eli, we all wore blue.

My dress was stunning. It was a light blue silk that matched my eyes and clung to my body, which is now a little softer, thanks to my recent pregnancy. I haven't bounced back from this pregnancy like I did when I was seventeen.

The back of the dress was open and stopped just above the small of my back. I kept my hair short but dyed it back to black.

It was the perfect day as I promised myself to my men, and they promised themselves to me. We committed ourselves to our family forever.

We may not have a marriage license, but we were pronounced husbands and wife by a pastor that Ace hired, who didn't object to marrying four people together.

After our wedding, the six of us took a family honeymoon to Disneyworld, and since we returned, our life has only improved.

For the first time in my life, I'm pleased. I'm not afraid anymore of what's to come. I'm no longer living in fear and looking over my shoulder. Instead, I'm living with a purpose.

King trails his fingers along the back of my arms, his solid erection pressing into my bottom. "Let's go to bed, wife. I have something I want to give you." I place a hand over my mouth to keep me from laughing and waking Ollie.

Rolling my eyes, I take my husband's hand and lead him out of the room, looking back at our son once more before I close the door and allow King to carry me down the hall into our bedroom.

During my pregnancy, I was tired of sleeping in a different bed every night. I didn't want to bed hop and room hop anymore, so my guys surprised me by expanding the master bedroom and getting a custom-made bed for us.

Now, our room is fucking huge, big enough for the four of us.

King shuts and locks the door behind us and tosses me onto the bed. I giggle as I bounce on the mattress.

Sitting up, I lock eyes with Rowen, who's sitting on his side of the bed with the remote in his hand as he aimlessly flips through the channels on TV. One look at me, and he's putting the remote away and crawling toward me, a smirk curling his lips.

Ace walks out of the bathroom with a towel wrapped around his waist, his chest glistening with water, fresh from his shower.

"Ah, looks like we're going to play tonight." He rips his towel off, walking toward the bed with a look of hunger in his eyes.

It takes seconds for King to strip me from my clothing and undress himself.

Once naked, King kisses over my soft body, taking time to worship the silver stretch marks on my hips and thighs, trailing his tongue along every single line.

It's been a year since Ollie was born, and I haven't dropped the final fifteen pounds of baby weight. When the doctor cleared me for sex after six weeks, I'd been nervous about how my guys would react to my body. They're used to me being petite and fit, and I'm not anymore. Instead of the abs I once had, I now have a soft stomach and a belly roll when I sit.

When they saw my new body, they all three worshiped me more than ever, never once making me feel insecure. I think they love my body more now than they did before.

King kisses his way up my hot skin and enters me quickly, filling me to the hilt and taking my breath away, my lips falling apart. Ace takes the opportunity to fill my mouth.

As King fucks me, Rowen slips behind Ace and fucks him, and then we're all coming together and falling into an exhausted heap of flesh and limbs.

With my men beside me, and my children sleeping peacefully down the hall, I can't help but smile, remembering what it took to get here to this moment.

I'd never change anything about our story because everything we've done has led us to this exact moment.

I escaped the dollhouse of horrors that Sebastian kept me locked in. I escaped and burned my past life to the ground. Now, I stand in the ashes of who I used to be.

All the heartache, betrayal, and trials we've faced have been worth it.

No matter what, in the end, it'll always be us. We'll always be together.

We were meant to be together from the very beginning.

Our story isn't over, things are just changing, and we're preparing to enter a new chapter in our lives.

As for our children, their lives and stories are just beginning.

# EPILOGUE

*Olivia*

### FOUR YEARS LATER

"Uh-oh. Somebody's waiting and angry," Daddy King says to me with a low laugh as we pull into the driveway of our home and see Mom waiting in the doorframe with her hands on her hips, tapping her foot rapidly, and a scowl on her face.

I had hoped to make it without anyone finding out, but I'd never be that lucky. When I was called into the principal's office, I knew exactly what he would say, so I sent a quick text to Daddy K, asking him to pick me up.

Of my three dads, King is the one who's the most easygoing. He doesn't let me get away with shit, but he doesn't bust me by telling Mom and grounding me like she tries to do.

Mom tries, but it always fails.

I'm her baby girl, and as long as my grades are good and I'm honest, she's happy.

She's the number one person I can talk to about anything and never receive a lecture or judgment. No matter what I do, she always has my back.

The last time I got in trouble, she got into it with the principal, which is why I had to call Daddy K to pick me up. Mom is no longer allowed on school grounds.

She always defends me, but I did something stupid this time, and she will be furious. This isn't like the other times I've gotten in trouble at school.

Mom has one rule, get an education. She wants me to have everything she never had, and a proper education is one of those things.

I hate that I let her down. She'll be so disappointed in me.

I had hoped she wouldn't find out, but unfortunately for me, the school called home. Daddy K was already on the way to pick me up when principal Brewer called Mom.

Daddy R sent me a heads-up text telling me my mom was furious and would be waiting for me. True to his word, she is. She's waiting at the door, and I'm unsure what her reaction will be.

Mom has made many visits to the school these last few years, especially these last few months. After Principal Brewer informed her I'd be suspended for two days, she'd tell me how important it is to get a good education, then we'd get to the car and go for Starbucks and pedicures.

Mom hates Principal Brewer. She knows the grumpy old man likes to pick on me and make something out of nothing, so she takes what he says with a grain of salt. He doesn't appreciate the fact I have three dads, and he's been very vocal about his opinions on our family, which is partly why Mom hates him.

Until now, it's only been either one or two-day suspensions. I've never been in as much trouble as I am now, which is why I'm concerned about how she will act.

The car stops, and I gulp, staring at her through the window.

Daddy K gets out of the car, walks to Mom, and presses a kiss on her forehead; it's as if that one action just visibly takes away all the anger she's feeling. Her hands fall to her sides, and she looks up at her lover with a smile, kissing him on the lips.

He whispers something in her ear that makes her laugh, her dimples prominent.

I love when she laughs. She's so beautiful and looks carefree in those moments. She carries a lot of invisible scars and has had a tough life, which is why I try and make things easy for her by getting good grades and doing what I'm told.

The only trouble I cause my parents is when it comes to my friends. Well, former friends. As of today, they can go straight to hell.

Finally getting the courage, I climb out of the car and walk toward my mom. "Good luck, princess," Daddy K says with a chuckle, stepping inside the house.

"Seriously, Olivia Elizabeth? Expulsion?" Mom fumes, throwing her hands in the air. "What the hell happened?"

"It wasn't my weed," I defend, pulling my backpack straps over my shoulders.

"Whose was it?" She's not suggesting anything; she's genuinely asking. Mom always believes me because I never lie. I'm always honest, even when it's difficult.

"Becca's. She put it in my locker right before Principal Brewer did locker checks. He got a tip that someone was smoking weed in the girl's bathroom, so she tried to hide it in my locker," I explain, my shoulders sagging. Becca's one of the two friends I have. *Had.*

Now, thanks to the stunt she pulled, she's on my shit list and no longer my friend.

"I knew I never liked that girl." Mom sighs, pulling me into her arms for a hug. I inhale her comforting scent—vanilla coconut. "She's a little bitch," she mumbles under her breath.

I pull back and look at her with a laugh. "Mom, you can't call a seventeen-year-old a bitch."

"Yes, I can. I just did." She wraps her arm around my shoulders and leads me inside.

"Don't worry, my sweet girl. We'll find another school for you to go to. I'm tired of dealing with Principal Little Dick anyway."

Daddy R walks into the living room with a smile on his face. "Hey, little warrior." He pulls me in for a hug, kissing my forehead.

"I've got good news. You've been accepted into Bowler Academy and start Monday morning," he says, wrapping an arm around Mom and me both.

I gulp and look at him with wide eyes.

Bowler Academy is the most prestigious private school in the state. Mom had tried to get me enrolled when I first started high school, but even with all the money my parents have, there's still a mile-long waiting list that they couldn't bypass.

"How?" My stomach fills with knots. I'm not sure how to feel. I've asked about being homeschooled in the past, but my parents always deny me, even though one of them is usually always home.

A lot has changed over the past four years after Daddy Eli died.

I've experienced losing two people I loved at a young age, and that's enough to make any child feel a little jaded.

Sure, I've been to therapy, but I've never been the same after the death of my mom Rachel, and dad, Eli. I keep that part of me hidden and maintain a happy smiling face for my parents.

After Daddy Eli died, and Mom found out she was pregnant with Ollie, she made King, Rowen, and Ace get their shit together and go straight edge. She said she wouldn't watch another man she loves die, and they were quick to bow down to her feet and quit doing illegal shit.

For her.

For me.

For Oliver.

Now, we're boring and your typical all-American family.

"Don't worry about the how. Just promise that you'll get back on track and stop going down this path you're currently on. Promise me, Olivia." His eyes are sad with desperation.

My parents love me. They want what's best for me and don't want to see me continuing down the self-destructive path I'm on.

I'm not a bad kid, but I make bad decisions—a lot of them.

It started with Tyler, the football team's captain. He took notice of me my freshman year, and after giving him my virginity behind the bleachers on the football field, he spread rumors and then ignored me.

Then it continued with Becca and Candice, who got me involved with partying and drinking.

After meeting them, that's when things really started going downhill. Since then, it's been one thing after another, it seems.

"You'll make better friends, sweet girl. Perhaps this is a good thing and exactly what you need to get back on track," my mom says, her bright blue eyes gentle and full of hope.

"Yeah, Mom. I hope you're right. I think a new school will be good for me." I force a smile, hoping she doesn't see the lie written all over my face.

She's hoping that Bowler Academy will be my fresh start, but I know that it won't be because the person who hates me most in the world is there, and he's vowed to make my life a living hell if he were to see my face again.

Come Monday morning, my life will never be the same.

Ace's story will be coming soon!

**Signed copies available!**

Do you want to own a signed copy
of this book?

Order yours today:
www.kylafayebooks.com

# ALSO BY KYLA FAYE

# ACKNOWLEDGMENTS

Phew! The long-awaited second book is finally complete! I hadn't planned on taking this long to complete this book, but as we all know, sometimes life fucks us up, and things don't always go as planned.

I appreciate everyone's patience, and I promise you will not have to wait as long to read about Ace.

I'll keep this short because writing acknowledgments isn't my favorite thing to do, and Ace is currently speaking to me, so I need to hurry and get started on his story.

As always, I want to start by thanking my readers. Without all of you, this book would not have been possible. From the day I published Dollhouse until the day I announced Ashes, I've received constant support and encouragement from my incredible readers. I often had self-doubt about writing about such dark topics, but my readers and the book community were all there to remind me that they love dark shit as much as I do. It still amazes me that people in the world enjoy my words and eagerly wait for the next release. Thank you.

Next, I'd like to thank my husband. He's my number one supporter, and I would've never published my first book if it weren't for him. So, thank you, babe, for always being my number one fan and believing in me even when I don't always believe in myself. You know the stress I was under working on releasing two books, and you made it easy for me to focus and supported me daily. You are so fucking amazing, and I'll forever be in love with you.

As I've said before, it truly takes an entire village to publish a book, so let me thank mine.

To my editors, Tori and Zee, THANK YOU!!!!! Tori is new to

the Down We Go series, but she jumped head first into my jumbled writing and worked her magic to make my trash less trashy ;) Jk. She's terrific, and I'm lucky to have such a fantastic editor!

Zee, buddy, you're an OG and always my number one. I'm not sorry for keeping you in suspense for an entire year.

To my beta and ARC readers, you will forever be the bee's knees.

To the lovely team at Books and Moods, thank you for creating such a stunning cover and making my interior beautiful yet again. Y'all are crazy talented!

To everyone else who played a role in this release, I thank you from the bottom of my heart. Every DM, like, comment, share, edit, everything, has been incredible. It still blows my mind that I get to do what I love. Childhood me from a small middle-of-nowhere town is stunned right now, unable to believe that she's getting to live her dream.

Okay, so I'll end things before I get emotional and sappy.

Once again, THANK YOU to every single person who has played a role in this and who has chosen to read. You're amazing.

Fyi, be on the lookout. Three more books are coming in this series! ;)

XO,
KF

# ABOUT THE AUTHOR

Kyla Faye is a twenty-something author of dark, adult erotic, and contemporary romance. When she's not reading about romance, she's writing about it, trying to give a voice to the characters that live inside her head. She has a caffeine addiction and always has a candle burning.

You can find her on social media.

Instagram.com/authorkylafaye

Facebook.com/authorkylafaye

Goodreads.com/authorkylafaye

Tiktok.com/@authorkylafaye

Printed in Great Britain
by Amazon

17781222R00228